H. Beam Piper

Murder in the Gunroom

OK Publishing 2021

H. Beam Piper
MURDER IN THE GUNROOM

Published by

MUSAICUM
Books

- Advanced Digital Solutions & High-Quality book Formatting -

musaicumbooks@okpublishing.info

2021 OK Publishing

ISBN 978-80-272-7821-3

Contents

Chapter 1	11
Chapter 2	14
Chapter 3	18
Chapter 4	22
Chapter 5	25
Chapter 6	29
Chapter 7	33
Chapter 8	37
Chapter 9	39
Chapter 10	47
Chapter 11	54
Chapter 12	59
Chapter 13	63
Chapter 14	67
Chapter 15	72
Chapter 16	76
Chapter 17	80
Chapter 18	86
Chapter 19	88
Chapter 20	94
Chapter 21	99

TO

Colonel Henry W. Shoemaker
an old and valued friend, who was
promised this dedication, with an entirely different novel in mind, twenty-two years ago.

The Lane Fleming collection of early pistols and revolvers was one of the best in the country. When Fleming was found dead on the floor of his locked gunroom, a Confederate-made Colt-type percussion .36 revolver in his hand, the coroner's verdict was "death by accident." But Gladys Fleming had her doubts. Enough at any rate to engage Colonel Jefferson Davis Rand-better known just as Jeff-private detective and a pistol-collector himself, to catalogue, appraise, and negotiate the sale of her late husband's collection.

There were a number of people who had wanted the collection. The question was: had anyone wanted it badly enough to kill Fleming? And if so, how had he done it? Here is a mystery, told against the fascinating background of old guns and gun-collecting, which is rapid-fire without being hysterical, exciting without losing its contact with reason, and which introduces a personable and intelligent new private detective. It is a story that will keep your nerves on a hair trigger even if you don't know the difference between a cased pair of Paterson .34's and a Texas .40 with a ramming-lever.

Chapter 1

It was hard to judge Jeff Rand's age from his appearance; he was certainly over thirty and considerably under fifty. He looked hard and fit, like a man who could be a serviceable friend or a particularly unpleasant enemy. Women instinctively suspected that he would make a most satisfying lover. One might have taken him for a successful lawyer (he had studied law, years ago), or a military officer in mufti (he still had a Reserve colonelcy, and used the title occasionally, to impress people who he thought needed impressing), or a prosperous businessman, as he usually thought of himself. Most of all, he looked like King Charles II of England anachronistically clad in a Brooks Brothers suit.

At the moment, he was looking rather like King Charles II being bothered by one of his mistresses who wanted a peerage for her husband.

"But, Mrs. Fleming," he was expostulating. "There surely must be somebody else....After all, you'll have to admit that this isn't the sort of work this agency handles."

The would-be client released a series of smoke-rings and watched them float up toward the air-outlet at the office ceiling. It spoke well for Rand's ability to subordinate esthetic to business considerations that he was trying to give her a courteous and humane brush-off. She made even the Petty and Varga girls seem credible. Her color-scheme was blue and gold; blue eyes, and a blue tailored outfit that would have looked severe on a less curvate figure, and a charmingly absurd little blue hat perched on a mass of golden hair. If Rand had been Charles II, she could have walked out of there with a duchess's coronet, and Nell Gwyn would have been back selling oranges.

"Why isn't it?" she countered. "Your door's marked *Tri-State Detective Agency, Jefferson Davis Rand, Investigation and Protection.* Well, I want to know how much the collection's worth, and who'll pay the closest to it. That's investigation, isn't it? And I want protection from being swindled. And don't tell me you can't do it. You're a pistol-collector, yourself; you have one of the best small collections in the state. And you're a recognized authority on early pistols; I've read some of your articles in the *Rifleman*. If you can't handle this, I don't know who can."

Rand's frown deepened. He wondered how much Gladys Fleming knew about the principles of General Semantics. Even if she didn't know anything, she was still edging him into an untenable position. He hastily shifted from the attempt to identify his business with the label, "private detective agency."

"Well, here, Mrs. Fleming," he explained. "My business, including armed-guard and protected-delivery service, and general investigation and protection work, requires some personal supervision, but none of it demands my exclusive attention. Now, if you wanted some routine investigation made, I could turn it over to my staff, maybe put two or three men to work on it. But there's nothing about this business of yours that I could delegate to anybody; I'd have to do it all myself, at the expense of neglecting the rest of my business. Now, I could do what you want done, but it would cost you three or four times what you'd gain by retaining me."

"Well, let me decide that, Colonel," she replied. "How much would you have to have?"

"Well, this collection of your late husband's consists of some twenty-five hundred pistols and revolvers, all types and periods," Rand said. "You want me to catalogue it, appraise each item, issue lists, and negotiate with prospective buyers. The cataloguing and appraisal alone would take from a week to ten days, and it would be a couple more weeks until a satisfactory sale could be arranged. Why, say five thousand dollars; a thousand as a retainer and the rest on completion."

That, he thought, would settle that. He was expecting an indignant outcry, and hardened his heart, like Pharaoh. Instead, Gladys Fleming nodded equably.

"That seems reasonable enough, Colonel Rand, considering that you'd have to be staying with us at Rosemont, away from your office," she agreed. "I'll give you a check for the thousand now, with a letter of authorization."

Rand nodded in return. Being thoroughly conscious of the fact that he could only know a thin film of the events on the surface of any situation, he was not easily surprised.

"Very well," he said. "You've hired an arms-expert. I'll be in Rosemont some time tomorrow afternoon. Now, who are these prospective purchasers you mentioned, and just how prospective, in terms of United States currency, are they?"

"Well, for one, there's Arnold Rivers; he's offering ten thousand for the collection. I suppose you know of him; he has an antique-arms business at Rosemont."

"I've done some business with him," Rand admitted. "Who else?"

"There's a commission-dealer named Carl Gwinnett, who wants to handle the collection for us, for twenty per cent. I'm told that that isn't an unusually exorbitant commission, but I'm not exactly crazy about the idea."

"You shouldn't be, if you want your money in a hurry," Rand told her. "He'd take at least five years to get everything sold. He wouldn't dump the whole collection on the market at once, upset prices, and spoil his future business. You know, two thousand five hundred pistols of the sort Mr. Fleming had, coming on the market in a lot, could do just that. The old-arms market isn't so large that it couldn't be easily saturated."

"That's what I'd been thinking....And then, there are some private collectors, mostly friends of Lane's —Mr. Fleming's —who are talking about forming a pool to buy the collection for distribution among themselves," she continued.

"That's more like it," Rand approved. "If they can raise enough money among them, that is. They won't want the stuff for resale, and they may pay something resembling a decent price. Who are they?"

"Well, Stephen Gresham appears to be the leading spirit," she said. "The corporation lawyer, you know. Then, there is a Mr. Trehearne, and a Mr. MacBride, and Philip Cabot, and one or two others."

"I know Gresham and Cabot," Rand said. "They're both friends of mine, and I have an account with Cabot, Joyner & Teale, Cabot's brokerage firm. I've corresponded with MacBride; he specializes in Colts....You're the sole owner, I take it?"

"Well, no." She paused, picking her words carefully. "We may just run into a little trouble, there. You see, the collection is part of the residue of the estate, left equally to myself and my two stepdaughters, Nelda Dunmore and Geraldine Varcek. You understand, Mr. Fleming and I were married in 1941; his first wife died fifteen years before."

"Well, your stepdaughters, now; would they also be my clients?"

"Good Lord, no!" That amused her considerably more than it did Rand. "Of course," she continued, "they're just as interested in selling the collection for the best possible price, but beyond that, there may be a slight divergence of opinion. For instance, Nelda's husband, Fred Dunmore, has been insisting that we let him handle the sale of the pistols, on the grounds that he is something he calls a businessman. Nelda supports him in this. It was Fred who got this ten-thousand-dollar offer from Rivers. Personally, I think Rivers is playing him for a sucker. Outside his own line, Fred is an awful innocent, and I've never trusted this man Rivers. Lane had some trouble with him, just before..."

"Arnold Rivers," Rand said, when it was evident that she was not going to continue, "has the reputation, among collectors, of being the biggest crook in the old-gun racket, a reputation he seems determined to live up-or down-to. But here; if your stepdaughters are co-owners, what's my status? What authority, if any, have I to do any negotiating?"

Gladys Fleming laughed musically. "That, my dear Colonel, is where you earn your fee," she told him. "Actually, it won't be as hard as it looks. If Nelda gives you any argument, you can count on Geraldine to take your side as a matter of principle; if Geraldine objects first, Nelda will help you steam-roll her into line. Fred Dunmore is accustomed to dealing with a lot of yes-men at the plant; you shouldn't have any trouble shouting him down. Anton Varcek won't be interested, one way or another; he has what amounts to a pathological phobia about firearms of any sort. And Humphrey Goode, our attorney, who's executor of the estate, will welcome you with open arms, once he finds out what you want to do. That collection has him talking to himself, already. Look; if you come out to our happy home in the early afternoon, before Fred and Anton get back from the plant, we ought to ram through some sort of agreement with Geraldine and Nelda."

"You and whoever else sides with me will be a majority," Rand considered. "Of course, the other one may pull a Gromyko on us, but ...I think I'll talk to Goode, first."

"Yes. That would be smart," Gladys Fleming agreed. "After all, he's responsible for selling the collection." She crossed to the desk and sat down in Rand's chair while she wrote out the check and a short letter of authorization, then she returned to her own seat.

"There's another thing," she continued, lighting a fresh cigarette. "Because of the manner of Mr. Fleming's death, the girls have a horror of the collection almost-but not quite-as strong as their desire to get the best possible price for it."

"Yes. I'd heard that Mr. Fleming had been killed in a firearms accident, last November," Rand mentioned.

"It was with one of his collection-pieces," the widow replied. "One he'd bought just that day; a Confederate-made Colt-type percussion .36 revolver. He'd brought it home with him, simply delighted with it, and started cleaning it at once. He could hardly wait until dinner was over to get back to work on it.

"We'd finished dinner about seven, or a little after. At about half-past, Nelda went out somewhere in the coupé. Anton had gone up to his laboratory, in the attic-he's one of these fortunates whose work is also his hobby; he's a biochemist and dietitian-and Lane was in the gunroom, on the second floor, working on his new revolver. Fred Dunmore was having a bath, and Geraldine and I had taken our coffee into the east parlor. Geraldine put on the radio, and we were listening to it.

"It must have been about 7:47 or 7:48, because the program had changed and the first commercial was just over, when we heard a loud noise from somewhere upstairs. Neither of us thought of a shot; my own first idea was of a door slamming. Then, about five minutes later, we heard Anton, in the upstairs hall, pounding on a door, and shouting: 'Lane! Lane! Are you all right?' We ran up the front stairway, and found Anton, in his rubber lab-apron, and Fred, in a bathrobe, and barefooted, standing outside the gunroom door. The door was locked, and that in itself was unusual; there's a Yale lock on it, but nobody ever used it.

"For a minute or so, we just stood there. Anton was explaining that he had heard a shot and that nobody in the gunroom answered. Geraldine told him, rather impatiently, to go down to the library and up the spiral. You see," she explained, "the library is directly under the gunroom, and there's a spiral stairway connecting the two rooms. So Anton went downstairs and we stood waiting in the hall. Fred was shivering in his bathrobe; he said he'd just jumped out of the bathtub, and he had nothing on under it. After a while, Anton opened the gunroom door from the inside, and stood in the doorway, blocking it. He said: 'You'd better not come in. There's been an accident, but it's too late to do anything. Lane's shot himself with one of those damned pistols; I always knew something like this would happen.'

"Well, I simply elbowed him out of the way and went in, and the others followed me. By this time, the uproar had penetrated to the rear of the house, and the servants-Walters, the butler, and Mrs. Horder, the cook-had joined us. We found Lane inside, lying on the floor, shot through the forehead. Of course, he was dead. He'd been sitting on one of these old cobblers' benches of the sort that used to be all the thing for cocktail-tables; he had his tools and polish and oil and rags on it. He'd fallen off it to one side and was lying beside it. He had a revolver in his right hand, and an oily rag in his left."

"Was it the revolver he'd brought home with him?" Rand asked.

"I don't know," she replied. "He showed me this Confederate revolver when he came home, but it was dirty and dusty, and I didn't touch it. And I didn't look closely at the one he had in his hand when he was ...on the floor. It was about the same size and design; that's all I could swear to." She continued: "We had something of an argument about what to do. Walters, the butler, offered to call the police. He's English, and his mind seems to run naturally to due process of law. Fred and Anton both howled that proposal down; they wanted no part of the police. At the same time, Geraldine was going into hysterics, and I was trying to get her quieted down. I took her to her room and gave her a couple of sleeping-pills, and then went back to the gunroom. While I was gone, it seems that Anton had called our family doctor, Dr. Yardman, and then Fred called Humphrey Goode, our lawyer. Goode lives next door to us, about two hundred yards away, so he arrived almost at once. When the doctor came, he called the coroner, and when he arrived, about an hour later, they all went into a huddle and decided that it was an obvious accident and that no inquest would be necessary. Then somebody, I'm not sure who, called an undertaker. It was past eleven when he arrived, and for once, Nelda got home early. She was just coming in while they were carrying Lane out in a basket. You can imagine how horrible that was for her; it was days before she was over the shock. So she'll be just as glad as anybody to see the last of the pistol-collection."

Through the recital, Rand had sat silently, toying with the ivory-handled Italian Fascist dagger-of-honor that was doing duty as a letter-opener on his desk. Gladys Fleming wasn't, he was sure, indulging in any masochistic self-harrowing; neither, he thought, was she talking to relieve her mind. Once or twice there had been a small catch in her voice, but otherwise the narration had been a piece of straight reporting, neither callous nor emotional. Good reporting, too; carefully detailed. There had been one or two inclusions of inferential matter in the guise of description, but that was to be looked for and discounted. And she had remembered, at the end, to include her ostensible reason for telling the story.

"Yes, it must have been dreadful," he sympathized. "Odd, though, that an old hand with guns like Mr. Fleming would have an accident like that. I met him, once or twice, and was at your home to see his collection, a couple of years ago. He impressed me as knowing firearms pretty thoroughly.... Well, you can look for me tomorrow, say around two. In the meantime, I'll see Goode, and also Gresham and Arnold Rivers."

Chapter 2

After ushering his client out the hall door and closing it behind her, Rand turned and said:
"All right, Kathie, or Dave; whoever's out there. Come on in."
Then he went to his desk and reached under it, snapping off a switch. As he straightened, the door from the reception-office opened and his secretary, Kathie O'Grady, entered, loading a cigarette into an eight-inch amber holder. She was a handsome woman, built on the generous lines of a Renaissance goddess; none of the Renaissance masters, however, had ever employed a model so strikingly Hibernian. She had blue eyes, and a fair, highly-colored complexion; she wore green, which went well with her flaming red hair, and a good deal of gold costume-jewelry.
Behind her came Dave Ritter. He was Rand's assistant, and also Kathie's lover. He was five or six years older than his employer, and slightly built. His hair, fighting a stubborn rearguard action against baldness, was an indeterminate mousy gray-brown. It was one of his professional assets that nobody ever noticed him, not even in a crowd of one; when he wanted it to, his thin face could assume the weary, baffled expression of a middle-aged book-keeper with a wife and four children on fifty dollars a week. Actually, he drew three times that much, had no wife, admitted to no children. During the war, he and Kathie had kept the Tri-State Agency in something better than a state of suspended animation while Rand had been in the Army.
Ritter fumbled a Camel out of his shirt pocket and made a beeline for the desk, appropriating Rand's lighter and sharing the flame with Kathie.
"You know, Jeff," he said, "one of the reasons why this agency never made any money while you were away was that I never had the unadulterated insolence to ask the kind of fees you do. I was listening in on the extension in the file-room; I could hear Kathie damn near faint when you said five grand."

"Yes; five thousand dollars for appraising a collection they've been offered ten for, and she only has a third-interest," Kathie said, retracting herself into the chair lately vacated by Gladys Fleming. "If that makes sense, now..."

"Ah, don't you get it, Kathleen Mavourneen?" Ritter asked. "She doesn't care about the pistols; she wants Jeff to find out who fixed up that accident for Fleming. You heard that big, long shaggy-dog story about exactly what happened and where everybody was supposed to have been at the time. I hope you got all that recorded; it was all told for a purpose."

Rand had picked up the outside phone and was dialing. In a moment, a girl's voice answered.

"Carter Tipton's law-office; good afternoon."

"Hello, Rheba; is Tip available?"

"Oh, hello, Jeff. Just a sec; I'll see." She buzzed another phone. "Jeff Rand on the line," she announced.

A clear, slightly Harvard-accented male voice took over.

"Hello, Jeff. Now what sort of malfeasance have you committed?"

"Nothing, so far-cross my fingers," Rand replied. "I just want a little information. Are you busy?...Okay, I'll be up directly."

He replaced the phone and turned to his disciples.

"Our client," he said, "wants two jobs done on one fee. Getting the pistol-collection sold is one job. Exploring the whys and wherefores of that quote accident unquote is the other. She has a hunch, and probably nothing much better, that there's something sour about the accident. She expects me to find evidence to that effect while I'm at Rosemont, going over the collection. I'm not excluding other possibilities, but I'll work on that line until and unless I find out differently. Five thousand should cover both jobs."

"You think that's how it is?" Kathie asked.

"Look, Kathie. I got just as far in Arithmetic, at school, as you did, and I suspect that Mrs. Fleming got at least as far as long division, herself. For reasons I stated, I simply couldn't have handled that collection business for anything like a reasonable fee, so I told her five thousand, thinking that would stop her. When it didn't, I knew she had something else in mind, and when she went into all that detail about the death of her husband, she as good as told me that was what it was. Now I'm sorry I didn't say ten thousand; I think she'd have bought it at that price just as cheerfully. She thinks Lane Fleming was murdered. Well, on the face of what she told me, so do I."

"All right, Professor; expound," Ritter said.

"You heard what he was supposed to have shot himself with," Rand began. "A Colt-type percussion revolver. You know what they're like. And I know enough about Lane Fleming to know how much experience he had with old arms. I can't believe that he'd buy a pistol without carefully examining it, and I can't believe that he'd bring that thing home and start working on it without seeing the caps on the nipples and the charges in the chambers, if it had been loaded. And if it had been, he would have first taken off the caps, and then taken it apart and drawn the charges. And she says he started working on it as soon as he got home-presumably around five-and then took time out for dinner, and then went back to work on it, and more than half an hour later, there was a shot and he was killed." Rand blew a Bronx cheer. "If that accident had been the McCoy, it would have happened in the first five minutes after he started working on that pistol. No, in the first thirty seconds. And then, when they found him, he had the revolver in his right hand, and an oily rag in his left. I hope both of you noticed that little touch."

"Yeah. When I clean a gat, I generally have it in my left hand, and clean with my right," Ritter said.

"Exactly. And why do you use an oily rag?" Rand inquired.

Ritter looked at him blankly for a half-second, then grinned ruefully.

"Damn, I never thought of that," he admitted. "Okay, he was bumped off, all right."

"But you use oily rags on guns," Kathie objected. "I've seen both of you, often enough."

"When we're all through, honey," Ritter told her.

"Yes. When he brought home that revolver, it was in neglected condition," Rand said. "Either surface-rusted, or filthy with gummed oil and dirt. Even if Mrs. Fleming hadn't mentioned that point, the length of time he spent cleaning it would justify such an inference. He would have taken it apart, down to the smallest screw, and cleaned everything carefully, and then put it together again, and then, when he had finished, he would have gone over the surface with an oiled rag, before hanging it on the wall. He would certainly not have surface-oiled it before removing the charges, if there ever were any. I assume the revolver he was found holding, presumably the one with which he was killed, was another one. And I would further assume that the killer wasn't particularly familiar with the subject of firearms, antique, care and maintenance of."

"And with all the hollering and whooping and hysterics-throwing, nobody noticed the switch," Ritter finished. "Wonder what happened to the one he was really cleaning."

"That I may possibly find out," Rand said. "The general incompetence with which this murder was committed gives me plenty of room to hope that it may still be lying around somewhere."

"Well, have you thought that it might just be suicide?" Kathie asked.

"I have, very briefly; I dismissed the thought, almost at once," Rand told her. "For two reasons. One, that if it had been suicide, Mrs. Fleming wouldn't want it poked into; she'd be more than willing to let it ride as an accident. And, two, I doubt if a man who prided himself on his gun-knowledge, as Fleming did, would want his self-shooting to be taken for an accident. I'm damn sure I wouldn't want my friends to go around saying: 'What a dope; didn't know it was loaded!' I doubt if he'd even expect people to believe that it had been an accident." He shook his head. "No, the only inference I can draw is that somebody murdered Fleming, and then faked evidence intended to indicate an accident." He rose. "I'll be back, in a little; think it over, while I'm gone."

Carter Tipton had his law-office on the floor above the Tri-State Detective Agency. He handled all Rand's not infrequent legal involvements, and Rand did all his investigating and witness-chasing; annually, they compared books to see who owed whom how much. Tipton was about five years Rand's junior, and had been in the Navy during the war. He was frequently described as New Belfast's leading younger attorney and most eligible bachelor. His dark, conservatively cut clothes fitted him as though they had been sprayed on, he wore gold-rimmed glasses, and he was so freshly barbered, manicured, valeted and scrubbed as to give the impression that he had been born in cellophane and just unwrapped. He leaned back in his chair and waved his visitor to a seat.

"Tip, do you know anything about this Fleming family, out at Rosemont?" Rand began, getting out his pipe and tobacco.

"The Premix-Foods Flemings?" Tipton asked. "Yes, a little. Which one of them wants you to frame what on which other one?"

"That'll do for a good, simplified description, to start with," Rand commented. "Why, my client is Mrs. Gladys Fleming. As to what she wants...."

He told the young lawyer about his recent interview and subsequent conclusions.

"So you see," he finished, "she won't commit herself, even with me. Maybe she thinks I have more official status, and more obligations to the police, than I have. Maybe she isn't sure in her own mind, and wants me to see, independently, if there's any smell of something dead in the woodpile. Or, she may think that having a private detective called in may throw a scare into somebody. Or maybe she thinks somebody may be fixing up an accident for her, next, and she wants a pistol-totin' gent in the house for a while. Or any combination thereof. Personally, I deplore these clients who hire you to do one thing and expect you to do another, but with five grand for sweetening, I can take them."

"Yes. You know, I've heard rumors of suicide, but this is the first whiff of murder I've caught."
He hesitated slightly. "I must say, I'm not greatly surprised. Lane Fleming's death was very
convenient to a number of people. You know about this Premix Company, don't you?"

"Vaguely. They manufacture ready-mixed pancake flour, and ready-mixed ice-cream and pud-
ding powders, and this dehydrated vegetable soup-pour on hot water, stir, and serve-don't they?
My colored boy, Buck, got some of the soup, once, for an experiment. We unanimously voted
not to try it again."

"They put out quite a line of such godsends to the neophyte in the kitchen, the popularity of
which is reflected in a steadily rising divorce-rate," Tipton said. "They advertise very extensively,
including half an hour of tear-jerking drama on a national hookup during soap-opera time. Your
client, the former Gladys Farrand, was on the air for Premix for a couple of years; that's how
Lane Fleming first met her."

"So you think some irate and dyspeptic husband went to the source of his woes?" Rand
inquired.

"Well, not exactly. You see, Premix is only Little Business, as the foods industry goes, but
they have something very sweet. So sweet, in fact, that one of the really big fellows, National
Milling & Packaging, has been going to rather extreme lengths to effect a merger. Mill-Pack,
par 100, is quoted at around 145, and Premix, par 50, is at 75 now, and Mill-Pack is offering a
two-for-one-share exchange, which would be a little less than four-for-one in value. I might
add, for what it's worth, that this Stephen Gresham you mentioned is Mill-Pack's attorney,
negotiator, and general Mr. Fixit; he has been trying to put over this merger for Mill-Pack."

"I'll bear that in mind, too," Rand said.

"Naturally, all this is not being shouted from the housetops," Tipton continued. "Fact is, it's
a minor infraction of ethics for me to mention it to you."

"I'll file it in the burn-box," Rand promised. "What was the matter; didn't Premix want
to merge?"

"Lane Fleming didn't. And since he held fifty-two per cent of the common stock himself,
try and do anything about it."

"Anything short of retiring Fleming to the graveyard, that is," Rand amended. "That would
do for a murder-motive, very nicely....What were Fleming's objections to the merger?"

"Mainly sentimental. Premix was his baby, or, at least, his kid brother. His father started
mixing pancake flour back before the First World War, and Lane Fleming peddled it off a spring
wagon. They worked up a nice little local trade, and finally a state-wide wholesale business.
They incorporated in the early twenties, and then, after the old man died, Lane Fleming hired
an advertising agency to promote his products, and built up a national distribution, and took
on some sidelines. Then, during the late Mr. Chamberlain's 'Peace in our time,' he picked
up a refugee Czech chemist and foods-expert named Anton Varcek, who whipped up a lot of
new products. So business got better and better, and they made more money to spend on
advertising to get more money to buy more advertising to make more money, like Bill Nye's
Puritans digging clams in the winter to get strength to hoe corn in the summer to get strength
to dig clams in the winter.

"So Premix became a sort of symbol of achievement to Fleming. Then, he was one of these
old-model paternalistic employers, and he was afraid that if he relinquished control, a lot of
his old retainers would be turned out to grass. And finally, he was opposed in principle to concentration of business ownership. He claimed it made business more vulnerable to government
control and eventual socialization."

"I'm not sure he didn't have something there," Rand considered. "We get all our corporate
eggs in a few baskets, and they're that much easier for the planned-economy boys to grab....
Just who, on the Premix side, was in favor of this merger?"

"Just about everybody but Fleming," Tipton replied. "His two sons-in-law, Fred Dunmore
and Varcek, who are first and second vice presidents. Humphrey Goode, the company attorney,
who doubles as board chairman. All the directors. All the New York banking crowd who are

interested in Premix. And all the two-share tinymites. I don't know who inherits Fleming's voting interest, but I can find out for you by this time tomorrow."

"Do that, Tip, and bill me for what you think finding out is worth," Rand said. "It'll be a novel reversal of order for you to be billing me for an investigation.... Now, how about the family, as distinct from the company?"

"Well, there's your client, Gladys Fleming. She married Lane Fleming about ten years ago, when she was twenty-five and he was fifty-five. In spite of the age difference, I understand it was a fairly happy marriage. Then, there are two daughters by a previous marriage, Nelda Dunmore and Geraldine Varcek, and their respective husbands. They all live together, in a big house at Rosemont. In the company, Dunmore is Sales, and Varcek is Production. They each have a corner of the mantle of Lane Fleming in one hand and a dirk in the other. Nelda and Geraldine hate each other like Greeks and Trojans. Nelda is the nymphomaniac sister, and Geraldine is the dipsomaniac. From time to time, temporary alliances get formed, mainly against Gladys; all of them resent the way she married herself into a third-interest in the estate. You're going to have yourself a nice, pleasant little stay in the country."

"I'm looking forward to it." Rand grimaced. "You mentioned suicide rumors. Such as, and who's been spreading them?"

"Oh, they are the usual bodyless voices that float about," Tipton told him. "Emanating, I suspect, from sources interested in shaking out the less sophisticated small shareholders before the merger. The story is always approximately the same: That Lane Fleming saw his company drifting reefward, was unwilling to survive the shipwreck, and performed *seppuku*. The family are supposed to have faked up the accident afterward. I dismiss the whole thing as a rather less than subtle bit of market-manipulation chicanery."

"Or a smoke screen, to cover the defects in camouflaging a murder as an accident," Rand added.

Tipton nodded. "That could be so, too," he agreed. "Say somebody dislikes the looks of that accident, and starts investigating. Then he runs into all this miasma of suicide rumors, and promptly shrugs the whole thing off. Fleming killed himself, and the family made a few alterations and are passing it off as an accident. The families of suicides have been known to do that."

"Yes. Regular defense-in-depth system; if the accident line is penetrated, the suicide line is back of it," Rand said. "Well, in the last few years, we've seen defenses in depth penetrated with monotonous regularity. I've jeeped through a couple, myself, to interrogate the surviving ex-defenders. It's all in having the guns and armor to smash through with."

Chapter 3

Humphrey Goode was sixty-ish, short and chunky, with a fringe of white hair around a bald crown. His brow was corrugated with wrinkles, and he peered suspiciously at Rand through a pair of thick-lensed, black-ribboned glasses. His wide mouth curved downward at the corners in an expression that was probably intended to be stern and succeeded only in being pompous. His office was dark, and smelled of dusty books.

"Mr. Rand," he began accusingly, "when your secretary called to make this appointment, she informed me that you had been retained by Mrs. Gladys Fleming."

"That's correct." Rand slowly packed tobacco into his pipe and lit it. "Mrs. Fleming wants me to look after some interests of hers, and as you're executor of her late husband's estate, I thought I ought to talk to you, first of all."

Goode's eyes narrowed behind the thick glasses.

"Mr. Rand, if you're investigating the death of Lane Fleming, you're wasting your time and Mrs. Fleming's money," he lectured. "There is nothing whatever for you to find out that is not already public knowledge. Mr. Fleming was accidentally killed by the discharge of an old revolver he was cleaning. I don't know what foolish feminine impulse led Mrs. Fleming to employ you, but you'll do nobody any good in this matter, and you may do a great deal of harm."

"Did my secretary tell you I was making an investigation?" Rand demanded incredulously. "She doesn't usually make mistakes of that sort."

The wrinkles moved up Goode's brow like a battalion advancing in platoon front. He looked even more narrowly at Rand, his suspicion compounded with bewilderment.

"Why should I investigate the death of Lane Fleming?" Rand continued. "As far as I know, Mrs. Fleming is satisfied that it was an accident. She never expressed any other belief to me. Do you think it was anything else?"

"Why, of course not!" Goode exclaimed. "That's just what I was telling you. I —" He took a fresh start. "There have been rumors-utterly without foundation, of course-that Mr. Fleming committed suicide. They are, I may say, nothing but malicious fabrications, circulated for the purpose of undermining public confidence in Premix Foods, Incorporated. I had thought that perhaps Mrs. Fleming might have heard them, and decided, on her own responsibility, to bring you in to scotch them; I was afraid that such a step might, by giving these rumors fresh currency, defeat its intended purpose."

"Oh, nothing of the sort!" Rand told him. "I'm not in the least interested in how Mr. Fleming was killed, and the question is simply not involved in what Mrs. Fleming wants me to do."

He stopped there. Goode was looking at him sideways, sucking in one corner of his mouth and pushing out the other. It was not a facial contortion that impressed Rand favorably; it was too reminiscent of a high-school principal under whom he had suffered, years ago, in Vicksburg, Mississippi. Rand began to suspect that Goode might be just another such self-righteous, opinionated, egotistical windbag. Such men could be dangerous, were usually quite unscrupulous, and were almost always unpleasant to deal with.

"Then why," the lawyer demanded, "did Mrs. Fleming employ you?"

"Well, as you know," Rand began, "the Fleming pistol-collection, now the joint property of Mrs. Fleming and her two stepdaughters, is an extremely valuable asset. Mr. Fleming spent the better part of his life gathering it. At one time or another, he must have owned between four and five thousand different pistols and revolvers. The twenty-five hundred left to his heirs represent the result of a systematic policy of discriminating purchase, replacement of inferior items, and general improvement. It's one of the largest and most famous collections of its kind in the country."

"Well?" Goode was completely out of his depth by now. "Surely Mrs. Fleming doesn't think...?"

"Mrs. Fleming thinks that expert advice is urgently needed in disposing of that collection," Rand replied, carefully picking his words to fit what he estimated to be Goode's probable semantic reactions. "She has the utmost confidence in your ability and integrity, as an attorney; however, she realized that you could hardly describe yourself as an antique-arms expert. It happens that I am an expert in antique firearms, particularly pistols. I have a collection of my own, I am the author of a number of articles on the subject, and I am recognized as something of an authority. I know arms-values, and understand market conditions. Furthermore, not being a dealer, or connected with any museum, I have no mercenary motive for undervaluing the collection. That's all there is to it; Mrs. Fleming has retained me as a firearms-expert, in connection with the collection."

Goode was looking at Rand as though the latter had just torn off a mask, revealing another and entirely different set of features underneath. The change seemed to be a welcome one, but he was evidently having trouble adjusting to it. Rand grinned inwardly; now he was going to have to find himself a new set of verbal labels and identifications.

"Well, Mr. Rand, that alters the situation considerably," he said, with noticeably less hostility. He was still a bit resentful; people had no right to confuse him by jumping about from one category to another, like that. "Now understand, I'm not trying to be offensive, but it seems a little unusual for a private detective also to be an authority on antique firearms."

"Mr. Fleming was an authority on antique firearms, and he was a manufacturer of foodstuffs," Rand parried, carefully staying inside Goode's Aristotelian system of categories and verbal identifications. "My own business does not occupy all my time, any more than his did, and I doubt if an interest in the history and development of deadly weapons is any more incongruous in a criminologist than in an industrialist. But if there's any doubt in your mind as to my qualifications, you can check with Colonel Taylor, at the State Museum, or with the editor of the *American Rifleman.*"

"I see." Goode nodded. "And as you point out, being a sort of non-professional expert, you should be free from mercenary bias." He nodded again, taking off his glasses and polishing them on an outsize white handkerchief. "Frankly, now that I understand your purpose, Mr. Rand, I must say that I am quite glad that Mrs. Fleming took this step. I was perplexed about how to deal with that collection. I realized that it was worth a great deal of money, but I haven't the vaguest idea how much, or how it could be sold to the best advantage....At a rough guess, Mr. Rand, how much do you think it ought to bring?"

Rand shook his head. "I only saw it twice, the last time two years ago. Ask me that after I've spent a day or so going over it, and I'll be able to give you an estimate. I will say this, though: It's probably worth a lot more than the ten thousand dollars Arnold Rivers has offered for it."

That produced an unexpected effect. Goode straightened in his chair, gobbling in surprised indignation.

"Arnold Rivers? Has he had the impudence to try to buy the collection?" he demanded. "Where did you hear that?"

"From Mrs. Fleming. I understand he made the offer to Fred Dunmore. That's his business, isn't it?"

"I believe the colloquial term is 'racket,'" Goode said. "Why, that man is a notorious swindler! Mr. Rand, do you know that only a week before his death, Mr. Fleming instructed me to bring suit against him, and also to secure his indictment on criminal charges of fraud?"

"I didn't know that, but I'm not surprised," Rand answered. "What did he burn Fleming with?"

"Here; I'll show you." Goode rose from his seat and went to a rank of steel filing-cabinets behind the desk. In a moment, he was back, with a large manila envelope under his arm, and a huge pistol in either hand. "Here, Mr. Rand," he chuckled. "We'll just test your firearms knowledge. What do you make of these?"

Rand took the pistols and looked at them. They were wheel locks, apparently sixteenth-century South German; they were a good two feet in over-all length, with ball-pommels the size of oranges, and long steel belt-hooks. The stocks were so covered with ivory inlay that the wood showed only in tiny interstices; the metal-work was lavishly engraved and gold-inlaid. To the trigger-guards were attached tags marked *Fleming vs. Rivers.*

Rand examined each pistol separately, then compared them. Finally, he took a six-inch rule from his pocket and made measurements, first with one edge and then with the other.

"Well, I'm damned," he said, laying them on the desk. "These things are the most complete fakes I ever saw-locks, stocks, barrels and mountings. They're supposed to be late sixteenth-century; I doubt if they were made before 1920. As far as I can see or measure, there isn't the slightest difference between them, except on some of the decorative inlay. The whole job must have been miked in ten-thousandths, and what's more, whoever made them used metric measurements. You'll find pairs of English dueling pistols as early as 1775 that are almost indistinguishable, but in 1575, when these things were supposed to have been made, a gunsmith was working fine when he was working in sixteenth-inches. They just didn't have the measuring instruments, at that time, to do closer work. I won't bother taking these things apart, but if I did, I'd bet all Wall Street to Junior's piggy-bank that I'd find that the screws were machine-threaded and the working-parts interchanged. I've heard about fakes like these," —he named a famous, recently liquidated West Coast collection —"but I'd never hoped to see an example like this."

Goode gave a hacking chuckle. "You'll do as an arms-expert, Mr. Rand," he said. "And you'd win the piggy-bank. It seems that after Mr. Fleming bought them, he took them apart, and found, just as you say, that the screw-threads had been machine-cut, and that the working-parts were interchangeable from one pistol to the other. There were a lot of papers accompanying them —I have them here-purporting to show that they had been sold by some Austrian nobleman, an anti-Nazi refugee, in whose family they had been since the reign of Maximilian II. They are, of course, fabrications. I looked up the family in the *Almanach de Gotha*; it simply never existed. At first, Mr. Fleming had been inclined to take the view that Rivers had been equally victimized with himself. However, when Rivers refused to take back the pistols and refund the purchase price, he altered his opinion. He placed them in my hands, instructing me to bring suit and also start criminal action; he was in a fearful rage about it, and swore that he'd drive Rivers out of business. However, before I could start action, Mr. Fleming was killed in that accident, and as he was the sole witness to the fact of the sale, and as none of the heirs was interested, I did nothing about it. In fact, I advised them that action against Rivers would cost the estate more than they could hope to recover in damages." He picked up one of the pistols and examined it. "Now, I don't know what to do about these."

"Take them home and hang them over the mantel," Rand advised. "If I'm going to have anything to do with selling the collection, I don't want anything to do with them."

Goode was peering at the ivory inlay on the underbelly of the stock.

"They are beautiful, and I don't care when they were made," he said. "I think, if nobody else wants them, I'll do just that.... Now, Mr. Rand, what had you intended doing about the collection?"

"Well, that's what I came to see you about, Mr. Goode. As I understand it, it is you who are officially responsible for selling the collection, and the proceeds would be turned over to you for distribution to Mrs. Fleming, Mrs. Dunmore and Mrs. Varcek. Is that correct?"

"Yes. The collection, although in the physical possession of Mrs. Fleming, is still an undistributed asset."

"I thought so." Rand got out Gladys Fleming's letter of authorization and handed it to Goode. "As you'll see by that, I was retained by, and only by, Mrs. Fleming," he said. "I am assuming that her interests are identical with those of the other heirs, but I realize that this is true only to a very limited extent. It's my understanding that relations between the three ladies are not the most pleasant."

Goode produced a short, croaking laugh. "Now there's a cautious understatement," he commented. "Mr. Rand, I feel that you should know that all three hate each other poisonously."

"That was rather my impression. Now, I expect some trouble, from Mrs. Dunmore and/or Mrs. Varcek, either or both of whom are sure to accuse me of having been brought into this by Mrs. Fleming to help her defraud the others. That, of course, is not the case; they will all profit equally by my participation in this. But I'm going to have trouble convincing them of that."

"Yes. You will," Goode agreed. "Would you rather carry my authorization than Mrs. Fleming's?"

"Yes, indeed, Mr. Goode. To tell the truth, that was why I came here, for one reason. You will not be obligated in any way by authorizing me to act as your agent —I'm getting my fee from Mrs. Fleming-but I would be obligated to represent her only as far as her interests did not improperly conflict with those of the other heirs, and that's what I want made clear."

Goode favored the detective with a saurian smile. "You're not a lawyer, too, Mr. Rand?" he asked.

"Well, I am a member of the Bar in the State of Mississippi, though I never practiced," Rand admitted. "Instead of opening a law-office, I went into the F.B.I., in 1935, and then opened a private agency a couple of years later. But if I had to, which God forbid, I could go home tomorrow and hang out my shingle."

"You seem to have had quite an eventful career," Goode remarked, with a queer combination of envy and disapproval. "I understand that, until recently, you were an officer in the Army

Intelligence, too....I'll have your authorization to act for me made out immediately; to list and appraise the collection, and to negotiate with prospective purchasers. And by the way," he continued, "did I understand you to say that you had heard some of these silly rumors to the effect that Lane Fleming had committed suicide?"

"Oh, that's what's always heard, under the circumstances," Rand shrugged. "A certain type of sensation-loving mind..."

"Mr. Rand, there is not one scintilla of truth in any of these scurrilous stories!" Goode declared, pumping up a fine show of indignation. "The Premix Company is in the best possible financial condition; a glance at its books, or at its last financial statement, would show that. I ought to know, I'm chairman of the board of directors. Just because there was some talk of retrenchment, shortly before Mr. Fleming's death..."

"Oh, no responsible person pays any attention to that sort of talk," Rand comforted him. "My armed-guard and armored-car service brings me into contact with a lot of the local financial crowd. None of them is taking these rumors seriously."

"Well, of course, nobody wants the responsibility of starting a panic, even a minor one, but people are talking, and it's hurting Premix on the market," Goode gloomed. "And now, people will hear of Mrs. Fleming's having retained you, and will assume, just as I did at first, that you are making some kind of an investigation. I hope you will make a prompt denial, if you hear any talk like that." He pressed a button on his desk. "And now, I'll get a letter of authorization made out for you, Mr. Rand..."

Chapter 4

Stephen Gresham was in his early sixties, but he could have still worn his World War I uniform without anything giving at the seams, and buckled the old Sam Browne at the same hole. As Rand entered, he rose from behind his desk and advanced, smiling cordially.

"Why, hello, Jeff!" he greeted the detective, grasping his hand heartily. "You haven't been around for months. What have you been doing, and why don't you come out to Rosemont to see us? Dot and Irene were wondering what had become of you."

"I'm afraid I've been neglecting too many of my old friends lately," Rand admitted, sitting down and getting his pipe out. "Been busy as the devil. Fact is, it was business that finally brought me around here. I understand that you and some others are forming a pool to buy the Lane Fleming collection."

"Yes!" Gresham became enthusiastic. "Want in on it? I'm sure the others would be glad to have you in with us. We're going to need all the money we can scrape together, with this damned Rivers bidding against us."

"I'm afraid you will, at that, Stephen," Rand told him. "And not necessarily on account of Rivers. You see, the Fleming estate has just employed me to expertize the collection and handle the sale for them." Rand got his pipe lit and drawing properly. "I hate doing this to you, but you know how it is."

"Oh, of course. I should have known they'd get somebody like you in to sell the collection for them. Humphrey Goode isn't competent to handle that. What we were all afraid of was a public auction at some sales-gallery."

Rand shook his head. "Worst thing they could do; a collection like that would go for peanuts at auction. Remember the big sales in the twenties?...Why, here; I'm going to be in Rosemont, staying at the Fleming place, working on the collection, for the next week or so. I suppose your crowd wouldn't want to make an offer until I have everything listed, but I'd like to talk to your associates, in a group, as soon as possible."

"Well, we all know pretty much what's in the collection," Gresham said. "We were neighbors of his, and collectors are a gregarious lot. But we aren't anxious to make any premature offers.

We don't want to offer more than we have to, and at the same time, we don't want to underbid and see the collection sold elsewhere."

"No, of course not." Rand thought for a moment. "Tell you what; I'll give you and your friends the best break I can in fairness to my clients. I'm not obliged to call for sealed bids, or anything like that, so when I've heard from everybody, I'll give you a chance to bid against the highest offer in hand. If you want to top it, you can have the collection for any kind of an overbid that doesn't look too suspiciously nominal."

"Why, Jeff, I appreciate that," Gresham said. "I think you're entirely within your rights, but naturally, we won't mention this outside. I can imagine Arnold Rivers, for instance, taking a very righteous view of such an arrangement."

"Yes, so can I. Of course, if he'd call me a crook, I'd take that as a compliment," Rand said. "I wonder if I could meet your group, say tomorrow evening? I want to be in a position to assure the Fleming family and Humphrey Goode that you're all serious and responsible."

"Well, we're very serious about it," Gresham replied, "and I think we're all responsible. You can look us up, if you wish. Besides myself, there is Philip Cabot, of Cabot, Joyner & Teale, whom you know, and Adam Trehearne, who's worth about a half-million in industrial shares, and Colin MacBride, who's vice president in charge of construction and maintenance for Edison-Public Power & Light, at about twenty thousand a year, and Pierre Jarrett and his fiancée, Karen Lawrence. Pierre was a Marine captain, invalided home after being wounded on Peleliu; he writes science-fiction for the pulps. Karen has a little general-antique business in Rosemont. They intend using their share of the collection, plus such culls and duplicates as the rest of us can consign to them, to go into the arms business, with a general-antique sideline, which Karen can manage while Pierre's writing.... Tell you what; I'll call a meeting at my place tomorrow evening, say at eight thirty. That suit you?"

That, Rand agreed, would be all right. Gresham asked him how recently he had seen the Fleming collection.

"About two years ago; right after I got back from Germany. You remember, we went there together, one evening in March."

"Yes, that's right. We didn't have time to see everything," Gresham said. "My God, Jeff! Twenty-five wheel locks! Ten snaphaunces. And every imaginable kind of flintlock-over a hundred U.S. Martials, including the 1818 Springfield, all the S. North types, a couple of Virginia Manufactory models, and-he got this since the last time you saw the collection—a real Rappahannock Forge flintlock. And about a hundred and fifty Colts, all models and most variants. Remember that big Whitneyville Walker, in original condition? He got that one in 1924, at the Fred Hines sale, at the old Walpole Galleries. And seven Paterson Colts, including a couple of cased sets. And anything else you can think of. A Hall flintlock breech-loader; an Elisha Collier flintlock revolver; a pair of Forsythe detonator-lock pistols.... Oh, that's a collection to end collections."

"By the way, Humphrey Goode showed me a pair of big ball-butt wheel locks, all covered with ivory inlay," Rand mentioned.

Gresham laughed heartily. "Aren't they the damnedest ever seen, though?" he asked. "Made in Germany, about 1870 or '80, about the time arms-collecting was just getting out of the family-heirloom stage, wouldn't you say?"

"I'd say made in Japan, about 1920," Rand replied. "Remember, there were a couple of small human figures on each pistol, a knight and a huntsman? Did you notice that they had slant eyes?" He stopped laughing, and looked at Gresham seriously. "Just how much more of that sort of thing do you think I'm going to have to weed out of the collection, before I can offer it for sale?" he asked.

Gresham shook his head. "They're all. They were Lane Fleming's one false step. Ordinarily, Lane was a careful buyer; he must have let himself get hypnotized by all that ivory and gold, and all that documentation on crested notepaper. You know, Fleming's death was an undeserved stroke of luck for Arnold Rivers. If he hadn't been killed just when he was, he'd have run Rivers out of the old-arms business."

"I notice that Rivers isn't advertising in the *American Rifleman* any more," Rand observed.

"No; the National Rifle Association stopped his ad, and lifted his membership card for good measure," Gresham said. "Rivers sold a rifle to a collector down in Virginia, about three years ago, while you were still occupying Germany. A fine, early flintlock Kentuck, that had been made out of a fine, late percussion Kentuck by sawing off the breech-end of the barrel, rethreading it for the breech-plug, drilling a new vent, and fitting the lock with a flint hammer and a pan-and-frizzen assembly, and shortening the fore-end to fit. Rivers has a gunsmith over at Kingsville, one Elmer Umholtz, who does all his fraudulent conversions for him. I have an example of Umholtz's craftsmanship, myself. The collector who bought this spurious flintlock spotted what had been done, and squawked to the Rifle Association, and to the postal authorities."

"Rivers claimed, I suppose, that he had gotten it from a family that had owned it ever since it was made, and showed letters signed 'D. Boone' and 'Davy Crockett' to prove it?"

"No, he claimed to have gotten it in trade from some wayfaring collector," Gresham replied. "He convinced Uncle Whiskers, but the N.R.A. took a slightly dimmer view of the transaction, so Rivers doesn't advertise in the *Rifleman* any more."

"Wasn't there some talk about Whitneyville Walker Colts that had been made out of 1848 Model Colt Dragoons?" Rand asked.

"Oh Lord, yes! This fellow Umholtz was practically turning them out on an assembly-line, for a while. Rivers must have sold about ten of them. You know, Umholtz is a really fine gunsmith; I had him build a deer-rifle for Dot, a couple of years ago-Mexican-Mauser action, Johnson barrel, chambered for .300 Savage; Umholtz made the stock and fitted a scope-sight — it's a beautiful little rifle. I hate to see him prostitute his talents the way he does by making these fake antiques for Rivers. You know, he made one of these mythical heavy .44 six-shooters of the sort Colt was supposed to have turned out at Paterson in 1839 for Colonel Walker's Texas Rangers-you know, the model he couldn't find any of in 1847, when he made the real Walker Colt. That story you find in Sawyer's book."

"Why, that story's been absolutely disproved," Rand said. "There never was any such revolver."

"Not till Umholtz made one," Gresham replied. "Rivers sold it to," —he named a moving-picture bigshot —"for twenty-five hundred dollars. His story was that he picked it up in Mexico, in 1938; traded a .38-special to some halfbreed goat-herder for it."

"This fellow who bought it, now; did he see Belden and Haven's Colt book, when it came out in 1940?"

"Yes, and he was plenty burned up, but what could he do? Rivers was dug in behind this innocent-purchase-and-sale-in-good-faith Maginot Line of his. You know, that bastard took me, once, just one-tenth as badly, with a fake U.S. North & Cheney Navy flintlock 1799 Model that had been made out of a French 1777 Model." The lawyer muttered obscenely.

"Why didn't you sue hell out of him?" Rand asked. "You might not have gotten anything, but you'd have given him a lot of dirty publicity. That's all Fleming was expecting to do about those wheel locks."

"I'm not Fleming. He could afford litigation like that; I can't. I want my money, and if I don't get it in cash, I'm going to beat it out of that dirty little swindler's hide," Gresham replied, an ugly look appearing on his face.

"I wouldn't blame you. You could find plenty of other collectors who'd hold your coat while you were doing it," Rand told him. Then he inquired, idly: "What sort of a pistol was it that Lane Fleming is supposed to have shot himself with?"

Gresham frowned. "I really don't know; I didn't see it. It's supposed to have been a Confederate Leech & Rigdon .36; you know, one of those imitation Colt Navy Models that were made in the South during the Civil War."

Rand nodded. He was familiar with the type.

"The story is that Fleming found it hanging back of the counter at some roadside lunch-stand, along with a lot of other old pistols, and talked the proprietor into letting it go for a few dollars," Gresham continued. "It was supposed to have been loaded at the time, and went off while Fleming was working on it, at home." He shook his head. "I can't believe that, Jeff. Lane Fleming would know a loaded revolver when he saw one. I believe he deliberately shot himself, and the family faked the accident and fixed the authorities. The police never made any investigation; it was handled by the coroner alone. And our coroner, out in Scott County, is eminently fixable, if you go about it right; a pitiful little nonentity with a tremendous inferiority complex."

"But good Lord, why?" Rand demanded. "I never heard of Fleming having any troubles worth killing himself over."

Gresham lowered his voice. "Jeff, I'm not supposed to talk about this, but the fact is that I believe Fleming was about to lose control of the Premix Company," he said. "I have, well, sources of inside information. This is in confidence, so don't quote me, but certain influences were at work, inside the company, toward that end." He inspected the tip of his cigar and knocked off the ash into the tray at his elbow. "Lane Fleming's death is on record as accidental, Jeff. It's been written off as such. It would be a great deal better for all concerned if it were left at that."

Chapter 5

Rand drove slowly through Rosemont, the next day, refreshing his memory of the place. It was one of the many commuters' villages strung out for fifty miles along the railroad lines radiating from New Belfast, and depended for its support upon a population scattered over a five-mile radius at estates and country homes. Obviously a planned community, it was dominated by a gray-walled, green-roofed railroad station which stood on its passenger-platform like a captain in front of four platoons of gray-walled, green-roofed houses and stores aligned along as many converging roads. There was a post office, uniform with the rest of the buildings; an excessive quantity of aluminum trimming dated it somewhere in the middle Andrew W. Mellon period. There were four gas stations, a movie theater, and a Woolworth store with a red front that made it look like some painted hussy who had wandered into a Quaker Meeting.

Over the door of one of the smaller stores, Rand saw a black-lettered white sign: *Antiques*. There was a smoke-gray Plymouth coupé parked in front of it.

Instead of turning onto the road to the Fleming estate, he continued along Route 19 for a mile or so beyond the village, until he came to a red brick pseudo-Colonial house on the right. He pulled to the side of the road and got out, turning up the collar of his trench coat. The air was raw and damp, doubly unpleasant after the recent unseasonable warmth. An apathetically persistent rain sogged the seedling-dotted old fields on either side, and the pine-woods beyond, and a high ceiling of unbroken dirty gray gave no promise of clearing. The mournful hoot of a distant locomotive whistle was the only sound to pierce the silence. For a moment, Rand stood with his back to the car, looking at the gallows-like sign that proclaimed this to be the business-place of Arnold Rivers, Fine Antique and Modern Firearms for the Discriminating Collector.

The house faced the road with a long side; at the left, a porch formed a continuation under a deck roof, and on the right, an ell had been built at right angles, extending thirty feet toward the road. Although connected to the house by a shed roof, which acquired a double pitch and became a gable roof where the ell projected forward, it was, in effect, a separate building, with its own front door and its own door-path. Its floor-level was about four feet lower than that of the parent structure.

A Fibber McGee door-chime clanged as Rand entered. Closing the door behind him, he looked around. The room, some twenty feet wide and fifty long, was lighted by an almost continuous row of casement windows on the right, and another on the left for as far as the ell extended beyond the house. They were set high, a good five feet from lower sill to floor, and there was no ceiling; the sloping roof was supported by bare timber rafters. Racks lined the walls, under the windows, holding long-guns and swords; the pistols and daggers and other small items were displayed on a number of long tables. In the middle of the room, glaring at the front door, was a brass four-pounder on a ship's carriage; a Philippine *latanka*, muzzle tilted upward, stood beside it. Where the ell joined the house under the shed roof, there was a fireplace, and a short flight of steps to a landing and a door out of the dwelling, and some furniture —a davenport, three or four deep chairs facing the fire, a low cocktail-table, a cellarette, and, in the far corner, a big desk.

As Rand went toward the rear, a young man rose from one of the chairs, laid aside a magazine, and advanced to meet him. He didn't exactly harmonize with all the lethal array around him; he would have looked more at home presiding over an establishment devoted to ladies' items. His costume ran to pastel shades, he had large and soulful blue eyes and prettily dimpled cheeks, and his longish blond hair was carefully disordered into a windblown effect.

"Oh, good afternoon," he greeted. "Is there anything in particular you're interested in, or would you like to just look about?"

"Mostly look about," Rand said. "Is Mr. Rivers in?"

"Mr. Rivers is having luncheon. He'll be finished before long, if you care to wait....Have you ever been here before?"

"Not for some time," Rand said. "When I was here last, there was a young fellow named Jordan, or Gordon, or something like that."

"Oh. He was before my time." The present functionary introduced himself as Cecil Gillis. Rand gave his name and shook hands with him. Young Gillis wanted to know if Rand was a collector.

"In a small way. General-pistol collector," Rand told him. "Have you many Colts, now?"

There was a whole table devoted to Colts. No spurious Whitneyville Walkers; after all, a dealer can sell just so many of such top-drawer rarities before the finger of suspicion begins leveling itself in his direction, and Arnold Rivers had long ago passed that point. There were several of the commoner percussion models, however, with lovely, perfect bluing that was considerably darker than that applied at the Colt factory during the 'fifties and 'sixties of the last century. The silver plating on backstraps and trigger-guards was perfect, too, but the naval-battle and stagecoach-holdup engravings on the cylinders were far from clear-in one case, completely obliterated. The cylinder of one 1851 Navy bore serial numbers that looked as though they had been altered to conform to the numbers on other parts of the weapon. Many of the Colts, however, were entirely correct, and all were in reasonably good condition.

Rand saw something that interested him, and picked it up.

"That isn't a real Colt," the exquisite Mr. Gillis told him. "It's a Confederate copy; a Leech & Rigdon."

"So I see. I have a Griswold & Grier, but no Leech & Rigdon."

"The Griswold & Grier; that's the one with the brass frame," Cecil Gillis said. "Surprising how many collectors think all Confederate revolvers had brass frames, because of the Griswold & Grier, and the Spiller & Burr....That's an unusually fine specimen, Mr. Rand. Mr. Rivers got it sometime in late December or early January; from a gentleman in Charleston, I understand. I believe it had been carried during the Civil War by a member of the former owner's family."

Rand looked at the tag tied to the trigger-guard; it was marked, in letter-code, with three different prices. That was characteristic of Arnold Rivers's business methods.

"How much does Mr. Rivers want for this?" he asked, handing the revolver to young Gillis.

The clerk mentally decoded the three prices and vacillated for a moment over them. He had already appraised Rand, from his twenty-dollar Stetson past his Burberry trench coat to his

English hand-sewn shoes, and placed him in the pay-dirt bracket; however, from some remarks Rand had let drop, he decided that this customer knew pistols, and probably knew values.

"Why, that is sixty dollars, Mr. Rand," he said, with the air of one conferring a benefaction. Maybe he was, at that, Rand decided; prices had jumped like the very devil since the war.

"I'll take it." He dug out his billfold and extracted three twenties. "Nice clean condition; clean it up yourself?"

"Why, no. Mr. Rivers got it like this. As I said, it's supposed to have been a family heirloom, but from the way it's been cared for, I would have thought it had been in a collection," the clerk replied. "Shall I wrap it for you?"

"Yes, if you please." Rand followed him to the rear, laying aside his coat and hat. Gillis got some heavy paper out of a closet and packaged it, then hunted through a card-file in the top drawer of the desk, until he found the card he wanted. He made a few notes on it, and was still holding it and the sixty dollars when he rejoined Rand by the fire.

In spite of his effeminate appearance and over-refined manner, the young fellow really knew arms. The conversation passed from Confederate revolvers to the arms of the Civil War in general, and they were discussing the changes in tactics occasioned by the introduction of the revolver and the repeating carbine when the door from the house opened and Arnold Rivers appeared on the landing.

He looked older than when Rand had last seen him. His hair was thinner on top and grayer at the temples. Never particularly robust, he had lost weight, and his face was thinner and more hollow-cheeked. His mouth still had the old curve of supercilious insolence, and he was still smoking with the six-inch carved ivory cigarette-holder which Rand remembered.

He looked his visitor over carefully from the doorway, decided that he was not soliciting magazine subscriptions or selling Fuller brushes, and came down the steps. As he did, he must have recognized Rand; he shifted the cigarette-holder to his left hand and extended his right.

"Mr. Rand, isn't it?" he asked. "I thought I knew you. It's been some years since you've been around here."

"I've been a lot of places in the meantime," Rand said.

"You were here last in October, '41, weren't you?" Rivers thought for a moment. "You bought a Highlander, then. By Alexander Murdoch, of Doune, wasn't it?"

"No; Andrew Strahan, of Edzel," Rand replied.

Rivers snapped his fingers. "That's right! I sold both of those pistols at about the same time; a gentleman in Chicago got the Murdoch. The Strahan had a star-pierced lobe on the hammer. Did you ever get anybody to translate the Gaelic inscription on the barrel?"

"You've a memory like Jim Farley," Rand flattered. "The inscription was the clan slogan of the Camerons; something like: *Sons of the hound, come and get flesh!* I won't attempt the original."

"Mr. Rand just bought 6524, the Leech & Rigdon .36," Gillis interjected, handing Rivers the card and the money. Rivers looked at both, saw how much Rand had been taken for, and nodded.

"A nice item," he faintly praised, as though anything selling for less than a hundred dollars was so much garbage. "Considering the condition in which Confederate arms are usually found, it's really first-rate. I think you'll like it, Mr. Rand."

The telephone rang, Cecil Gillis answered it, listened for a moment, and then said: "For you, Mr. Rivers; long distance from Milwaukee."

Rivers's face lit with the beatific smile of a cat at a promising mouse-hole. "Ah, excuse me, Mr. Rand." He crossed to the desk, picked up the phone and spoke into it. "This is Arnold Rivers," he said, much as Edward Murrow used to say, *This-is London!* The telephone sputtered for a moment. "Ah, yes indeed, Mr. Verral. Quite well, I thank you. And you?...No, it hasn't been sold yet. Do you wish me to ship it to you?...On approval; certainly....Of course it's an original flintlock; I didn't list it as re-altered, did I?...No, not at all; the only replacement is the small spring inside the patchbox....Yes, the rifling is excellent....Of course; I'll ship it at once....Good-by, Mr. Verral."

He hung up and turned to his hireling, fairly licking his chops.

"Cecil, Mr. Verral, in Milwaukee, whose address we have, has just ordered 6288, the F. Zorger flintlock Kentuck. Will you please attend to it?"

"Right away, Mr. Rivers." Gillis went to one of the racks under the windows and selected a long flintlock rifle, carrying it out the door at the rear.

"I issued a list, a few days ago," Rivers told Rand. "When Cecil comes back, I'll have him get you a copy. I've been receiving calls ever since; this is the twelfth long-distance call since Tuesday."

"Business must be good," Rand commented. "I understand you've offered to buy the Lane Fleming collection. For ten thousand dollars."

"Where did you hear that?" Rivers demanded, looking up from the drawer in which he was filing the card on the Leech & Rigdon.

"From Mrs. Fleming." Rand released a puff of pipe smoke and watched it draw downward into the fireplace. "I've been retained to handle the sale of that collection; naturally, I'd know who was offering how much."

Rivers's eyes narrowed. He came around the desk, loading another cigarette into his holder.

"And just why, might I ask, did Mrs. Fleming think it in order to employ a detective in a matter like that?" he wanted to know.

Rand let out more smoke. "She didn't. She employed an arms-expert, a Colonel Jefferson Davis Rand, U.S.A., O.R.C., who is a well-known contributor to the *American Rifleman* and the *Infantry Journal* and *Antiques* and the old *Gun Report*. You've read some of his articles, I believe?"

"Then you're not making an investigation?"

"What in the world is there to investigate?" Rand asked. "I'm just selling a lot of old pistols for the Fleming estate."

"I thought Fred Dunmore was doing that."

"So did Fred. You're both wrong, though. I am." He got out Goode's letter of authorization and handed it to Rivers, who read it through twice before handing it back. "You see anything in that about Fred Dunmore, or any of the other relatives-in-law?" he asked.

"Well, I didn't understand; I'm glad to know what the situation really is." Rivers frowned. "I thought you were making some kind of an investigation, and as I'm the only party making any serious offer to buy those pistols, I wanted to know what there was to investigate."

"Do you consider ten thousand dollars to be a serious offer?" Rand asked. "And aren't you forgetting Stephen Gresham and his friends?"

"Oh, those people!" Rivers scoffed. "Mr. Rand, you certainly don't expect them to be able to handle anything like this, do you?"

"Well, the banks speak well of them," Rand replied. "Some of them have good listings in Dun & Bradstreet's, too."

"Well, so do I," Rivers reported. "I can top any offer that crowd makes. What do you expect to get out of them, anyhow?"

"I haven't talked price with them, yet. A lot more than ten thousand dollars, anyhow."

Rivers forced a laugh. "Now, Mr. Rand! That was just an opening offer. I thought Fred Dunmore was handling the collection." He grimaced. "What do you think it's really worth?"

Rand shrugged. "It probably has a dealer's piece-by-piece list-value of around seventy thousand. I'm not nuts enough to expect anything like that in a lump sum, but please, let's not mention ten thousand dollars in this connection any more. That's on the order of Lawyer Marks bidding seventy-five cents for Uncle Tom; it's only good for laughs."

"Well, how much more than that do you think Gresham and his crowd will offer?"

"I haven't talked price with them, yet," Rand repeated. "I mean to, as soon as I can."

"Well, you get their offer, and I'll top it," Rivers declared. "I'm willing to go as high as twenty-five thousand for that collection; they won't go that high."

Although he just managed not to show it, Rand was really surprised. Even a consciousness of abstracting had not prepared him for the shock of hearing Arnold Rivers raise his own offer to something resembling an acceptable figure. A good case, he reflected, could be made of that for the actuality of miracles.

He rose, picking up his trench coat.

"Well! That's something like it, now," he said. "I'll see you later; I don't know how long it's going to take me to get a list prepared, and circularize the old-arms trade. I should hear from everybody who's interested in a few weeks. You can be sure I'll keep your offer in mind."

He slipped into the coat and put on his hat, and then picked up the package containing the Confederate revolver. Rivers had risen, too; he was watching Rand nervously. When Rand tucked the package under his arm and began drawing on his gloves, Rivers cleared his throat.

"Mr. Rand, I'm dreadfully sorry," he began, "but I'll have to return your money and take back that revolver. It should not have been sold." He got Rand's sixty dollars out of his pocket as though he expected it to catch fire, and held it out.

Rand favored him with a display of pained surprise.

"Why, I can't do that," he replied. "I bought this revolver in good faith, and you accepted payment and were satisfied with the transaction. The sale's been made, now."

Rivers seemed distressed. It was probably the first time he had ever been on the receiving end of that routine, and he didn't like it.

"Now you're being unreasonable, Mr. Rand," he protested. "Look here; I'll give you seventy-five dollars' credit on anything else in the shop. You certainly can't find fault with an offer like that."

"I don't want anything else in the shop; I want this revolver you sold me." Rand gave him a look of supercilious insolence that was at least a two hundred per cent improvement on Rivers at his most insolent. "You know, I'll begin to acquire a poor idea of your business methods before long," he added.

Rivers laughed ruefully. "Well, to tell the truth, I just remembered a customer of mine who specializes in Confederate arms, who would pay me at least eighty for that item," he admitted. "I thought..."

Rand shook his head. "I have a special fondness for Confederate arms, myself. One of my grandfathers was in Mosby's Rangers, and the other was with Barksdale, to say nothing of about a dozen great-uncles and so on."

"Well, you're entirely within your rights, Mr. Rand," Rivers conceded. "I should apologize for trying to renege on a sale, but....Well, I hope to see you again, soon." He followed Rand to the door, shaking hands with him. "Don't forget; I'm willing to pay anything up to twenty-five thousand for the Fleming collection."

Chapter 6

The Fleming butler-Walters, Rand remembered Gladys Fleming having called him-became apologetic upon learning who the visitor was.

"Forgive me, Colonel Rand, but I'm afraid I must put you to some inconvenience, sir," he said. "You see, we have no chauffeur, at present, and I don't drive very well, myself. Would you object to putting up your own car, sir? The garage is under the house, at the rear; just follow the driveway around. I'll go through the house and meet you there for the luggage. I'm dreadfully sorry to put you to the trouble, but...."

"Oh, that's all right," Rand comforted him. "Just as soon do it, myself, now, anyhow. I expect to be in and out with the car while I'm here, and I'd better learn the layout of the garage now."

"You may back in, sir, or drive straight in and back out," the butler told him. "One way's about as easy as the other."

Rand returned to his car, driving around the house. A row of doors opened out of the basement garage; Walters, who must have gone through the house on the double, was waiting for him. Having what amounted to a conditioned reflex to park his car so that he could get it out as fast as possible, he cut over to the right, jockeyed a little, and backed in. There were already two cars in the garage; a big maroon Packard sedan, and a sand-colored Packard station-wagon, standing side by side. Rand put his Lincoln in on the left of the sedan.

"Bags in the luggage-compartment; it isn't locked," he told the butler, making sure that the glove-compartment, where he had placed the Leech & Rigdon revolver, was locked. As he got out, the servant went to the rear of the car and took out the Gladstone and the B-4 bag Rand had brought with him.

"If you don't mind entering the house from the rear, sir, we can go up those steps, there, and through the rear hall," the butler suggested, almost as though he were making some indecent and criminal proposal.

Rand told him to forget the protocol and lead the way. The butler picked up the bags and conducted him up a short flight of concrete steps to a landing and a door opening into a short hall above. An open door from this gave access to a longer hall, stretching to the front of the house, and there was a third door, closed, which probably led to the servants' domain.

Rand followed his guide through the open door and into the long hall, which passed under an arch to extend to the front door. There was a door on either side, about midway to the arch under the front stairway; the one on the right was the dining-room, Walters explained, and the one on the left was the library. He seemed to be still suffering from the ignominy of admitting a house-guest through any but the main portal.

Emerging into the front hallway, he put down the bags, took Rand's hat and coat and laid them on top of the luggage, and then went to an open doorway on the right, standing in it and coughing delicately, before announcing that Colonel Rand was here.

Gladys Fleming, wearing a pale blue frock, came forward as Rand entered the parlor, her hand extended. The two other women in the big parlor remained motionless. They would be the sisters, Geraldine Varcek and Nelda Dunmore. Rand didn't wonder that they resented Gladys so bitterly; economic considerations aside, girls seldom enthuse over a stepmother so near their own age who is so much more beautiful.

"Good afternoon, Colonel Rand," Gladys said. "This is Mrs. Varcek." She indicated a very pale blonde who sat slumped in a deep chair beside a low cocktail-table, a highball in her hand. "And Mrs. Dunmore." She was the brunette with the full bust and hips, in the short black skirt and the tight white sweater, who was standing by the fireplace.

"H'lo." The blonde-Geraldine-smiled shyly at him. She had big blue eyes, and delicately tinted rose-petal lips that seemed to be trying not to laugh at some private joke. She wasn't exactly blotto, but she had evidently laid a good foundation for a first-class jag. After all, it was only two thirty in the afternoon.

The other sister-Nelda-didn't say anything. She merely stood and stared at Rand distrustfully. Rand doubted that she ordinarily gave men the hostile eye. The full, dark-red lips; the lush figure; the way she draped it against the side of the fireplace, to catch the ruddy light on her more interesting curves and bulges-there was a bimbo just made to be leered at, and she probably resented it like hell if she weren't.

Rand gave them a general good-afternoon, then turned to Gladys. "I had a talk with Goode, yesterday afternoon," he said. "I have his authorization to handle all the details. As soon as I get an itemized list, I'll circularize dealers and other possible buyers and ask for offers."

"Is that all?" Nelda demanded angrily of Gladys. "Why Fred's done all that already!"

"Is that correct, Mrs. Fleming?" Rand asked, for the record.

"I told you, yesterday, what's been done," Gladys replied. "Fred has talked to one dealer, Arnold Rivers. There has been no inventory of any sort made."

"Mr. Rivers is offering us ten thousand dollars," Nelda retorted. "I don't see why you had to bring this Colonel What's-his-name into it, at all. You think he can get us a better offer? If you do, you're crazy!"

"Ten thousand dollars, for a collection that ought to sell for five times that, in Macy's basement!" Geraldine hooted. "How much is Rivers slipping Fred, on the side?"

"Oh, go back to your bottle!" Nelda cried. "You're too drunk to know what you're talking about!"

"They tell me Colonel Rand is a detective, too," Geraldine continued. "Maybe he can find out why Fred never talked to Stephen Gresham, or Carl Gwinnett, or anybody else except this Rivers. How much *is* Fred getting out of Rivers, anyhow?"

"My God, Geraldine, shut up!" Nelda howled. Then she decided to take direct notice of Rand's presence. "Colonel Rand, I'm sorry to say that, in her present condition, my sister doesn't know what she's saying. It's bad enough for my stepmother to bring an outsider into what's obviously a family matter, but when my sister begins making these ridiculous accusations..."

"What's ridiculous about them?" Geraldine demanded, dumping another two ounces of whiskey into her glass and freshening it with the siphon. "I think Rivers's offering ten thousand dollars for the collection, and Fred's thinking we'd accept it, are the only ridiculous things about it."

"That's rather what I told Rivers, this afternoon," Rand put in. "He seemed a bit upset about my being brought into this, too, but he finally admitted that he was willing to pay up to twenty-five thousand dollars for the collection, and if he buys it, that's exactly what it's going to cost him."

"*What?*" Nelda fairly screamed. Her hands opened and closed spasmodically: she was using a dark-red nail-tint that made Rand think of blood-dripping talons.

"Mr. Arnold Rivers told me, this afternoon, and I quote: I'm willing to pay up to twenty-five thousand dollars for that collection, unquote," Rand said. "And I can tell you now that twenty-five thousand dollars is just what he will pay for it, unless I can find somebody who's willing to pay more, which is not at all improbable."

"H'ray!" Geraldine waved her glass and toasted Rand with it. "And twenty-five G ain't hay, brother!"

Gladys smiled quickly at Rand, then turned to Nelda. "Now I hope you see why I thought it wise to bring in somebody who knows something about old arms," she said.

Nelda evidently saw; there was apparently nothing stupid about her. "And Fred was going to take a miserable ten thousand dollars!" The way she said it, ten thousand sounded like a fairly generous headwaiter's tip. "Did Rivers actually tell you he'd pay twenty-five?"

Rand gave, as nearly verbatim as possible, his conversation with the dealer. "And he can afford it, too," he finished. "He can make a nice profit on the collection, at that figure."

"My God, do you mean the pistols are worth more than that, even?" she wanted to know, aghast.

"Certainly, if you're a dealer with an established business, and customers all over the country, and want to take five or six years to make your profit," Rand replied. "If you aren't, and want your money in a hurry, no."

"That's why I was against turning the collection over to Gwinnett on a commission basis," Gladys said. "It would take him five years to get everything sold."

Nelda left the fireplace and advanced toward Rand. "Colonel, I owe you an apology," she said. "I had no idea Father's pistols were worth anywhere near that much. I don't suppose Fred did, either." She frowned. Wait till she gets Fred alone, Rand thought; I'd hate to be in his spot.... "You say you're acting on Humphrey Goode's authority?"

"That's right. I'll negotiate the sale, but the money will be paid directly to him, for distribution according to the terms of your father's will." Rand got out Goode's letter and handed it to Nelda.

She read it carefully. "I see." She seemed greatly relieved; she was looking at Rand, now, as she was accustomed to look at men, particularly handsome six-footers who were broad across the shoulders and narrow at the hips and resembled King Charles II. She was probably wondering if Rand was equal to Old Rowley in another important respect. "I didn't understand ...I thought...." A dirty look, aimed at Gladys, explained what she had thought. Then her glance fell on the bottle and siphon on the table beside Geraldine's chair, and she changed the subject by inquiring if Colonel Rand mightn't like a drink.

"Well, let's go up to the gunroom," Gladys suggested. "We can have our drink up there, while Colonel Rand's looking at the pistols.... Coming with us, Geraldine?"

Geraldine rose, not too steadily, her glass still in her hand, and took Rand's left arm. Gladys, seeing Nelda moving in on the detective's right, took his other arm. Nelda was barely successful in suppressing a look of murderous anger. The double doorway into the hall was just wide enough for Rand and his two flankers to pass through; Nelda had to fall in a couple of paces rear of center, and wasn't able to come up into line until they were in the hall upstairs.

"There's the gunroom." Gladys pointed. "And that's your room, over there." As she spoke, Walters came out of the doorway she had indicated.

"Your bags are unpacked, sir," he reported. Then he told Rand where he would find his things, and where the bath was.

There was a brief discussion of drinks. The butler received his instructions and went down the stairway; Rand broke up the feminine formation around him and ushered the ladies ahead of him into the gunroom.

It was much as he remembered it from his visit of two years before. There was a desk in one corner, and back of it a short workbench and tool-cabinet. There was a long table in the middle of the room, its top covered with green baize, upon which many flat rectangular boxes of hardwood rested-some walnut, some rosewood, some quartered oak. Each would contain a pistol or pair of pistols, with cleaning and loading tools. In the corner farthest from the desk, he saw the head of the spiral stairway from the library below, mentioned by Gladys Fleming. There were ashstands and a couple of cocktail-tables, and a number of chairs, and the old maple cobbler's bench on which Lane Fleming had died. The only books in the room were in a small case over the workbench; they were all arms-books.

Then he looked at the walls. On both ends, and on the long inside wall, the pistols hung, hundreds and hundreds of them, the cream of a lifetime's collecting. Horizontal white-painted boards had been fixed to the walls about four feet from the floor, and similar boards had been placed five feet above them. Between, narrow vertical strips, as wide as a lath but twice as thick, were set. Rows of pistols were hung, the barrels horizontal, on pairs of these strips, with screwhooks at grip and muzzle. There were about a hundred such vertical rows of pistols.

Rand was still looking at them when the butler brought in the drinks; when Gladys told the servant that that would be all, he went out, rather reluctantly, by the spiral stairs to the library.

"Well, what do you think of them, Colonel Rand?" Gladys asked.

Rand tasted his whiskey and looked around. "It's one of the finest collections in the country," he said. "I may even be able to find somebody who'll top Rivers's offer, but don't be disappointed if I don't.... By the way, did anybody help Mr. Fleming keep this stuff clean? The room seems dry, but even so, they'd need an occasional wiping-off."

"Oh, Walters was always in here, going over the pistols," Nelda said. "He's been in here every day, lately."

"I wonder if you could spare him to help me a little? I'll need somebody who knows his way around here, at first."

"Why, of course," Gladys agreed. "He isn't very busy in the mornings, or in the afternoons till close to dinner-time. Are you going to start work today?"

"I'll have to. I'm going to see Stephen Gresham and his associates this evening, and I'll want to know what I'm talking about."

They spent about fifteen minutes over their drinks, talking about the collection. Rand and Gladys did most of the talking, in spite of Nelda's best efforts to monopolize the conversation. Geraldine, after a few minutes, retired into her private world and only roused herself when her sister and stepmother were about to leave. When they went out, Gladys promised to send Walters up directly; Rand heard her speaking to him at the foot of the main stairway.

Chapter 7

When Walters entered, Rand had his pipe lit and was walking slowly around the room, laying out the work ahead of him. Roughly, the earliest pieces were on the extreme left, on the short north wall of the room, and the most recent ones on the right, at the south end. This was, of course, only relatively true; the pistols seemed to have been classified by type in vertical rows, and chronologically from top to bottom in each row. The collection seemed to consist of a number of intensely specialized small groups, with a large number of pistols of general types added. For instance, about midway on the long east wall, there were some thirty-odd all-metal pistols, from wheel lock to percussion. There was a collection of U.S. Martials, with two rows of the regulation pistols, flintlock and percussion, of foreign governments, placed on the left, and the collection of Colts on the right. After them came the other types of percussion revolvers, and the later metallic-cartridge types.

It was an arrangement which made sense, from the arms student's point of view, and Rand decided that it would make sense to the dealers and museums to whom he intended sending lists. He would save time by listing them as they were hung on the walls. Then, there were the cases between the windows on the west wall, containing the ammunition collection-examples of every type of fixed-pistol ammunition-and the collection of bullet-molds and powder flasks and wheel lock spanners and assorted cleaning and loading accessories. All that stuff would have to be listed, too.

"I beg your pardon, sir," Walters broke in, behind him. "Mrs. Fleming said that you wanted me."

"Oh, yes." Rand turned. "Is this the whole thing? What's on the walls, here?"

"Yes, sir. There is also a wall-case containing a number of modern pistols and revolvers, and several rifles and shotguns, in the room formerly occupied by Mr. Fleming, but they are not part of the collection, and they are now the personal property of Mrs. Fleming. I understand that she intends selling at least some of them, on her own account. Then, there is a quantity of ammunition and ammunition-components in that closet under the workbench-cartridges, primed cartridge-shells, black and smokeless powder, cartridge-primers, percussion caps-but they are not part of the collection, either. I believe Mrs. Fleming wants to sell most of that, too."

"Well, I'll talk to her about it. I may want to buy some of the ammunition for myself," Rand said. "So I only need to bother with what's on the walls, in this room?...By the way, did Mr. Fleming keep any sort of record of his collection? A book, or a card-index, or anything like that?"

"Why no, sir." Walters was positive. Then he hedged. "If he did, I never saw or heard of anything of the sort. Mr. Fleming knew everything in this room. I've seen him, downstairs, when somebody would ask him about something, close his eyes as though trying to visualize and then give a perfect description of any pistol in the collection. Or else, he could enumerate all the pistols of a certain type; say, all the Philadelphia Deringers, or all the Allen pepperboxes, or all the rim-fire Smith & Wesson tip-back types. He had a remarkable memory for his pistols, although it was not out of the ordinary otherwise, sir."

Rand nodded. Any collector-at least, any collector who was a serious arms-student —could do that, particularly if he were a good visualizer and kept his stuff in some systematic order. At the moment, he could have named and described any or all of his own modest collection of two hundred-odd pistols and revolvers.

"I was hoping he'd kept a record," he said. "A great many collectors do, and it would have helped me quite a bit." He made up his mind to compile such a record, himself, when he got back to New Belfast. It would be a big help to Carter Tipton, when it came time to settle his own estate, and a man on whom the Reaper has scored as many near-misses as on Jeff Rand should begin to think of such things. "And how about writing materials? And is there a typewriter available?"

There was: a cased portable was on the floor beside the workbench. Walters showed him which desk drawers contained paper and other things. There was, Rand noticed, a loaded .38 Colt Detective Special, in the upper right-hand desk drawer.

"And these phones," the butler continued, indicating them. "This one is a private outside phone; it doesn't connect with any other in the house. The other is an extension. It has a buzzer; the outside phone has a regular bell."

Rand thanked him for the information. Then, picking up a note-pad and pencil, he started on the left of the collection, meaning to make a general list and rough approximation of value for use in talking to Gresham's friends that evening. Tomorrow he would begin on the detailed list for use in soliciting outside offers.

Twenty-five wheel locks: four heavy South German dags, two singles and a pair; three Saxon pistols, with sharply dropped grips, a pair and one single; five French and Italian sixteenth-century pistols; a pair of small pocket or sash pistols; a pair of French petronels, and an extremely long seventeenth-century Dutch pistol with an ivory-covered stock and a carved ivory Venus-head for a pommel; eight seventeenth-century French, Italian and Flemish pistols. Rand noted them down, and was about to pass on; then he looked sharply at one of them.

It was nothing out of the ordinary, as wheel locks go; a long Flemish weapon of about 1640, the type used by the Royalist cavalry in the English Civil War. There were two others almost like it, but this one was in simply appalling condition. The metal was rough with rust, and apparently no attempt had been made to clean it in a couple of centuries. There was a piece cracked out of the fore-end, the ramrod was missing, as was the front ramrod-thimble, both the trigger-guard and the butt-cap were loose, and when Rand touched the wheel, it revolved freely if sluggishly, betraying a broken spring or chain.

The vertical row next to it seemed to be all snaphaunces, but among them Rand saw a pair of Turkish flintlocks. Not even good Turkish flintlocks; a pair of the sort of weapons hastily thrown together by native craftsmen or imported ready-made from Belgium for bazaar sale to gullible tourists. Among the fine examples of seventeenth-century Brescian gunmaking above and below it, these things looked like a pair of Dogpatchers in the Waldorf's Starlight Room. Rand contemplated them with distaste, then shrugged. After all, they might have had some sentimental significance; say souvenirs of a pleasantly remembered trip to the Levant.

A few rows farther on, among some exceptionally fine flintlocks, all of which pre-dated 1700, he saw one of those big Belgian navy pistols, *circa* 1800, of the sort once advertised far and wide by a certain old-army-goods dealer for $6.95. This was a particularly repulsive specimen of its breed; grimy with hardened dust and gummed oil, maculated with yellow-surface-rust, the brasswork green with corrosion. It was impossible to shrug off a thing like that. From then on, Rand kept his eyes open for similar incongruities.

They weren't hard to find. There was a big army pistol, of Central European origin and in abominable condition, among a row of fine multi-shot flintlocks. Multi-shot ... Stephen Gresham had mentioned an Elisha Collier flintlock revolver. It wasn't there. It should be hanging about where this post-Napoleonic German thing was.

There was no Hall breech-loader, either, but there was a dilapidated old Ketland. There were many such interlopers among the U.S. Martials: an English ounce-ball cavalry pistol, a French 1777 and a French 1773, a couple more $6.95 bargain-counter specials, a miserable altered S. North 1816. Among the Colts, there was some awful junk, including a big Spanish hinge-frame .44 and a Belgian imitation of a Webley R.I.C. Model. There weren't as many Paterson Colts as Gresham had spoken of, and the Whitneyville Walker was absent. It went on like that; about a dozen of the best pistols which Rand remembered having seen from two years ago were gone, and he spotted at least twenty items which the late Lane Fleming wouldn't have hung in his backyard privy, if he'd had one.

Well, that was to be expected. The way these pistols were arranged, the absence of one from its hooks would have been instantly obvious. So, as the good stuff had moved out, these disreputable changelings had moved in.

"You had rather a shocking experience here, in Mr. Fleming's death," Rand said, over his shoulder, to the butler.

"Oh, yes indeed, sir!" Walters seemed relieved that Rand had broken the silence. "A great loss to all of us, sir. And so unexpected."

He didn't seem averse to talking about it, and went on at some length. His story closely paralleled that of Gladys Fleming.

"Mr. Varcek called the doctor immediately," he said. "Then Mr. Dunmore pointed out that the doctor would be obliged to notify either the coroner or the police, so he called Mr. Goode, the family solicitor. That was about twenty minutes after the shot. Mr. Goode arrived directly; he was here in about ten minutes. I must say, sir, I was glad to see him; to tell the truth, I had been afraid that the authorities might claim that Mr. Fleming had shot himself deliberately."

Somebody else doesn't like the smell of that accident, Rand thought. Aloud, he said:

"Mr. Goode lives nearby, then, I take it?"

"Oh, yes, sir. You can see his house from these windows. Over here, sir."

Rand looked out the window. The rain-soaked lawn of the Fleming residence ended about a hundred yards to the west; beyond it, an orchard was beginning to break into leaf, and beyond the orchard and another lawn stood a half-timbered Tudor-style house, somewhat smaller than the Fleming place. A path led down from it to the orchard, and another led from the orchard to the rear of the house from which Rand looked.

"Must be comforting to know your lawyer's so handy," he commented. "And what do you think, Walters? Are you satisfied, in your own mind, that Mr. Fleming was killed accidentally?"

The servant looked at him seriously. "No, sir; I'm not," he replied. "I've thought about it a great deal, since it happened, sir, and I just can't believe that Mr. Fleming would have that revolver, and start working on it, without knowing that it was loaded. That just isn't possible, if you'll pardon me, sir. And I can't understand how he would have shot himself while removing the charges. The fact is, when I came up here at quarter of seven, to call him for cocktails, he had the whole thing apart and spread out in front of him." The butler thought for a moment. "I believe Mr. Dunmore had something like that in mind when he called Mr. Goode."

"Well, what happened?" Rand asked. "Did the coroner or the doctor choke on calling it an accident?"

"Oh no, sir; there was no trouble of any sort about that. You see, Dr. Yardman called the coroner, as soon as he arrived, but Mr. Goode was here already. He'd come over by that path you saw, to the rear of the house, and in through the garage, which was open, since Mrs. Dunmore was out with the coupé. They all talked it over for a while, and the coroner decided that there would be no need for any inquest, and the doctor wrote out the certificate. That was all there was to it."

Rand looked at the section of pistol-rack devoted to Colts.

"Which one was it?" he asked.

"Oh it's not here, sir," Walters replied. "The coroner took it away with him."

"And hasn't returned it yet? Well, he has no business keeping it. It's part of the collection, and belongs to the estate."

"Yes, sir. If I may say so, I thought it was a bit high-handed of him, taking it away, myself, but it wasn't my place to say anything about it."

"Well, I'll make it mine. If that revolver's what I'm told it is, it's too valuable to let some damned county-seat politician walk off with." A thought occurred to him. "And if I find that he's disposed of it, this county's going to need a new coroner, at least till the present incumbent gets out of jail."

The buzzer of the extension phone went off like an annoyed rattlesnake. Walters scooped it up, spoke into it, listened for a moment, and handed it to Rand.

"For you, sir; Mrs. Fleming."

"Colonel Rand, Carl Gwinnett, the commission-dealer I told you about is here," Gladys told him. "Do you want to talk to him?"

"Why, yes. Do I understand, now, that you and the other ladies want cash, and don't want the collection peddled off piecemeal?...All right, send him up. I'll talk to him."

A few minutes later, a short, compact-looking man of forty-odd entered the gunroom, shifting a brief case to his left hand and extending his right. Rand advanced to meet him and shook hands with him.

"You're Colonel Rand? Enjoyed your articles in the *Rifleman*," he said. "Mrs. Fleming tells me you're handling the sale of the collection for the estate."

"That's right, Mr. Gwinnett. Mrs. Fleming tells me you're interested."

"Yes. Originally, I offered to sell the collection for her on a commission basis, but she didn't seem to care for the idea, and neither do the other ladies. They all want spot cash, in a lump sum."

"Yes. Mrs. Fleming herself might have been interested in your proposition, if she'd been sole owner. You could probably get more for the collection, even after deducting your commission, than I'll be able to, but the collection belongs to the estate, and has to be sold before any division can be made."

"Yes, I see that. Well, how much would the estate, or you, consider a reasonable offer?"

"Sit down, Mr. Gwinnett," Rand invited. "What would you consider a reasonable offer, yourself? We're not asking any specific price; we're just taking bids, as it were."

"Well, how much have you been offered, to date?"

"Well, we haven't heard from everybody. In fact, we haven't put out a list, or solicited offers, except locally, as yet. But one gentleman has expressed a willingness to pay up to twenty-five thousand dollars."

Gwinnett's face expressed polite skepticism. "Colonel Rand!" he protested. "You certainly don't take an offer like that seriously?"

"I think it was made seriously," Rand replied. "A respectable profit could be made on the collection, even at that price."

Gwinnett's eyes shifted over the rows of horizontal barrels on the walls. He was almost visibly wrestling with mental arithmetic, and at the same time trying to keep any hint of his notion of the collection's real value out of his face.

"Well, I doubt if I could raise that much," he said. "Might I ask who's making this offer?"

"You might; I'm afraid I couldn't tell you. You wouldn't want me to publish your own offer broadcast, would you?"

"I think I can guess. If I'm right, don't hold your head in a tub of water till you get it," Gwinnett advised. "Making a big offer to scare away competition is one thing, and paying off on it is another. I've seen that happen before, you know. Fact is, there's one dealer, not far from here, who makes a regular habit of it. He'll make some fantastic offer, and then, when everybody's been bluffed out, he'll start making objections and finding faults, and before long he'll be down to about a quarter of his original price."

"The practice isn't unknown," Rand admitted.

"I'll bet you don't have this twenty-five thousand dollar offer on paper, over a signature," Gwinnett pursued. "Well, here." He opened his brief case and extracted a sheet of paper, handing it to Rand. "You can file this; I'll stand back of it."

Rand looked at the typed and signed statement to the effect that Carl Gwinnett agreed to pay the sum of fifteen thousand dollars for the Lane Fleming pistol-collection, in its entirety, within thirty days of date. That was an average of six dollars a pistol. There had been a time, not too long ago, when a pistol-collection with an average value of six dollars, particularly one as large as the Fleming collection, had been something unusual. For one thing, arms values had increased sharply in the meantime. For another, Lane Fleming had kept his collection clean of the two-dollar items which dragged down so many collectors' average values. Except for the two-dozen-odd mysterious interlopers, there wasn't a pistol in the Fleming collection that wasn't worth at least twenty dollars, and quite a few had values expressible in three figures.

"Well, your offer is duly received and filed, Mr. Gwinnett," Rand told him, folding the sheet and putting it in his pocket. "This is better than an unwitnessed verbal statement that somebody is willing to pay twenty-five thousand. I'll certainly bear you in mind."

"You can show that to Arnold Rivers, if you want to," Gwinnett said. "See how much he's willing to commit himself to, over his signature."

Chapter 8

Pre-dinner cocktails in the library seemed to be a sort of household rite —a self-imposed Truce of Bacchus before the resumption of hostilities in the dining-room. It lasted from six forty-five to seven; everybody sipped Manhattans and kept quiet and listened to the radio newscast. The only new face, to Rand, was Fred Dunmore's.

It was a smooth, pinkly-shaven face, decorated with octagonal rimless glasses; an entirely unremarkable face; the face of the type that used to be labeled "Babbitt." The corner of Rand's mind that handled such data subconsciously filed his description: forty-five to fifty, one-eighty, five feet eight, hair brown and thinning, eyes blue. To this he added the Rotarian button on the lapel, and the small gold globule on the watch chain that testified that, when his age and weight had been considerably less, Dunmore had played on somebody's basketball team. At that time he had probably belonged to the Y.M.C.A., and had thought that Mussolini was doing a splendid job in Italy, that H. L. Mencken ought to be deported to Russia, and that Prohibition was here to stay. At company sales meetings, he probably radiated an aura of synthetic good-fellowship.

As Rand followed Walters down the spiral from the gunroom, the radio commercial was just starting, and Geraldine was asking Dunmore where Anton was.

"Oh, you know," Dunmore told her, impatiently. "He had to go to Louisburg, to that Medical Association meeting; he's reading a paper about the new diabetic ration."

He broke off as Rand approached and was introduced by Gladys, who handed both men their cocktails. Then the news commentator greeted them out of the radio, and everybody absorbed the day's news along with their Manhattans. After the broadcast, they all crossed the hall to the dining-room, where hostilities began almost before the soup was cool enough to taste.

"I don't see why you women had to do this," Dunmore huffed. "Rivers has made us a fair offer. Bringing in an outsider will only give him the impression that we lack confidence in him."

"Well, won't that be just too, too bad!" Geraldine slashed at him. "We mustn't ever hurt dear Mr. Rivers's feelings like that. Let him have the collection for half what it's worth, but never, never let him think we know what a God-damned crook he is!"

Dunmore evidently didn't think that worth dignifying with an answer. Doubtless he expected Nelda to launch a counter-offensive, as a matter of principle. If he did, he was disappointed.

"Well?" Nelda demanded. "What did you want us to do; give the collection away?"

"You don't understand," Dunmore told her. "You've probably heard somebody say what the collection's worth, and you never stopped to realize that it's only worth that to a dealer, who can sell it item by item. You can't expect..."

"We can expect a lot more than ten thousand dollars," Nelda retorted. "In fact, we can expect more than that from Rivers. Colonel Rand was talking to Rivers, this afternoon. Colonel Rand doesn't have any confidence in Rivers at all, and he doesn't care who knows it."

"You were talking to Arnold Rivers, this afternoon, about the collection?" Dunmore demanded of Rand.

"That's right," Rand confirmed. "I told him his ten thousand dollar offer was a joke. Stephen Gresham and his friends can top that out of one pocket. Finally, he got around to admitting that he's willing to pay up to twenty-five thousand."

"I don't believe it!" Dunmore exclaimed angrily. "Rivers told me personally, that neither he nor any other dealer could hope to handle that collection profitably at more than ten thousand."

"And you believed that?" Nelda demanded. "And you're a business man? *My God!*"

"He's probably a good one, as long as he sticks to pancake flour," Geraldine was generous enough to concede. "But about guns, he barely knows which end the bullet comes out at. Ten thousand was probably his idea of what we'd think the pistols were worth."

Dunmore ignored that and turned to Rand. "Did Arnold Rivers actually tell you he'd pay twenty-five thousand dollars for the collection?" he asked. "I can't believe that he'd raise his own offer like that."

"He didn't raise his offer; I threw it out and told him to make one that could be taken seriously." Rand repeated, as closely as he could, his conversation with the arms-dealer. When he had finished, Dunmore was frowning in puzzled displeasure.

"And you think he's actually willing to pay that much?"

"Yes, I do. If he handles them right, he can double his money on the pistols inside of five years. I doubt if you realize how valuable those pistols are. You probably defined Mr. Fleming's collection as a 'hobby' and therefore something not to be taken seriously. And, aside from the actual profit, the prestige of handling this collection would be worth a good deal to Rivers, as advertising. I haven't the least doubt that he can raise the money, or that he's willing to pay it."

Dunmore was still frowning. Maybe he hated being proved wrong in front of the women of the family.

"And you think Gresham and his friends will offer enough to force him to pay the full amount?"

Rand laughed and told him to stop being naïve. "He's done that, himself, and what's more, he knows it. When he told me he was willing to go as high as twenty-five thousand, he fixed the price. Unless somebody offers more, which isn't impossible."

"But maybe he's just bluffing." Dunmore seemed to be following Gwinnett's line of thought. "After he's bluffed Gresham's crowd out, maybe he'll go back to his original ten thousand offer."

"Fred, please stop talking about that ten thousand dollars!" Geraldine interrupted. "How much did Rivers actually tell you he'd pay? Twenty-five thousand, like he did Colonel Rand?"

Dunmore turned in his chair angrily. "Now, look here!" he shouted. "There's a limit to what I've got to take from you...."

He stopped short, as Nelda, beside him, moved slightly, and his words ended in something that sounded like a smothered moan. Rand suspected that she had kicked her husband painfully under the table. Then Walters came in with the meat course, and firing ceased until the butler had retired.

"By the way," Rand tossed into the conversational vacuum that followed his exit, "does anybody know anything about a record Mr. Fleming kept of his collection?"

"Why, no; can't say I do," Dunmore replied promptly, evidently grateful for the change of subject. "You mean, like an inventory?"

"Oh, Fred, you do!" Nelda told him impatiently. "You know that big gray book Father kept all his pistols entered in."

"It was a gray ledger, with a black leather back," Gladys said. "He kept it in the little bookcase over the workbench in the gunroom."

"I'll look for it," Rand said. "Sure it's still there? It would be a big help to me."

The rest of the dinner passed in relative tranquillity. The conversation proceeded in fairly safe channels. Dunmore was anxious to avoid any further reference to the sum of ten thousand dollars; when Gladys induced Rand to talk about his military experiences, he lapsed into preoccupied silence. Several times, Geraldine and Nelda aimed halfhearted feline swipes at one another, more out of custom than present and active rancor. The women seemed to have erected a temporary tri-partite *Entente*-more-or-less-*Cordiale*.

Finally, the meal ended, and the diners drifted away from the table. Rand went to his room for a few moments, then went to the gunroom to get the notes he had made. Fred Dunmore was using the private phone as he entered.

"Well, never mind about that, now," he was saying. "We'll talk about it when I see you.... Yes, of course; so am I.... Well, say about eleven.... Be seeing you."

He hung up and turned to Rand. "More God-damned union trouble," he said. "It's enough to make a saint lose his religion! Our factory-hands are organized in the C.I.O., and our warehouse, sales, and shipping personnel are in the A.F. of L., and if they aren't fighting the company, they're fighting each other. Now they have some damn kind of a jurisdictional dispute.... I don't know what this country's coming to!" He glared angrily through his octagonal glasses for a moment. Then his voice took on an ingratiating note. "Look here, Colonel; I just didn't understand the situation, until you explained it. I hope you aren't taking anything that sister-in-law of mine said seriously. She just blurts out the first thing that comes into her so-called mind; why, only yesterday she was accusing Gladys of bringing you into this to help her gyp the rest of us. And before that..."

"Oh, forget it." Rand dismissed Geraldine with a shrug. "I know she was talking through a highball glass. As far as selling the collection is concerned, you just let Rivers sell you a bill of something you hadn't gotten a good look at. He's a smart operator, and he's crooked as a wagon-load of blacksnakes. Maybe you never realized just how much money Fleming put into this collection; naturally you wouldn't realize how much could be gotten out of it again. A lot of this stuff has been here for quite a while, and antiques of any kind tend to increase in value."

"Well, I want you to know that I'm just as glad as anybody if you can get a better price out of him than I could." Dunmore smiled ruefully. "I guess he's just a better poker player than I am."

"Not necessarily. He could see your hand, and you couldn't see his," Rand told him.

"You going to see Gresham and his friends, this evening?" Dunmore asked. "Well, when you get back, if you find four cars in the garage, counting the station-wagon, lock up after you've put your own car away. If you find only three, then you'll know that Anton Varcek's still out, so leave it open for him. That's the way we do here; last one in locks up."

Chapter 9

Rand found another car, a smoke-gray Plymouth coupé, standing on the left of his Lincoln when he went down to the garage. Running his car outside and down to the highway, he settled down to his regular style of driving —a barely legal fifty m.p.h., punctuated by bursts of absolutely felonious speed whenever he found an unobstructed straightaway. Entering Rosemont, he slowed and went through the underpass at the railroad tracks, speeding again when he was clear of the village. A few minutes later, he was turning into the crushed-limestone drive that led up to the buff-brick Gresham house.

A girl met him at the door, a cute little redhead in a red-striped dress, who gave him a smile that seemed to start on the bridge of her nose and lift her whole face up after it. She held out her hand to him.

"Colonel Rand!" she exclaimed. "I'll bet you don't remember me."

"Sure I do. You're Dot," Rand said. "At least, I think you are; the last time I saw you, you were in pigtails. And you were only about so high." He measured with his hand. "The last time I was here, you were away at school. You must be old enough to vote, by now."

"I will, this fall," she replied. "Come on in; you're the first one here. Daddy hasn't gotten back from town yet. He called and said he'd be delayed till about nine." In the hall she took his hat and coat and guided him toward the parlor on the right.

"Oh, Mother!" she called. "Here's Colonel Rand!"

Rand remembered Irene Gresham, too; an over-age dizzy blonde who was still living in the Flaming Youth era of the twenties. She was an extremely good egg; he liked her very much. After all, insisting upon remaining an F. Scott Fitzgerald character was a harmless and amusing foible, and it was no more than right that somebody should try to keep the bright banner of Jazz Age innocence flying in a grim and sullen world. He accepted a cigarette, shared the flame of his lighter with mother and daughter, and submitted to being gushed over.

"...and, honestly, Jeff, you get handsomer every year," Irene Gresham rattled on. "Dot, doesn't he look just like Clark Gable in *Gone with the Wind*? But then, of course, Jeff really *is* a Southerner, so..."

The doorbell interrupted this slight *non sequitur*. She broke off, rising.

"Sit still, Jeff; I'm just going to see who it is. You know, we're down to only one servant now, and it seems as if it's always her night off, or something. I don't know, honestly, what I'm going to do...."

She hurried out of the room. Voices sounded in the hall; a man's and a girl's.

"That's Pierre and Karen," Dot said. "Let's all go up in the gunroom, and wait for the others there."

They went out to meet the newcomers. The man was a few inches shorter than Rand, with gray eyes that looked startlingly light against the dark brown of his face. He wasn't using a cane, but he walked with a slight limp. Beside him was a slender girl, almost as tall as he was, with dark brown hair and brown eyes. She wore a rust-brown sweater and a brown skirt, and low-heeled walking-shoes.

Irene Gresham went into the introductions, the newcomers shook hands with Rand and were advised that the style of address was "Jeff," rather than "Colonel Rand," and then Dot suggested going up to the gunroom. Irene Gresham said she'd stay downstairs; she'd have to let the others in.

"Have you seen this collection before?" Pierre Jarrett inquired as he and Rand went upstairs together.

"About two years ago," Rand said. "Stephen had just gotten a cased dueling set by Wilkinson, then. From the Far West Hobby Shop, I think."

"Oh, he's gotten a lot of new stuff since then, and sold off about a dozen culls and duplicates," the former Marine said. "I'll show you what's new, till the others come."

They reached the head of the stairs and started down the hall to the gunroom, in the wing that projected out over the garage. Along the way, the girls detached themselves for nose-powdering.

Unlike the room at the Fleming home, Stephen Gresham's gunroom had originally been something else —a nursery, or play-room, or party-room. There were windows on both long sides, which considerably reduced the available wall-space, and the situation wasn't helped any by the fact that the collection was about thirty per cent long-arms. Things were pretty badly crowded; most of the rifles and muskets were in circular barracks-racks, away from the walls.

"Here, this one's new since you were here," Pierre said, picking a long musket from one of the racks and handing it to Rand. "How do you like this one?"

Rand took it and whistled appreciatively. "Real European matchlock; no, I never saw that. Looks like North Italian, say 1575 to about 1600."

"That musket," Pierre informed him, "came over on the *Mayflower*."

"Really, or just a gag?" Rand asked. "It easily could have. The *Mayflower* Company bought their muskets in Holland, from some seventeenth-century forerunner of Bannerman's, and Europe was full of muskets like this then, left over from the wars of the Holy Roman Empire and the French religious wars."

"Yes; I suppose all their muskets were obsolete types for the period," Pierre agreed. "Well, that's a real *Mayflower* arm. Stephen has the documentation for it. It came from the Charles

Winthrop Sawyer collection, and there were only three ownership changes between the last owner and the *Mayflower* Company. Stephen only paid a hundred dollars for it, too."

"That was practically stealing," Rand said. He carried the musket to the light and examined it closely. "Nice condition, too; I wouldn't be afraid to fire this with a full charge, right now." He handed the weapon back. "He didn't lose a thing on that deal."

"I should say not! I'd give him two hundred for it, any time. Even without the history, it's worth that."

"Who buys history, anyhow?" Rand wanted to know. "The fact that it came from the Sawyer collection adds more value to it than this *Mayflower* business. Past ownership by a recognized authority like Sawyer is a real guarantee of quality and authenticity. But history, documented or otherwise-hell, only yesterday I saw a pair of pistols with a wonderful three-hundred-and-fifty-year documented history. Only not a word of it was true; the pistols were made about twenty years ago."

"Those wheel locks Fleming bought from Arnold Rivers?" Pierre asked. "God, wasn't that a crime! I'll bet Rivers bought himself a big drink when Lane Fleming was killed. Fleming was all set to hang Rivers's scalp in his wigwam.... But with Stephen, the history does count for something. As you probably know, he collects arms-types that figured in American history. Well, he can prove that this individual musket was brought over by the Pilgrims, so he can be sure it's an example of the type they used. But he'd sooner have a typical Pilgrim musket that never was within five thousand miles of Plymouth Rock than a non-typical arm brought over as a personal weapon by one of the *Mayflower* Company."

"Oh, none of us are really interested in the individual history of collection weapons," Rand said. "You show me a collection that's full of known-history arms, and I'll show you a collection that's either full of junk or else cost three times what it's worth. And you show me a collector who blows money on history, and nine times out of ten I'll show you a collector who doesn't know guns. I saw one such collection, once; every item had its history neatly written out on a tag and hung onto the trigger-guard. The owner thought that the patent-dates on Colts were model-dates, and the model-dates on French military arms were dates of fabrication."

Pierre wrinkled his nose disgustedly. "God, I hate to see a collection all fouled up with tags hung on things!" he said. "Or stuck over with gummed labels; that's even worse. Once in a while I get something with a label pasted on it, usually on the stock, and after I get it off, there's a job getting the wood under it rubbed up to the same color as the rest of the stock."

"Yes. I picked up a lovely little rifled flintlock pistol, once," Rand said. "American; full-length curly-maple stock; really a Kentucky rifle in pistol form. Whoever had owned it before me had pasted a slip of paper on the underside of the stock, between the trigger-guard and the lower ramrod thimble, with a lot of crap, mostly erroneous, typed on it. It took me six months to remove the last traces of where that thing had been stuck on."

"What do you collect, or don't you specialize?"

"Pistols; I try to get the best possible specimens of the most important types, special emphasis on British arms after 1700 and American arms after 1800. What I'm interested in is the evolution of the pistol. I have a couple of wheel locks, to start with, and three miguelet-locks and an Italian snaphaunce. Then I have a few early flintlocks, and a number of mid-eighteenth-century types, and some late flintlocks and percussion types. And about twenty Colts, and so on through percussion revolvers and early cartridge types to some modern arms, including a few World War II arms."

"I see; about the same idea Lane Fleming had," Pierre said. "I collect personal combat-arms, firearms and edge-weapons. Arms that either influenced fighting techniques, or were developed to meet special combat conditions. From what you say, you're mainly interested in the way firearms were designed and made; I'm interested in the conditions under which they were used. And Adam Trehearne, who'll be here shortly, collects pistols and a few long-arms in wheel lock, proto-flintlock and early flintlock, to 1700. And Philip Cabot collects U.S. Martials, flintlock to automatic, and also enemy and Allied Army weapons from all our wars. And Colin MacBride collects nothing but Colts. Odd how a Scot, who's only been in this country twenty years, should become interested in so distinctively American a type."

"And I collect anything I can sell at a profit, from Chinese matchlocks to tommy-guns," Karen Lawrence interjected, coming into the room with Dot Gresham.

Pierre grinned. "Karen is practically a unique specimen herself; the only general-antique dealer I've ever seen who doesn't hate the sight of a gun-collector."

"That's only because I'm crazy enough to want to marry one," the girl dealer replied. "Of all the miserly, unscrupulous, grasping characters ..." She expressed a doubt that the average gun-collector would pay more than ten cents to see his Lord and Savior riding to hounds on a Bren-carrier. "They don't give a hoot whose grandfather owned what, and if anything's battered up a little, they don't think it looks quaint, they think it looks lousy. And they've never heard of inflation; they think arms ought still to sell for the sort of prices they brought at the old Mark Field sale, back in 1911."

"What were you looking at?" Dot asked Rand, then glanced at the musket in Pierre's hands. "Oh, Priscilla."

Karen laughed. "Dot not only knows everything in the collection; she knows it by name. Dot, show Colonel Rand Hester Prynne."

"Hester coming up," Gresham's daughter said, catching another musket out of the same rack from which Pierre had gotten the matchlock and passing it over to Rand. He grasped the heavy piece, approving of the easy, instinctive way in which the girl had handled it. "Look on the barrel," she told him. "On top, right at the breech."

The gun was a flintlock, or rather, a dog-lock; sure enough, stamped on the breech was the big "A" of the Company of Workmen Armorers of London, the seventeenth-century gun-makers' guild.

"That's right," he nodded. "That's Hester Prynne, all right; the first American girl to make her letter."

There were footsteps in the hall outside, and male voices.

"Adam and Colin," Pierre recognized them before they entered.

Both men were past fifty. Colin MacBride was a six-foot black Highlander; black eyes, black hair, and a black weeping-willow mustache, from under which a stubby pipe jutted. Except when he emptied it of ashes and refilled it, it was a permanent fixture of his weather-beaten face. Trehearne was somewhat shorter, and fair; his sandy mustache, beginning to turn gray at the edges, was clipped to micrometric exactness.

They shook hands with Rand, who set Hester back in her place. Trehearne took the matchlock out of Pierre's hands and looked at it wistfully.

"Some chaps have all the luck," he commented. "What do you think of it, Mr. Rand?" Pierre, who had made the introductions, had respected the detective's present civilian status. "Or don't you collect long-arms?"

"I don't collect them, but I'm interested in anything that'll shoot. That's a good one. Those things are scarce, too."

"Yes. You'll find a hundred wheel locks for every matchlock, and yet there must have been a hundred matchlocks made for every wheel lock."

"Matchlocks were cheap, and wheel locks were expensive," MacBride suggested. He spoke with the faintest trace of Highland accent. "Naturally, they got better care."

"It would take a Scot to think of that," Karen said. "Now, you take a Scot who collects guns, and you have something!"

"That's only part of it," Rand said. "I believe that by the last quarter of the seventeenth century, most of the matchlocks that were lying around had been scrapped, and the barrels used in making flintlocks. Hester Prynne, over there, could easily have started her career as a matchlock. And then, a great many matchlocks went into the West African slave and ivory trade, and were promptly ruined by the natives."

"Yes, and I seem to recall having seen Spanish and French miguelet muskets that looked as though they had been altered directly from matchlock, retaining the original stock and even the original lock-plate," Trehearne added.

"So have I, come to think of it." Rand stole a glance at his wrist-watch. It was nine five; he was wishing Stephen Gresham would put in an appearance.

MacBride and Trehearne joined Pierre and the girls in showing him Gresham's collection; evidently they all knew it almost as well as their own. After a while, Irene Gresham ushered in Philip Cabot. He, too, was past middle age, with prematurely white hair and a thin, scholarly face. According to Hollywood type-casting, he might have been a professor, or a judge, or a Boston Brahmin, but never a stockbroker.

Irene Gresham wanted to know what everybody wanted to drink. Rand wanted Bourbon and plain water; MacBride voted for Jamaica rum; Trehearne and Cabot favored brandy and soda, and Pierre and the girls wanted Bacardi and Coca-Cola.

"And Stephen'll want rye and soda, when he gets here," Irene said. "Come on, girls; let's rustle up the drinks."

Before they returned, Stephen Gresham came in, lighting a cigar. It was just nine twenty-two.

"Well, I see everybody's here," he said. "No; where's Karen?"

Pierre told him. A few minutes later the women returned, carrying bottles and glasses; when the flurry of drink-mixing had subsided, they all sat down.

"Let's get the business over first," Gresham suggested. "I suppose you've gone over the collection already, Jeff?"

"Yes, and first of all, I want to know something. When was the last that any of you saw it?"

Gresham and Pierre had been in Fleming's gunroom just two days before the fatal "accident."

"And can you tell me if the big Whitneyville Colt was still there, then?" Rand asked. "Or the Rappahannock Forge, or the Collier flintlock, or the Hall?"

"Why, of course ... My God, aren't they there now?" Gresham demanded.

Rand shook his head. "And if Fleming still had them two days before he was killed, then somebody's been weeding out the collection since. Doing it very cleverly, too," he added. "You know how that stuff's arranged, and how conspicuous a missing pistol would be. Well, when I was going over the collection, I found about two dozen pieces of the most utter trash, things Lane Fleming wouldn't have allowed in the house, all hanging where some really good item ought to have been." He took a paper from his pocket and read off a list of the dubious items, interpolating comments on the condition, and a list of the real rarities which Gresham had mentioned the day before, which were now missing.

"All that good stuff was there the last time I saw the collection," Gresham said. "What do you say, Pierre?"

"I had the Hall pistol in my hands," Pierre said. "And I remember looking at the Rappahannock Forge."

Trehearne broke in to ask how many English dog-locks there were, and if the snaphaunce Highlander and the big all-steel wheel lock were still there. At the same time, Cabot was inquiring about the Springfield 1818 and the Virginia Manufactory pistols.

"I'll have a complete, itemized list in a few days," Rand said. "In the meantime, I'd like a couple of you to look at the collection and help me decide what's missing. I'm going to try to catch the thief, and then get at the fence through him."

"Think Rivers might have gotten the pistols?" Gresham asked. "He's the crookedest dealer I know of."

"He's the crookedest dealer anybody knows of," Rand amended. "The only thing, he's a little too anxious to buy the collection, for somebody who's just skimmed off the cream."

"Ten thousand dollars isn't much in the way of anxiety," Cabot said. "I'd call that a nominal bid, to avoid suspicion."

"The dope's changed a little on that." Rand brought him up to date. "Rivers's offer is now twenty-five thousand."

There was a stunned hush, followed by a gust of exclamations.

"Guid Lorrd!" The Scots accent fairly curdled on Colin MacBride's tongue. "We canna go over that!"

"I'm afraid not; twenty would be about our limit," Gresham agreed. "And with the best items gone ..." He shrugged.

Pierre and Karen were looking at each other in blank misery; their dream of establishing themselves in the arms business had blown up in their faces.

"Oh, he's talking through his hat!" Cabot declared. "He just hopes we'll lose interest, and then he'll buy what's left of the collection for a song."

"Maybe he knows the collection's been robbed," Trehearne suggested. "That would let him out, later. He'd accuse you or the Fleming estate of holding out the best pieces, and then offer to take what's left for about five thousand."

"Well, that would be presuming that he knows the collection has been robbed," Cabot pointed out. "And the only way he'd know that would be if he, himself, had bought the stolen pistols."

"Well, does anybody need a chaser to swallow that?" Trehearne countered. "I'm bloody sure I don't."

Karen Lawrence shook her head. "No, he'd pay twenty-five thousand for the collection, just as it stands, to keep Pierre and me out of the arms business. This end of the state couldn't support another arms-dealer, and with the reputation he's made for himself, he'd be the one to go under." She stubbed out her cigarette and finished her drink. "If you don't mind, Pierre, I think I'll go home."

"I'm not feeling very festive, myself, right now." The ex-Marine rose and held out his hand to Rand. "Don't get the idea, Jeff, that anybody here holds this against you. You have your clients' interests to look out for."

"Well, if this be treason make the most of it," Rand said, "but I hope Rivers doesn't go through with it. I'd like to see you people get the collection, and I'd hate to see a lot of nice pistols like that get into the hands of a damned swindler like Rivers....Maybe I can catch him with the hot-goods on him, and send him up for about three-to-five."

"Oh, he's too smart for that," Karen despaired. "He can get away with faking, but the dumbest jury in the world would know what receiving stolen goods was, and he knows it."

Dorothy and Irene Gresham accompanied Pierre and Karen downstairs. After they had gone, Gresham tried, not very successfully, to inject more life into the party with another round of drinks. For a while they discussed the personal and commercial iniquities of Arnold Rivers. Trehearne and MacBride, who had come together in the latter's car, left shortly, and half an hour later, Philip Cabot rose and announced that he, too, was leaving.

"You haven't seen my collection since before the war, Jeff," he said. "If you're not sleepy, why don't you stop at my place and see what's new? You're staying at the Flemings'; my house is along your way, about a mile on the other side of the railroad."

They went out and got into their cars. Rand kept Cabot's taillight in sight until the broker swung into his drive and put his car in the garage. Rand parked beside the road, took the Leech & Rigdon out of the glove-box, and got out, slipping the Confederate revolver under his trouser-band. He was pulling down his vest to cover the butt as he went up the walk and joined his friend at the front door.

Cabot's combination library and gunroom was on the first floor. Like Rand's own, his collection was hung on racks over low bookcases on either side of the room. It was strictly a collector's collection, intensely specialized. There were all but a few of the U.S. regulation single-shot pistols, a fair representation of secondary types, most of the revolvers of the Civil War, and all the later revolvers and automatics. In addition, there were British pistols of the Revolution and 1812, Confederate revolvers, a couple of Spanish revolvers of 1898, the Lugers and Mausers and Steyers of the first World War, and the pistols of all our allies, beginning with the French weapons of the Revolution.

"I'm having the devil's own time filling in for this last war," Cabot said. "I have a want-ad running in the *Rifleman*, and I've gotten a few: that Nambu, and that Japanese Model-14, and the Polish Radom, and the Italian Glisenti, and that Tokarev, and, of course, the P-'38 and the Canadian Browning; but it's going to take the devil's own time. I hope nobody starts another war, for a few years, till I can get caught up on the last one."

Rand was looking at the Confederate revolvers. Griswold & Grier, Haiman Brothers, Tucker & Sherrod, Dance Brothers & Park, Spiller & Burr-there it was: Leech & Rigdon. He tapped it on the cylinder with a finger.

"Wasn't it one of those things that killed Lane Fleming?" he asked.

"Leech & Rigdon? So I'm told." Cabot hesitated. "Jeff, I saw that revolver, not four hours before Fleming was shot. Had it in my hands; looked it over carefully." He shook his head. "It absolutely was not loaded. It was empty, and there was rust in the chambers."

"Then how the hell did he get shot?" Rand wanted to know.

"That I couldn't say; I'm only telling you how he didn't get shot. Here, this is how it was. It was a Thursday, and I'd come halfway out from town before I remembered that I hadn't bought a copy of *Time*, so I stopped at Biddle's drugstore, in the village, for one. Just as I was getting into my car, outside, Lane Fleming drove up and saw me. He blew his horn at me, and then waved to me with this revolver in his hand. I went over and looked at it, and he told me he'd found it hanging back of the counter at a barbecue-stand, where the road from Rosemont joins Route 22. There had been some other pistols with it, and I went to see them later, but they were all trash. The Leech & Rigdon had been the only decent thing there, and Fleming had talked it out of this fellow for ten dollars. He was disgustingly gleeful about it, particularly as it was a better specimen than mine."

"Would you know it, if you saw it again?" Rand asked.

"Yes. I remember the serials. I always look at serials on Confederate arms. The highest known serial number for a Leech & Rigdon is 1393; this one was 1234."

Rand pulled the .36 revolver from his pants-leg and gave it a quick glance; the number was 1234. He handed it to Cabot.

"Is this it?" he asked.

Cabot checked the number. "Yes. And I remember this bruise on the left grip; Fleming was saying that he was glad it would be on the inside, so it wouldn't show when he hung it on the wall." He carried the revolver to the desk and held it under the light. "Why, this thing wasn't fired at all!" he exclaimed. "I thought that Fleming might have loaded it, meaning to target it-he had a pistol range back of his house-but the chambers are clean." He sniffed at it. "Hoppe's Number Nine," he said. "And I can see traces of partly dissolved rust, and no traces of fouling. What the devil, Jeff?"

"It probably hasn't been fired since Appomattox," Rand agreed. "Philip, do you think all this didn't-know-it-was-loaded routine might be an elaborate suicide build-up, either before or after the fact?"

"Absolutely not!" There was a trace of impatience in Cabot's voice. "Lane Fleming wasn't the man to commit suicide. I knew him too well ever to believe that."

"I heard a rumor that he was about to lose control of his company," Rand mentioned. "You know how much Premix meant to him."

"That's idiotic!" Cabot's voice was openly scornful, now, and he seemed a little angry that Rand should believe such a story, as though his confidence in his friend's intelligence had been betrayed. "Good Lord, Jeff, where did you ever hear a yarn like that?"

"Quote, usually well-informed sources, unquote."

"Well, they were unusually ill-informed, that time," Cabot replied. "Take my word for it, there's absolutely nothing in it."

"So it wasn't an accident, and it wasn't suicide," Rand considered. "Philip, what is the prognosis on this merger of Premix and National Milling & Packaging, now that Lane Fleming's opposition has been, shall we say, liquidated?"

Cabot's head jerked up; he looked at Rand in shocked surprise.

"My God, you don't think...?" he began. "Jeff, are you investigating Lane Fleming's death?"

"I was retained to sell the collection," Rand stated. "Now, I suppose, I'll have to find out who's been stealing those pistols, and recover them, and jail the thief and the fence. But I was not retained to investigate the death of Lane Fleming. And I do not do work for which I am not paid," he added, with mendacious literalness.

"I see. Well, the merger's going through. It won't be official until the sixteenth of May, when the Premix stockholders meet, but that's just a formality. It's all cut and dried and in the bag now. Better let me pick you up a little Premix; there's still some lying around. You'll make a little less than four-for-one on it."

"I'd had that in mind when I asked you about the merger," Rand said. "I have about two thousand with you, haven't I?" He did a moment's mental arithmetic, then got out his checkbook. "Pick me up about a hundred shares," he told the broker. "I've been meaning to get in on this ever since I heard about it."

"I don't see how you did hear about it," Cabot said. "For obvious reasons, it's being kept pretty well under the hat."

Rand grinned. "Quote, usually well-informed sources, unquote. Not the sources mentioned above."

"Jeff, you know, this damned thing's worrying me," Cabot told him, writing a receipt and exchanging it for Rand's check. "I've been trying to ignore it, but I simply can't. Do you really think Lane Fleming was murdered by somebody who wanted to see this merger consummated and who knew that that was an impossibility as long as Fleming was alive?"

"Philip, I don't know. And furthermore, I don't give a damn," Rand lied. "If somebody wants me to look into it, and pays me my possibly exaggerated idea of what constitutes fair compensation, I will. And I'll probably come up with Fleming's murderer, dead or alive. But until then, it is simply no epidermis off my scrotum. And I advise you to adopt a similar attitude."

They changed the subject, then, to the variety of pistols developed and used by the opposing nations in World War II, and the difficulties ahead of Cabot in assembling even a fairly representative group of them. Rand promised to mail Cabot a duplicate copy of his list of the letter-code symbols used by the Nazis to indicate the factories manufacturing arms for them, as well as copies of some old wartime Intelligence dope on enemy small-arms. At a little past one, he left Cabot's home and returned to the Fleming residence.

There were four cars in the garage. The Packard sedan had not been moved, but the station-wagon was facing in the opposite direction. The gray Plymouth was in the space from which Rand had driven earlier in the evening, and a black Chrysler Imperial had been run in on the left of the Plymouth. He put his own car in on the right of the station-wagon, made sure that the Leech & Rigdon was locked in his glove-box, and closed and locked the garage doors. Then he went up into the house, through the library, and by the spiral stairway to the gunroom.

The garage had been open, he recalled, at the time of Lane Fleming's death. The availability of such an easy means of undetected ingress and egress threw the suspect field wide open. Anybody who knew the habits of the Fleming household could have slipped up to the gunroom, while Varcek was in his lab, Dunmore was in the bathroom, and Gladys and Geraldine were in the parlor. As he crossed the hall to his own room, Rand was thinking of how narrowly Arnold Rivers had escaped a disastrous lawsuit and criminal action by the death of Lane Fleming.

Chapter 10

When Rand came down to breakfast the next morning, he found Gladys, Nelda, and a man whom he decided, by elimination, must be Anton Varcek, already at the table. The latter rose as Rand entered, and bowed jerkily as Gladys verified the guess with an introduction.

He was about Rand's own age and height; he had a smooth-shaven, tight-mouthed face, adorned with bushy eyebrows, each of which was almost as heavy as Rand's mustache. It was a face that seemed tantalizingly familiar, and Rand puzzled for a moment, then nodded mentally. Of course he had seen a face like that hundreds of times, in newsreels and news-photos, and, once in pre-war Berlin, its living double. Rudolf Hess. He wondered how much deeper the resemblance went, and tried not to let it prejudice him.

Nelda greeted him with a trowelful of sweetness and a dash of bedroom-bait. Gladys waved him to a vacant seat at her right and summoned the maid who had been serving breakfast. After Rand had indicated his preference of fruit and found out what else there was to eat, he inquired where the others were.

"Oh, Fred's still dressing; he'll be down in a minute," Nelda told him. "And Geraldine won't; she never eats with her breakfast."

Varcek winced slightly at this, and shifted the subject by inquiring if Rand were a professional antiques-expert.

"No, I'm a lily-pure amateur," Rand told him. "Or was until I took this job. I have a collection of my own, and I'm supposed to be something of an authority. My business is operating a private detective agency."

"But you are here only as an arms-expert?" Varcek inquired. "You are not making any sort of detective investigation?"

"That's right," Rand assured him. "This is practically a paid vacation, for me. First time I ever handled anything like this; it's a real pleasure to be working at something I really enjoy, for a change."

Varcek nodded. "Yes, I can understand that. My own work, for instance. I would continue with my research even if I were independently wealthy and any sort of work were unnecessary."

"Tell Colonel Rand what you're working on now," Nelda urged.

Varcek gave a small mirthless laugh. "Oh, Colonel Rand would be no more interested than I would be in his pistols," he objected, then turned to Rand. "It is a series of experiments having to do with the chemical nature of life," he said. Another perfunctory chuckle. "No, I am not trying to re-create Frankenstein's monster. The fact is, I am working with fruit flies."

"Something about heredity?" Rand wanted to know.

Varcek laughed again, with more amusement. "So! One says: 'Fruit flies,' and immediately another thinks: 'Heredity.' It is practically a standard response. Only, in this case, I am investigating the effect of diet changes. I use fruit flies because of their extreme adaptability. If I find that I am on the right track, I shall work with mice, next."

"Fred Dunmore mentioned a packaged diabetic ration you'd developed," Rand mentioned.

"Oh, yes." Varcek shrugged. "Yes. Something like an Army field-ration, for diabetics to carry when traveling, or wherever proper food may be unobtainable. That is for the company; soon we put it on the market, and make lots of money. But this other, that is my own private work."

Dunmore had come in while Varcek was speaking and had seated himself beside his wife.

"Don't let him kid you, Colonel," he said. "Anton's just as keen about that dollar as the rest of us. I don't know what he's cooking up, up there in the attic, but I'll give ten-to-one we'll be selling it in twenty-five-cent packages inside a year, and selling plenty of them....Oh, and speaking about that dollar; how did you make out with Gresham and his friends?"

"I didn't. They'd expected to pay about twenty thousand for the collection; Rivers's offer has them stopped. And even if they could go over twenty-five, I think Rivers would raise them. He's afraid to let them get the collection; Pierre Jarrett and Karen Lawrence intended using their share of it to go into the old-arms business, in competition with him."

"Uh-huh, that's smart," Dunmore approved. "It's always better to take a small loss stopping competition than to let it get too big for you. You save a damn-sight bigger loss later."

"How soon do you think the pistols will be sold?" Gladys asked.

"Oh, in about a month, at the outside," Rand said, continuing to explain what had to be done first.

"Well, I'm glad of that," Varcek commented. "I never liked those things, and after what happened ... The sooner they can be sold, the better."

Breakfast finally ended, and Varcek and Dunmore left for the Premix plant. Rand debated for a moment the wisdom of speaking to Gladys about the missing pistols, then decided to wait until his suspicions were better verified. After a few minutes in the gunroom, going over Lane Fleming's arms-books on the shelf over the workbench without finding any trace of the book in which he had catalogued his collection, he got his hat and coat, went down to the garage, and took out his car.

It had stopped raining for the time being; the dingy sky showed broken spots like bits of bluing on a badly-rusted piece of steel. As he got out of his car in front of Arnold Rivers's red-brick house, he was wondering just how he was going to go about what he wanted to do. After all...

The door of the shop was unlocked, and opened with a slow clanging of the door-chime, but the interior was dark. All the shades had been pulled, and the lights were out. For a moment Rand stood in the doorway, adjusting his eyes to the darkness within and wondering where everybody was.

Then, in the path of light that fell inward from the open door, he saw two feet in tan shoes, toes up, at the end of tweed-trousered legs, on the floor. An instant later he stepped inside, pulled the door shut after him, and was using his pen-light to find the electric switch.

For a second or so after he snapped it nothing happened, and then the darkness was broken by the flickering of fluorescent tubes. When they finally lit, he saw the shape on the floor, arms outflung, the inverted rifle above it. For a seemingly long time he stood and stared at the grotesquely transfixed body of Arnold Rivers.

The dead man lay on his back, not three feet beyond the radius of the door, in a pool of blood that was almost dried and gave the room a sickly-sweet butchershop odor. Under the back of Rand's hand, Rivers's cheek was cold; his muscles had already begun to stiffen in *rigor mortis*. Rand examined the dead man's wounds. His coat was stained with blood and gashed in several places; driven into his chest by a downward blow, the bayonet of a short German service Mauser pinned him to the floor like a specimen on a naturalist's card. Beside the one in which the weapon remained, there were three stab-wounds in the chest, and the lower part of the face was disfigured by what looked like a butt-blow. Bending over, Rand could see the imprint of the Mauser butt-plate on Rivers's jaw; on the butt-plate itself were traces of blood.

The rifle, a regulation German infantry weapon, the long-familiar *Gewehr '98* in its most recent modification, was a Nazi product, bearing the eagle and encircled swastika of the Third Reich and the code-letters *lza* —the symbol of the Mauserwerke A.G. plant at Karlsruhe. It had doubtless been sold to Rivers by some returned soldier. In a rack beside the door were a number of other bolt-action military rifles —a Krag, a couple of Arisakas, a long German infantry rifle of the first World War, a Greek Mannlicher, a Mexican Mauser, a British short model Lee-Enfield. All had fixed bayonets; between the Lee-Enfield and one of the Arisakas there was a vacancy.

Rivers's carved ivory cigarette-holder was lying beside the body, crushed at the end as though it had been stepped on. A half-smoked cigarette had been in it; it, too, was crushed. There was no evidence of any great struggle, however; the attack which had ended the arms-dealer's life must have come as a complete surprise. He had probably been holding the cigarette-holder in his hand when the butt-blow had been delivered, and had dropped it and flung up his arms instinctively. Thereupon, his assailant had reversed his weapon and driven the bayonet into his chest. The first blow, no doubt, had been fatal-it could have been any of the three stabs in the chest-but the killer had given him two more, probably while he was on the floor. Then, grasping the rifle in both hands, he had stood over his victim and pinned the body to the floor. That last blow could have only been inspired by pure anger and hatred.

Yet, apparently, Rivers had been unaware of his visitor's murderous intentions, even while the rifle was being taken from the rack. Rand strolled back through the shop, looking about. Someone had been here with Rivers for some time; the dealer and another man had sat by the fire, drinking and smoking. On the low table was a fifth of Haig & Haig, a siphon, two glasses, a glass bowl containing water that had evidently melted from ice-cubes, and an ashtray. In the ashtray were a number of River's cigarette butts, all holder-crimped, and a quantity of ash, some of it cigar-ash. There was no cigar-butt, and no band or cellophane wrapper.

The fire on the hearth had burned out and the ashes were cold. They were not all wood-ashes; a considerable amount of paper-no, cardboard-had been burned there also. Poking gently with the point of a sword he took from a rack, Rand discovered that what had been burned had been a number of cards, about six inches by four, one of which had, somehow, managed to escape the flames with nothing more than a charred edge. Improvising tweezers from a pipe-cleaner, he picked this up and looked at it. It had been typewritten:

    4850:

    ENGLISH SCREW-BARREL F/L POCKET PISTOL.   *Queen Anne type, side hammer with pan attached to barrel, steel barrel and frame. Marked: Wilson, Minories, London. Silver masque butt-cap, hallmarked for 1723. 4-1/2" barrel; 9-1/4" O.A.; cal. abt .44. Taken in trade, 3/21/'38, from V. Sparling, for Kentuck #2538, along with 4851, 4852, 4853. App. cost, RLss; Replacement, do. NLss, OSss, LSss.*

To this had been added, in pen:

    Sold, R. Kingsley, St. Louis, Mo., Mail order, 12/20/'42, OSss.

Rand laid the card on the cocktail-table, along with the drinking equipment. At least, he knew what had gone into the fire: Arnold Rivers's card-index purchase and sales record. He doubted very strongly if that would have been burned while its owner was still alive. Going over to the desk, he checked; the drawer from which he had seen Cecil Gillis get the card for the Leech & Rigdon had been cleaned out.

Picking up the phone in an awkward, unnatural manner, he used a pencil from his pocket to dial a number with which he was familiar, a number that meant the same thing on any telephone exchange in the state.

"State Police, Corporal Kavaalen," a voice singsonged out of the receiver.

"My name is Rand," he identified himself. "I am calling from Arnold Rivers's antique-arms shop on Route 19, about a mile and a half east of Rosemont. I am reporting a homicide."

"Yeah, go ahead-Hey! Did you say homicide?" the other voice asked sharply. "Who?"

"Rivers himself. I called at his shop a few minutes ago, found the front door open, and walked in. I found Rivers lying dead on the floor, just inside the door. He had been killed with a Mauser rifle-not shot; clubbed with the butt, and bayoneted. The body is cold, beginning to stiffen; a pool of blood on the floor is almost completely dried."

"That's a good report, mister," the corporal approved. "You stick around; we'll be right along. You haven't touched anything, have you?"

"Not around the body. How long will it take you to get here?"

"About ten minutes. I'll tell Sergeant McKenna right away."

Rand hung up and glanced at his watch. Ten twenty-two; he gave himself seven minutes and went around the room rapidly, looking only at pistols. He saw nothing that might have come from the Fleming collection. Finally, he opened the front door, just as a white State Police car was pulling up at the end of the walk.

Sergeant Ignatius Loyola McKenna-customarily known and addressed as Mick-piled out almost before it had stopped. The driver, a stocky, blue-eyed Finn with a corporal's chevrons, followed him, and two privates got out from behind, dragging after them a box about the size and shape of an Army footlocker. McKenna was halfway up the drive before he recognized Rand. Then he stopped short.

"Well, Jaysus-me-beads!" He turned suddenly to the corporal. "My God, Aarvo; you said his name was Grant!"

"That's what I thought he said." Rand recognized the singsong accent he had heard on the phone. "You know him?"

"Know him?" McKenna stepped aside quickly, to avoid being overrun by the two privates with the equipment-box. He sighed resignedly. "Aarvo, this is the notorious Jefferson Davis Rand. Tri-State Agency, in New Belfast." He gestured toward the Finn. "Corporal Aarvo Kavaalen," he introduced. "And Privates Skinner and Jameson.... Well, where is it?"

"Right inside." Rand stepped backward, gesturing them in. "Careful; it's just inside the doorway."

McKenna and the corporal entered; the two privates set down their box outside and followed. They all drew up in a semicircle around the late Arnold Rivers and looked at him critically.

"Jesus!" Kavaalen pronounced the *J*-sound as though it were *Zh*; he gave all his syllables an equally-accented intonation. "Say, somebody gave him a good job!"

"Somebody's been seeing too many war-movies." McKenna got a cigarette out of his tunic pocket and lit it in Rand's pipe-bowl. "Want to confess now, or do you insist on a third degree with all the trimmings?"

Kavaalen looked wide-eyed at Rand, then at McKenna, and then back at Rand. Rand laughed.

"Now, Mick!" he reproved. "You know I never kill anybody unless I have a clear case of self-defense, and a flock of witnesses to back it up."

McKenna nodded and reassured his corporal. "That's right, Aarvo; when Jeff Rand kills anybody, it's always self-defense. And he doesn't generally make messes like this." He gave the body a brief scrutiny, then turned to Rand. "You looked around, of course; what do you make of it?"

"Last night, sometime," Rand reconstructed, "Rivers had a visitor. A man, who smoked cigars. He and Rivers were on friendly, or at least sociable, terms. They sat back there by the fire for some time, smoking and drinking. The shades were all drawn. I don't know whether that was standard procedure, or because this conference was something clandestine. Finally, Rivers's visitor got up to leave.

"Now, of course, he could have left, and somebody else could have come here later, been admitted, and killed Rivers. That's a possibility," Rand said, "but it's also an assumption without anything to support it. I rather like the idea that the man who sat back there drinking and smoking with Rivers was the killer. If so, Rivers must have gone with him to the door and was about to open it when this fellow picked up that rifle, probably from that rack, over there, and clipped him on the jaw with the butt. Then he gave him the point three times, the second and third probably while Rivers was down. Then he swung it up and slammed down with it, and left it sticking through Rivers and in the floor."

McKenna nodded. "Lights on when you got here?" he asked.

"No; I put them on when I came in. The killer must have turned them off when he left, but the deadlatch on the door wasn't set, and he doesn't seem to have bothered checking on that."

"Think he left right after he killed Rivers?"

Rand shook his head. "No, that was just the first part of it. After he'd finished Rivers, he went back to that desk and got all the cards Rivers used to record his transactions on-an individual card for every item. He destroyed the lot of them, or at least most of them, in the fireplace. Now, I'm only guessing, here, but I think he took out a card or cards in which he had some interest, and then dumped the rest in the fire to prevent anybody from being able to determine which ones he was interested in. I am further guessing that the cards which the killer wanted to suppress were in the 'sold' file. But I am not guessing about the destruction of the record-file; I found the fireplace full of ashes, found one card that had escaped unburned-you can be sure that one wasn't important-and found the drawer where the record-system was kept empty."

"Think he might have stolen something, and covered up by burning the cards?" McKenna asked.

Rand shook his head again. "I was here yesterday; bought a pistol from Rivers. That's how I noticed this card-index system. Of course, I didn't look at everything, while I was here, but I can't see where any quantity of arms have been removed, and Rivers didn't have any single item that was worth a murder. Fact is, no old firearm is. There are only a very few old arms that are worth over a thousand dollars, and most of them are well-known, unique specimens that would be unsaleable because every collector would know where it came from."

"We can check possible thefts with Rivers's clerk, when he gets here," McKenna said. "Now, suppose you show me these things you found, back at the rear ...Aarvo, you and the boys start taking pictures," he told the corporal, then he followed Rand back through the shop.

He tested the temperature of the water in the ice-bowl with his finger. He looked at the ashtray, and bent over and sniffed at each of the two glasses.

"I see one of them's been emptied out," he commented. "Want to bet it hasn't been wiped clean, too?"

"Huh-unh." Rand smiled slightly. "Even the tiny tots wipe off the cookie-jar, after they've raided it," he said.

A flash-bulb lit the front of the shop briefly. Corporal Kavaalen said something to the others. McKenna picked up the card Rand had found by the edges and looked at it.

"What in hell's this all about, Jeff?" he asked.

"Rivers made it out for one of his pistols. An English flintlock pocket-pistol; I can show you one almost like it, up front. He'd gotten it and three others, back in 1938, in trade for a Kentucky rifle. The numbers are reference-numbers; the letters are Rivers's private price-code. Those three at the end are, respectively, what he absolutely had to get for it, what he thought was a reasonable price, and the most he thought the traffic would stand. He sold it in 1942 for his middle price."

There was another flash by the door, then Kavaalen called out:

"Hey, Mick; we got two of the stiffs, now. All right if we pull out the bayonet for a close-up of his chest?"

"Sure. Better chalkline it, first; you'll move things jerking that bayonet out." He turned back to Rand. "You think, then, that maybe some card in that file would have gotten somebody in trouble, and he had to croak Rivers to get it, and then burned the rest of the cards for a cover-up?"

"That's the way it looks to me," Rand agreed. "Just because I can't think of any other possibility, though, doesn't mean that there aren't any others."

"Hey! You think he might have been selling modern arms to criminals, without reporting the sale?" McKenna asked.

"I wouldn't put it past him," Rand considered. "There was very little that I would put past that fellow. But I wouldn't think he'd be stupid enough to carry a record of such sales in his own file, though."

McKenna rubbed the butt of his .38 reflectively; that seemed to be his substitute for head-scratching, as an aid to cerebration.

"You said you were here yesterday, and bought a pistol," he began. "All right; I know about that collection of yours. But why were you back here bright and early this morning? You working on Rivers for somebody? If so, give."

Rand told him what he was working on. "Rivers wants to buy the Fleming collection. That was the reason I saw him yesterday. But the reason I came here, this morning, is that I find that somebody has stolen about two dozen of the best pistols out of the collection since Fleming's death, and tried to cover up by replacing them with some junk that Lane Fleming wouldn't have allowed inside his house. For my money, it's the butler. Now that Fleming's dead, he's the only one in the house who knows enough about arms to know what was worth stealing. He has constant access to the gunroom. I caught him in a lie about a book Fleming kept a record of his collection in, and now the book has vanished. And furthermore, and most important, if he'd been on the level, he would have spotted what was going on, long ago, and squawked about it."

"That's a damn good circumstantial case, Jeff," McKenna nodded. "Nothing you could take to a jury, of course, but mighty good grounds for suspicion.... You think Rivers could have been the fence?"

"He could have been. Whoever was higrading the collection had to have an outlet for his stuff, and he had to have a source of supply for the junk he was infiltrating into the collection as replacements. A crooked dealer is the answer to both, and Arnold Rivers was definitely crooked."

"You know that?" McKenna inquired. "For sure?"

Another flash lit the front of the shop. Rand nodded.

"For damn good and sure. I can show you half a dozen firearms in this shop that have been altered to increase their value. I don't mean legitimate restorations; I mean fraudulent alterations." He went on to tell McKenna about Rivers's expulsion from membership in the National Rifle Association. "And I know that he sold a pair of pistols to Lane Fleming, about a week before Fleming was killed, that were outright fakes. Fleming was going to sue the ears off Rivers about that; the fact is, until this morning, I'd been wondering if that mightn't have been why Fleming had that sour-looking accident. If he'd lived, he'd have run Rivers out of business."

"Hell, I didn't know that!" McKenna seemed worried. "Fleming used to target-shoot with our gang, and he knew too much about gats to pull a Russ Columbo on himself. I didn't like that accident, at the time, but I figured he'd pulled the Dutch, and the family were making out it was an accident. We never were called in; the whole thing was handled through the coroner's office. You really think Fleming could have been bumped?"

"Yes. I think he could have been bumped," Rand understated. "I haven't found any positive proof, but —" He told McKenna about his purchase, from Rivers, of the revolver that had been later identified as the one brought home by Fleming on the day of his death. "I still don't know how Rivers got hold of it," he continued. "Until I walked in here not half an hour ago and found Rivers dead on the floor, I'd had a suspicion that Rivers might have sneaked into the Fleming house, shot Fleming with another revolver, left it in Fleming's hand and carried away the one Fleming had been working on. The motive, of course, would have been to stop a lawsuit that would have put Rivers out of business and, not inconceivably, in jail. But now ..." He looked toward the front of the shop, where another photo-flash glared for an instant. "And don't suggest that Rivers got conscience-stricken and killed himself. Aside from the technical difficulties of pinning himself to the floor after he was dead, that explanation's out. Rivers had no conscience to be stricken with."

"Well, let's skip Fleming, for a minute," McKenna suggested. "You think this butler, at the Fleming place, was robbing the collection. And you say he could've sold the stuff he stole to Rivers. Well, when the family gets you in to work on the collection, Jeeves, or whatever his name is, realizes that you're going to spot what's been going on, and will probably suspect him. He knows you're no ordinary arms-expert; you're an agency dick. So he gets scared. If you catch up with Rivers, Rivers'll talk. So he comes over here, last night, and kills Rivers off before you can get to him. And while Rivers may not keep a record of the stuff he got from Jeeves, or whatever his name is —"

"Walters," Rand supplied.

"Walters, then. While he may not keep a record of what he bought from Walters, the chances are he does keep a record of the stuff Walters got from him, to use for replacements, so the card-file goes into the fire. How's that?"

The flare of another flash-bulb made distorted shadows dance over the walls.

"That would hang together, now," Rand agreed. "Of course, I haven't found anything here, except the revolver I bought yesterday, that came from the Fleming place, but I'll add this: As soon as Rivers found out I was working for the Fleming family, he tried to get that revolver back from me. Offered me seventy-five dollars' worth of credit on anything else in the shop if I'd give it back to him, not twenty minutes after I'd paid him sixty for it."

"See!" McKenna pounced. "Look; suppose you had a lot of hot stuff, in a place like this. You might take a chance on selling something that had gotten mixed in with your legitimate stuff, but would you want to sell it right back to where it had been stolen from?"

"No, I wouldn't. And if I were a butler who'd been robbing a valuable collection, and an agency man moved in and started poking around, I might get in a panic and do something extreme. That all hangs together, too."

While Rand was talking to McKenna, Private Jameson wandered back through the shop.

"Hey, Sarge, is there any way into the house from here?" he asked. "The outside doors are all locked, and I can't raise anybody."

Rand pointed out the flight of steps beside the fireplace. "I saw Rivers come out of the house that way, yesterday," he said.

The State Policeman went up the steps and tried the door; it opened, and he went through.

"Chances are Mrs. Rivers is away," McKenna said. "She's away a lot. They have a colored girl who comes in by the day, but she doesn't generally get here before noon. And the clerk doesn't get here till about the same time."

"You seem to know a lot about this household," Rand said.

"Yeah. We have this place marked up as a bad burglary- and stick-up hazard; we keep an eye on it. Rivers has all these guns, he does a big cash business, he always has a couple of hundred to a thousand on him-it's a wonder somebody hasn't made a try at this place long ago.... Tell you what, Jeff; say you check up on this butler at the Fleming place for us, and we'll check up here and see if we can find any of the stuff that was stolen. We can get together and compare notes. Maybe one or another of us may run across something about that accident of Fleming's, too."

"Suits me. I'll be glad to help you, and I'll be glad for any help you can give me on recovering those pistols. I haven't made any formal report on that, yet, because I'm not sure exactly what's missing, and I don't want any of that kind of publicity while I'm trying to sell the collection. It may be that the two matters are related; there are some points of similarity, which may or may not mean anything. And, of course, I just may find somebody who'll make it worth my time to get interested in this killing, while I'm at it."

McKenna chuckled. "That must hurt hell out of you, Jeff," he said. "A nice classy murder like this, and nobody to pay you to work on it."

"It does," Rand admitted. "I feel like an undertaker watching a man being swallowed by a shark."

"You want to stick around till this clerk of Rivers's gets here?" McKenna asked. "He should be here in about an hour and a half."

"No. I'd just as soon not be seen taking too much of an interest in this right now. Fact is, I'd just as soon not have my name mentioned at all in connection with this. You can charge the discovery of the body up to our old friend, Anonymous Tip, can't you?"

"Sure." McKenna accompanied Rand to the front door, past the white chalked outline that marked the original position of the body. The body itself, with ink-blackened fingertips, lay to one side, out of the way. Corporal Kavaalen was going through the dead man's pockets, and Skinner was working on the rifle with an insufflator.

"Well, we can't say it was robbery, anyhow," Kavaalen said. "He had eight C's in his billfold."

"Migawd, Sarge, is this damn rifle ever lousy with prints," Skinner complained. "A lot of Rivers's, and everybody else's who's been fooling with it around here, and half the *Wehrmacht*."

"Swell, swell!" McKenna enthused. "Maybe we can pass the case off on the War Crimes Commission."

Chapter 11

Mick McKenna had put his finger right on the sore spot. It did hurt Rand like hell; a nice, sensational murder and no money in it for the Tri-State Agency. Obviously, somebody would have to be persuaded to finance an investigation. Preferably some innocent victim of unjust suspicion; somebody who could best clear himself by unmasking the real villain....For "villain," Rand mentally substituted "public benefactor."

He was running over a list of possible suspects as he entered Rosemont. Passing the little antique shop he slowed, backed, read the name "Karen Lawrence" on the window, and then pulled over to the curb and got out. Crossing the sidewalk, he went up the steps to the door, entering to the jangling of a spring-mounted cowbell.

The girl dealer was inside, with a visitor, a sallow-faced, untidy-looking man of indeterminate age who was opening newspaper-wrapped packages on a table-top. Karen greeted Rand by name and military rank; Rand told her he'd just look around till she was through. She tossed him a look of comic reproach, as though she had counted on him to rid her of the man with the packages.

"Now, just you look at this-here, Miss Lawrence," the man was enthusing, undoing another package. "Here's something I know you'll want; I think this-here is real quaint! Just look, now!" He displayed some long, narrow, dark object, holding it out to her. "Ain't this-here an interestin' item, now, Miss Lawrence?"

"*Ooooooh!* What in heaven's name is that thing?" she demanded.

"That-there's a sword. A real African native sword. Look at that scabbard, now; made out of real crocodile-skin. A whole young crocodile, head, feet, an' all. I tell you, Miss Lawrence, that-there item is unique!"

"It's revolting! It's the most repulsive object that's ever been brought into this shop, which is saying quite a lot. Colonel Rand! If you don't have a hangover this morning, will you please come here and look at this thing?"

Rand laid down the Merril carbine he had been examining and walked over beside Karen. The man—whom Rand judged to be some rural free-lance antique-prospector —extended the object of the girl's repugnance. It was an African sword, all right, with a plain iron hilt and cross-guard. The design looked Berber, but the workmanship was low-grade, and probably attributable to some even more barbarous people. The scabbard was what was really surprising, if you liked that kind of surprises. It was an infant crocodile, rather indifferently smoke-cured; the sword simply went in between the creature's jaws and extended the length of the body and into the tail. Either end of a moldy-green leather thong had been fastened to the two front paws for a shoulder-baldric. When new, Rand thought, it must have given its wearer a really distinctive aroma, even for Africa. He drew the blade gingerly, looked at it, and sheathed it with caution.

"East African; Danakil, or Somali, or something like that," he commented. "Be damn good and careful not to scratch yourself on that; if you do, you'll need about a gallon of anti-tetanus shots."

"Y'think it might be poisoned?" the man with the dirty neck and the month-old haircut inquired eagerly. "See, Miss Lawrence? What I told you; a real African native sword. I got that-there from Hen Sourbaw, over at Feltonville; his uncle, the Reverend Sourbaw, that used to preach at Hemlock Gap Church, brung it from Africa, himself, about fifty years ago. He used to be a missionary, in his younger days....I can make you an awful good price on that-there item, Miss Lawrence."

"God forbid!" she exclaimed. "All my customers are heavy drinkers; I wouldn't want to answer for what might happen if some of them saw that thing, suddenly."

"Oh, well.... How about that-there little amethyst bottle, then?"

"Well ...I would give you seven dollars for that," she grudged.

"Y'would? Well, it's yours, then. An' how about them-there salt-cellars, an' that-there knife-box?"

Rand wandered back to examining firearms. Eventually, after buying the knife-box, Karen got rid of the man with the antiques. When he had gone, she found a pack of cigarettes, offered it to Rand and lit one for herself.

"Well, now you see why girls leave home and start antique shops," she said. "Never a dull moment.... Wasn't that sword the awfullest thing you ever saw, though?"

"Well, one of the ten awfullest," Rand conceded. "I just stopped in to give you some good news. You won't need to consider that offer of Arnold Rivers's, any more. He is no longer interested in the Fleming collection."

"He isn't?" An eager, happy light danced up in her eyes. "You saw him again this morning? What did he say?"

"He didn't say anything. He isn't talking any more, either. Fact is, he isn't even breathing any more."

"He.... You mean he's dead?" She was surprised, even shocked. The shock was probably a concession to good taste, but the surprise looked genuine. "When did he die? It must have been very sudden; I saw him a few days ago, and he looked all right. Of course, he's been having trouble with his lungs, but —"

"It was very sudden. Some time last night, some person or persons unknown gave him a butt-and-bayonet job with a German Mauser out of a rack in his shop. A most unpleasantly thorough job. I went to see him this morning, hoping to badger something out of him about those pistols that are missing from the Fleming collection, and found the body. I notified the State Police, and just came from there."

"For God's sake!" The shock was genuine, too, now. "Have the police any idea —?"

"Not the foggiest. If some of the Fleming pistols turn up at his place, I might think that had something to do with it. So far, though, they haven't. I gave the shop a once-over-lightly before the cops arrived, and couldn't find anything."

She tried to take a puff from her cigarette and found that she had broken it in her fingers. She lit a new one from the mangled butt.

"When did it happen?" She tried to make the question sound casual.

"That I couldn't say, either. Around midnight, would be my guess. They might be able to fix a no-earlier time." An idea occurred to him, and he smiled.

"But that's dreadful!" She really meant that. "It's a terrible thing to happen to anybody, being killed like that." She stopped just short of adding: "even Rivers." Instead, she continued: "But I can't say I'm really very sorry he's dead, Colonel."

"Outside of maybe his wife, and the gunsmith who made his fake Walker Colts and North & Cheney flintlocks, who is?" he countered. "Oh, yes; Cecil Gillis. He's about due for induction into the Army of the Unemployed, unless Mrs. Rivers intends carrying on the business."

Karen's eyes widened. "Cecil Gillis!" she exclaimed softly. "I wonder, now, if he has an alibi for last night!"

"Think he might need one?" Rand asked. "Of course I only saw him once, but he didn't strike me as a possible candidate. I can't seem to see young Gillis doing a messy job like this was, or going to all that manual labor when he could have used something neat, like a pistol or a dagger."

"Well, Cecil isn't quite the languishing flower he looks," Karen told him. "He does a lot of swimming, and he's one of the few people around here who can beat me at tennis. And he has a motive. Maybe two motives."

"Such as?" Rand prompted.

"Maybe you think Cecil is a—you know-one of those boys," she euphemized. "Well, he isn't. He takes a perfectly normal, and even slightly wolfish, interest in the female of his species. And while Arnold Rivers may have been a good provider from a financial standpoint, he wasn't quite up to his wife's requirements in another important respect. And Rivers was away a lot, on buying trips and so on, and when he was, nobody ever saw Cecil leave the Rivers place in the evenings. At least, that's the story; personally, I wouldn't know. Of course, where there's smoke, there may be nothing more than somebody with a stogie, but, then, there may be a regular conflagration."

"That would be a perfectly satisfactory motive, under some circumstances," Rand admitted. "And the other?"

"Cecil might have been doing funny things with the books, and Rivers might have caught him."

"That would also be a good enough motive." It would also, Rand thought, furnish an explanation for the burning of Rivers's record-cards. "I'll mention it to Mick McKenna; he's hard up for a good usable suspect. And by the way, the news of this killing will be out before evening, but in the meantime I wish you wouldn't mention it to anybody, or mention that I was in here to tell you about it."

"I won't. I'm glad you told me, though....Do you think there may be a chance that we can get the collection, now?"

"I wouldn't know why not. Rivers's offer was pretty high; there aren't many other dealers who would be able to duplicate it....Well, don't take any Czechoslovakian Stiegel."

He moved his car down the street to the Rosemont Inn, where he went into the combination bar and grill and had a Bourbon-and-water at the bar. Then he ordered lunch, and, while waiting for it, went into a phone-booth and dialed the number of Stephen Gresham's office in New Belfast.

"I'd hoped to catch you before you left for lunch," he said, when the lawyer answered. "There's been a new development in the Fleming business." He had decided to follow the same line as with Karen Lawrence. "You needn't worry about Arnold Rivers's offer, any more."

"Ha! So he backed out?"

"He was shoved out," Rand corrected. "On the sharp end of a Mauser bayonet, sometime last night. I found the body this morning, when I went to see him, and notified the State Police. They call it murder, but of course, they're just prejudiced. I'd call it a nuisance-abatement project."

"Look here, are you kidding?" Gresham demanded.

"I never kid about Those Who Have Passed On," Rand denied piously. Then he recited the already hackneyed description of what had happened to Rivers, with careful attention to all the gruesome details. "So I called copper, directly. Sergeant McKenna's up a stump about it, and looking in all directions for a suspect."

Gresham was silent for a moment, then swore softly.

"My God, Jeff! This is going to raise all kinds of hell!" He was silent for a moment. "Look here, can you see me, at my home, about two thirty this afternoon? I want to talk to you about this."

Rand smiled happily. This looked like what he had been angling for. Maybe Arnold Rivers hadn't died in vain, after all.

"Why, yes; I can make it," he replied.

"Good. See you there, then."

Rand assured him that he would be on hand. When he returned to his table, he found his lunch waiting for him. He sat down and ate with a good appetite. After finishing, he had another drink, and sat sipping it slowly and smoking his pipe; going over the story Gladys Fleming had told him, and the gossip he had gotten from Carter Tipton, and the other statements which had been made to him by different people about the death of Lane Fleming, and the conclusions he had reached about the theft of the pistols, and the killing of Arnold Rivers;

sorting out the inferences from the descriptions, and the descriptive statements of others from the things he himself had observed. When his glass was empty and his pipe burned out, he left a tip beside the ashtray, paid his check and went out.

He had two hours until his meeting with Stephen Gresham; he knew exactly where to spend them. The county seat was a normal twenty minutes' drive from Rosemont, but with the road relatively free from traffic he was able to cut that to fifteen. Parking his car in front of the courthouse, he went inside.

The coroner, one Jason Kirchner, was an inoffensive-looking little fellow with a Caspar Milquetoast mustache and an underslung jaw. He wore an Elks watchcharm, an Odd Fellows ring, and a Knights of Pythias lapel-pin. He looked at Rand's credentials, including the letter Humphrey Goode had given him, with some bewilderment.

"You're working for Mr. Goode?" he asked, rather needlessly. "Yes, I see; handling the sale of Mr. Fleming's pistols, for the estate. Yes. That must be interesting work, Mr. Rand. Now, what can I do for you?"

"Why, I understand you have an item from that collection, here in your office," Rand said. "The pistol with which Mr. Fleming shot himself. Regardless of its unpleasant associations, that pistol is a valuable collector's item, and one of the assets of the estate. If I'm to get full value for the collection, for the heirs, I'll have to have that, to sell with the rest of the weapons."

"Well, now, look here, Mr. Rand," Kirchner started to argue, "that revolver's a dangerous weapon. It's killed one man, already. I don't know as I ought to let it get out, where it might kill somebody else."

Rand estimated that this situation called for a modified version of his hard-boiled act.

"You think you can show cause why that revolver shouldn't be turned over to the Fleming estate?" he demanded. "Well, if I don't get it, right away, Mr. Goode will get a court order for it. You had no right to impound that revolver, in the first place; you removed it from the Fleming home illegally in the second place, since you had no intention of holding any formal inquest, and you're holding it illegally now. A court order might not be all we could get, either," he added menacingly. "Now, if you have any reason to suspect that Mr. Fleming committed suicide ... or was murdered, for instance..."

"Oh, my heavens, no!" Kirchner cried, horrified. "It was an accident, pure and simple; I so certified it. Death by accident, due to inadvertence of the deceased."

"Well, then," Rand said, "you have no right to hold that revolver, and I want it, right now. As Mr. Goode's agent, I'm responsible for that collection, of which the revolver you're holding is a part. That revolver is too valuable an asset to ignore. You certainly realize that."

"Well, I don't have any intention of exceeding my authority, of course," Kirchner disclaimed hastily. "And I certainly wouldn't want to go against Mr. Goode's wishes." Humphrey Goode must pull considerable weight around the courthouse, Rand surmised. "But you realize, that revolver's still loaded...."

"Oh, that's not your worry. I'll draw the charges, or, better, fire them out. It stood one shot, it can stand the other five."

"Well, would you mind if I called Mr. Goode on the phone?"

Rand did, decidedly. However, he shook his head negligently.

"Certainly not; go ahead and call him, by all means."

The coroner went away. In a few minutes he was back, carrying a revolver in both hands. Evidently Goode had given him the green light. He approached, handling the weapon with a caution that would have been excessive for a Mills grenade; after warning Rand again that it was loaded, he laid it gently on his desk.

It was a .36 Colt, one of the 1860 series, with the round barrel and the so-called "creeping" ramming-lever. Somebody had wound a piece of wire around it, back of the hammer and through the loading-aperture in front of the cylinder; as the hammer was down on a fired chamber, there was no way in God's world, short of throwing the thing into a furnace, in which it could be discharged, but Kirchner was shrinking away from it as though it might jump at his throat.

"I put the wire on," the coroner said. "I thought it might be safer that way."

"It'll be a lot safer after I've emptied it into the first claybank, outside town," Rand told him. "Sorry I had to be a little short with you, Mr. Kirchner, but you know how it is. I'm responsible to Mr. Goode for the collection, and this gun's part of it."

"Oh, that's all right; I really shouldn't have taken the attitude I did," Kirchner met him halfway. "After I talked to Mr. Goode, of course, I knew it was all right, but ... You see, I've been bothered a lot about that pistol, lately."

"Yes?" Rand succeeded in being negligent about it.

"Oh my, yes! The newspaper people wanted to take pictures of me holding it, and then, there was an antique-dealer who was here trying to buy it."

"Who was that-Arnold Rivers?"

"Why yes! Do you know him? He has an antique-shop on the other side of Rosemont; he doesn't sell anything but guns and swords and that sort of thing," Kirchner said. "He was here, making inquiries about it, and my clerk showed it to him, and then he started making offers for it-first ten dollars, and then fifteen, and then twenty; he got up as high as sixty dollars. I suppose it's worth a couple of hundred."

It was probably worth about thirty-five. Rand was intrigued by this second instance of an un-Rivers-like willingness to spare no expense to get possession of a .36-caliber percussion revolver.

"Did he have it in his hands?" he asked.

"Oh, yes; he looked it over carefully. I suppose he thought he could get a lot of money for it, because of the accident, and Mr. Fleming being such a prominent man," Kirchner suggested.

Rand allowed himself to be struck by an idea.

"Say, you know, that *would* make it worth more, at that!" he exclaimed. "What do you know! I never thought of that....Look, Mr. Kirchner; I'm supposed to get as much money for these pistols, for the heirs, as I can. How would you like to give me a letter, vouching for this as the pistol Mr. Fleming killed himself with? Put in how you found it in his hand, and mention the serial numbers, so that whoever buys it will know it's the same revolver." He picked up the Colt and showed Kirchner the serials, on the butt, and in front of the trigger-guard. "See, here it is: 2444."

Kirchner would be more than willing to oblige Mr. Goode's agent; he typed out the letter himself, looked twice at the revolver to make sure of the number, took Rand's word for the make, model, and caliber, signed it, and even slammed his seal down on it. Rand thanked him profusely, put the letter in his pocket, and stuck the Colt down his pants-leg.

About two miles from the county seat Rand stopped his car on a deserted stretch of road and got out. Unwinding the wire Kirchner had wrapped around the revolver, he picked up an empty beer-can from the ditch, set it against an embankment, stepped back about thirty feet and began firing. The first shot kicked up dirt a little over the can-Rand never could be sure just how high any percussion Colt was sighted-and the other four hit the can. He carried the revolver back to the car and put it into the glove-box with the Leech & Rigdon.

After starting the car, he snapped on the radio, in time for the two fifteen news-broadcast from the New Belfast station. As he had expected, the murder was out; the daily budget of strikes and Congressional investigations and international turmoil was enlivened by a more or less imaginative account of what had already been christened the "Rosemont Bayonet Murder." Rand resigned himself to the inevitable influx of reporters. Then he swore, as the newscaster continued:

"District Attorney Charles P. Farnsworth, of Scott County, who has taken charge of the investigation, says, and we quote: 'There is strong evidence implicating certain prominent persons, whom we are not, as yet, prepared to name, and if the investigation, now under way and making excellent progress, justifies, they will be apprehended and formally charged. No effort will be spared, and no consideration of personal prominence will be allowed to deter us from clearing up this dastardly crime....' "

Rand swore again, with weary bitterness, wondering how much trouble he was going to have with District Attorney Charles P. Farnsworth, as he pulled to a stop in Stephen Gresham's driveway.

Chapter 12

Gresham must have been waiting inside the door; as soon as Rand came up onto the porch, he opened it, and motioned the detective inside. Beyond a hasty greeting as Rand passed the threshold, he did not speak until they were seated in the gunroom upstairs. Then he came straight to the point.

"Jeff, can you spare the time from this work you're doing at the Flemings' to investigate this Rivers business?" he asked. "And how much would an investigation cost me? It's got to be a blitz job. I'm not interested in getting anybody convicted in court; I just want the case cleared up in a hurry."

"Well —" Rand puffed at the cigar Gresham had given him, watching the ash form on the end. "I don't work by the day, Stephen. I take a lump-sum fee, and, of course, it's to my interest to get a case cleared up as soon as I can. But I can't set any time limit on a job like this. This Rivers killing has more angles than *Nude Descending a Staircase*; I don't know how much work I'll have to do, or even what kind."

"Well, it'll have to be fast," Gresham told him urgently. "Look. I didn't kill Arnold Rivers. I hated his guts, and I think whoever did it ought to get a medal and a testimonial dinner, but I did not kill him. You believe me?"

"I'm inclined to," Rand replied. "In your law practice, you know what a lying client is letting himself in for. As my client, you wouldn't lie to me. You seem to think you may be suspected of purging Rivers. But why? Is there any reason, aside from that homemade North & Cheney he sold you, why anybody would think you'd killed him?"

"Great God, yes!" Gresham exclaimed. "Now look. I'm not worried about being railroaded for this. I didn't do it, and I can beat any case that half-assed ex-ambulance-chaser, Farnsworth, could dream up against me. But I can't afford even to be mentioned in connection with this. You know what that would do to me, in town. I just can't get mixed up in this, at all. I want you to see to it that I don't."

"That sounds like a large order." The ash was growing on Rand's cigar; he took another heavy drag at it. "But why necessarily you? Rivers had plenty of other enemies."

"Yes, but, dammit, they weren't all in his shop, last evening. Just me. And one other. The one who killed him."

"On your way out from town?" Rand inquired.

"Yes. I stopped at his place, about a quarter to nine. I was sore as hell about the hooking he gave me on that North & Cheney, falsely so-called, and I decided to stop and have it out with him. We had words, most of them unpleasant. I told him, for one thing, that Lane Fleming's death hadn't pulled his bacon off the fire, that I was going to start the same sort of action against him on my own account. But that isn't the point. The point is that when I was going in, this la-de-da clerk of his, Cecil Gillis, was coming out. He got into his car and drove away, leaving me alone with Rivers. He'll be the first one the police talk to, and he'll tell them all about it."

"That does put you back of the eight ball." Rand dropped the ash into a tray and looked at it curiously. It looked like the sort of ash he had seen at Rivers's shop, but he couldn't be sure. "But if it can be proved that Rivers was alive after nine twenty, when you got here, you'll be in the clear."

"I don't want to have to clear myself," Gresham insisted. "I don't want anything to do with it, at all. Here; I'll pay you a thousand down, and two more when you have the case completed;

I want you to get the murder cleared up before I can be publicly involved in it. I say publicly, because this damned Gillis has probably involved me with the police already."

"Well, Gillis isn't exactly in a state of pure sanctity, himself," Rand commented. "As a suspect, the smart handicappers are figuring him to run well inside the money. For instance, you know, there have been stories about him and Mrs. Rivers."

Gresham snapped his fingers. "Damned if there haven't, now!" he said. "You talk to Adam Trehearne. He did business with Rivers-there wasn't much in his line Rivers and Umholtz were able to fake-and different times he's gone to Rivers's shop and there'd be nobody around, and then Gillis would come in from the house, smelling of Chanel Number Five. Mrs. Rivers uses Chanel Number Five. Maybe you have something there. If Cecil thought he could marry the business, with Rivers out of the way....You'll take the case, won't you, Jeff?"

"Oh, certainly," Rand assured him. "Now, all they have on you is that there was ill-feeling between you and Rivers about that fake North & Cheney, and that you were in Rivers's shop yesterday evening?"

Rand's new client grimaced. "I wish that were all!" he said. "The worst part of it is the way Rivers was killed. See, back in Kaiser Willie's war, before I was assigned a company of my own, I was regimental bayonet-instruction officer. And after we got to France, I always carried a rifle and bayonet at the front; hell, I must have killed close to a dozen Krauts just the way Rivers was killed. And during Schicklgruber's war, I volunteered as bayonet instructor for the local Home Guard."

"My God!" Rand made a wry face. "There must be close to a hundred people around here who'd know that, and all of them are probably convinced that you killed Rivers, and are expressing that opinion at the top of their voices to all comers. You don't want a detective, you want a magician!" He took another drag at the cigar, and blew smoke through a circular gun-rack beside him. "What sort of a character is this Farnsworth, anyhow?" he asked. "Before the war, I had all the D.A.'s in the state typed and estimated, but since I got back —"

Gresham slandered the county prosecutor's legitimacy. "God-damn headline-hunting little egotist! He's running for re-election this year, too."

"One way, that could be bad. On the other hand, it might be easy to throw a scare into him....Stephen, when you were at Rivers's, were you smoking a cigar?"

Gresham shook his head. "No. I threw my cigar away when I got out of the car, and I didn't light another one till I got home. If you remember, I was lighting it when I came in here."

"Yes; so you were. Well, I don't suppose, in view of the state of relations between you and Rivers, that you had a drink with him, either?"

"I wouldn't drink that guy's liquor if I were dying of snakebite, and he wouldn't offer me a drink if he knew I was," Gresham declared.

"Well, did you notice, back near the fireplace, a low table with a fifth of Haig & Haig Pinch-bottle, and a couple of glasses, and a siphon, and so on, on it?"

"I saw the table. There was an ashtray on it, and a book —I think it was Gluckman's *United States Martial Pistols and Revolvers* —but no bottle, or siphon, or glasses."

"All right, then; it was the killer." Rand explained about the drinks, and the cigar-ashes. He went on to tell about the destruction of Rivers's record-cards.

"I don't get that." Gresham was puzzled. "Unless it was young Gillis, after all. He could have been knocking down on Rivers, and Rivers caught him at it."

"I'd thought of that," Rand admitted. "But I doubt if Rivers would sit down and drink with him, while accusing him of theft. And I can't seem to find anything around Rivers's place that looks as though it might have been stolen from the Fleming collection, either....Oh, and that reminds me: If you have time this afternoon, I wonder if you'd come along with me to the Flemings' and see just what's missing. I'll have to know that, in any case, and there's a good possibility that the thefts from the collection and the killing of Rivers are related."

"Yes, of course," Gresham agreed. "And suppose we take Pierre Jarrett along with us. He knows that collection as well as I do; he'll spot anything I miss. He works at home; I'll call him now. We can pick him up before we go to the Flemings'."

They went into Gresham's bedroom, where there was a phone, and Gresham talked to Pierre Jarrett. It was arranged that he should pick Jarrett up with his car and come to the Flemings', while Rand went there directly.

Then Rand used the phone to call his office in New Belfast. He talked to Dave Ritter, explaining the situation to date.

"I'm going to need some help," he continued. "I want you to come here and get a room at the Rosemont Inn, under your own name. I'll see you there about five thirty. And bring with you a suit of butler's livery, or reasonable facsimile. I believe there will be a vacancy in the Fleming household tomorrow or the next day, and I want you ready to take over. And bring a small gun with you; something you can wear under said livery. That .357 Colt of yours is a little too conspicuous. You'll find a .380 Beretta in the top right-hand drawer of my office desk, with a box of ammunition and a couple of spare clips."

"Right. I'll be at Rosemont Inn at five thirty," Ritter promised. "And say, Tip was in, this morning, with a lot of dope on the Fleming estate. Want me to let you have it now, or shall I give it to you when I see you?"

"You have notes? Bring them along; I'll be seeing you in a couple of hours."

He parted from Gresham, going out and getting in his car. As Gresham got his own car out of the garage and drove off toward Pierre Jarrett's house, Rand started in the opposite direction, toward Rosemont.

About a half-mile from Gresham's he caught an advancing gleam of white on the highway ahead of him and pulled to the side of the road, waiting until the State Police car drew up and stopped. In it were Mick McKenna, Aarvo Kavaalen, and a third man, a Nordic type, in an untidy brown suit.

"Hi, Jeff," McKenna greeted him, as Rand got out of his car and came across the road. "This is Gus Olsen, investigator for the D.A.'s office. Jeff Rand; Tri-State Agency," he introduced.

"Hey!" Olsen yelled. "We been lookin' for you! Where you been?"

Rand raised an eyebrow at McKenna.

"You just came from where we're going," the State Police sergeant surmised. "Was Gresham at home?"

"He was; he's gone now," Rand said. "He and another man are going to help me check up on what's missing from the Fleming collection."

"Hey!" Olsen exploded. "What I told you, now; he run ahead of us with a tip-off! Gresham's skipped out, now!"

"What is all this?" Rand wanted to know. "What's he screaming about, Mick?"

"Like he don't know!" Olsen vociferated. "He tipped off Gresham so's he could skip out; I'll bet he's in it with Gresham!"

"Pay no attention," McKenna advised. "He doesn't know what the score is; hell, he doesn't even know what teams are playing."

"Now you look here!" Olsen bawled. "We'll see what Mr. Farnsworth has to say about this. You're supposed to cooperate with us, not go fraternizin' with a lot of suspects. Why, it's plain as anything; him and Gresham's in it together. I bet that was why he come around, the first thing in the morning, to find the body!"

Kavaalen, behind the wheel, turned around and began jabbering at Olsen, in the back seat, in something that sounded like Swedish. Most Finns can speak Swedish, and Rand was wishing he could understand it. The corporal's remarks ran to about a paragraph, and must have been downright incendiary. At least, Olsen seemed to catch fire from them. He rose in his seat, waving his arms and howling back in the same language.

"Shut up, goddammit, *shut up!*" McKenna bellowed into his face. "Shut up before I sling your ass to hell out of this car! I'm talking, and I don't want any goddam jaw from you, Olsen. You either," he barked at Kavaalen, winking at him at the same time.

Silence fell with a heavy thump in the car.

"Well, now that the international crisis seems to have been averted, how's about letting me in on it, too?" Rand asked. "For instance, what about Gresham? What's he supposed to be a suspect for?"

"Ah, Olsen suspects him of chopping Rivers up," McKenna replied wearily. "See, we questioned this Cecil Gillis, and he told us that last evening, as he was leaving Rivers's, he saw Stephen Gresham drive up and go into the shop. I wanted to talk to him, myself; I thought he might account for the cigar-ashes, and the drink-fixings on that table. But when Farnsworth heard about the killing, he sent Olsen around, and when Olsen heard that Gresham had been there, he tried him and convicted him on the spot."

"Oh, obscenity! Is that what it's about?" Rand exclaimed in disgust. "Yes, Gresham told me about that. He didn't have the drink, and he wasn't smoking a cigar in the shop, and he left a little after nine. He got home at nine twenty-two. I can testify to that, myself; I was there at the time, and so were seven other people." Rand named them. "They dribbled away at different times during the evening, but Philip Cabot and I stayed till around eleven." He mentioned the approximate time at which the others had left. "What time was Rivers killed, or hasn't the time been fixed?"

"The M.E. says around ten to two," McKenna said.

"He could be wrong; them guys only guess, half the time," Olsen argued. "And besides, Gresham had it in for Rivers. And that ain't all, neither; he knew how to use a bayonet, too. I seen him, myself, during the war, showin' the Home Guard how to do it, just the way Rivers was killed!" he produced triumphantly.

McKenna used a dirty word. "So what? Anybody who's ever had infantry training knows that butt-stroke-and-lunge," he retorted. "I learned it myself, when I was a kid, in '24 and '25, in C.M.T.C. Hell, anybody who's ever seen a war-movie....If you hadn't lammed out of Sweden when you were sixteen, to duck conscription, you'd of known it, too."

"Well, maybe Olsen, or his boss, can explain why Gresham threw those record-cards in the fire," Rand contributed. "You know why Olsen says Gresham had it in for Rivers? Rivers sold Gresham a fake antique, a flint lock navy pistol that had been worked over into something else. Gresham was going to subpoena those records, when he brought suit against Rivers," Rand lied. "But I can explain why Cecil Gillis might have destroyed them, after killing Rivers, if he'd been cheating Rivers and Rivers caught him at it."

"Yeah, and that might explain why Gillis was in such a hurry to sic us onto Gresham, too," McKenna added. "I thought of something like that. And this high-brown girl that works for Rivers says that Gillis and Mrs. Rivers played all kinds of games together, when Rivers was away."

"Well, who's in charge of the investigation?" Rand wanted to know. "I heard, on the radio..."

"You're liable to hear anything on the radio, including slanders on Bing Crosby's horses. But for the record, I am in charge of this investigation. And don't anybody forget it, either," he added, in the direction of the rear seat.

"That's what I thought. Well, Stephen Gresham has just retained me to make an independent investigation," Rand said. "It is not that he lacks confidence in the State Police, or in you; he was afraid that other parties might get into the act and try to make political capital out of it. Which appears to have happened."

"Well, if Gresham retained you, I'm satisfied," McKenna said. "You can take care of that end of it. Glad you're in with us."

"Well, I ain't satisfied!" Olsen began yelling, again. "And Mr. Farnsworth won't be, neither. Why, this here private dick is like as not workin' for the very man that killed Rivers!"

McKenna turned slowly in his seat, to face Olsen.

"One time, ten years ago," he began, "Jeff Rand had a client who was guilty of the crime he hired Jeff to investigate. It was an arson case; this guy set fire to his own factory, and then got Jeff to run down a lot of fake clues he'd planted. I know about that; I was on the case, myself. That's where I first met Jeff, and he saved me from making a jackass out of myself. And what happened to this guy who'd hired Jeff was something that oughtn't to happen even to Molotov, and it happened because Jeff fixed it to happen. If anybody hires Jeff Rand, he's one of two things. He's either innocent, or else he's out of luck....I don't know why the hell I bother telling you this."

"Ten to two, you say," Rand considered. "Look. A couple of days ago, Rivers put out a new price-list to his regular customers. A lot of them, in different parts of the country, order by telephone, and some of them live in the West, where there's a couple of hours' time-difference. One of them, calling at, say, eight o'clock, local time, would get his call in at ten, Eastern Standard. If you checked the long-distance calls to Rivers's number last night, now, you might get something."

"Yeah. And if he took a call after nine twenty-two, that would let Gresham out. Even Farnsworth could figure that out. Sure. I'll check right away."

"Who's at Rivers's now?"

"Skinner and Jameson, of our gang. And Farnsworth, and some of his outfit. And the hell's own slew of reporters, of course," McKenna said. "Aarvo's going back there, in a little. We're still trying to locate Mrs. Rivers; we haven't been able to, yet. The maid says she went to New York day before yesterday."

"I'll probably be around at Rivers's, later in the day. I want to check on that Fleming angle."

"Uh-huh; I'll be there, in half an hour," Corporal Kavaalen said. "Be seeing you."

They exchanged so-longs, and Kavaalen backed, and made a U-turn, moving off in the direction of Rosemont. Olsen's voluble protests drifted back as the car receded. Rand returned to his own car and followed.

Chapter 13

Rand found Gladys alone in the library. As she rose to greet him, he came close to her, gesturing for silence with finger on lips.

"There's a perfect hell of a mess," he whispered. "Somebody murdered Arnold Rivers last night."

She looked at him in horror. "Murdered? Who was it? How did it...?"

"I haven't time to talk about that right now," he told her. "Stephen Gresham and Pierre Jarrett are on their way here, and I'd like you to keep the servants, and particularly Walters, out of earshot of the gunroom while they're here. It seems that a number of the best pistols have been stolen from the collection, sometime between the death of Mr. Fleming and the time I saw the collection yesterday. Stephen and Pierre are going to help me find out just what's been taken. I have an idea they might have been sold to Rivers. That may have been why he was killed-to prevent him from implicating the thief."

"You think somebody here-the servants?" she asked.

"I can't see how it could have been an outsider. The stuff wasn't all taken at once; it must have been moved out a piece at a time, and worthless pistols moved in and hung on the racks to replace valuable pistols taken." He had left the library door purposely open; when the doorbell rang, he heard it. "I'll let them in," he said. "You go and head Walters off."

Rand hurried to the front door and admitted Gresham and Pierre, hustling them down the hall, into the library, and up the spiral to the gunroom, while Gladys went to the foot of the front stairs. Through the open gunroom door, Rand could hear her speaking to Walters, as though sending him on some errand to the rear of the house. He closed the door and turned to the others.

"We'll have to make it fast," he said. "Mrs. Fleming can't hold the butler off all day. Let's start over here, and go around the racks."

They began at the left, with the wheel locks. Pierre put his finger immediately on the shabby and disreputable specimen Rand had first noticed.

"Phew! Is that one a stinker!" he said. "What used to be there was a nice late sixteenth- or early seventeenth-century North Italian pistol, all covered with steel filigree-work. A real beauty; much better than average."

"Those Turkish atrocities," Gresham pointed out. "They're filling in for a pair of Lazarino Cominazo snaphaunces that Lane Fleming paid seven hundred for, back in the mid-thirties, and didn't pay a cent too much for, even then. Worth an easy thousand, now. Remember the pair of Cominazo flintlocks illustrated in Pollard's *Short History of Firearms*? These were even better, and snaphaunces."

"Well, you go over the collection," Rand told them. "Note down anything you find missing." He handed them a pad of paper and a pencil from the desk. "I have something else to do, for a few minutes."

With that he left them scrutinizing the pistols on the wall, and went to the workbench in the corner, drawing the .36 Colt from under his waistband. Working rapidly, he dismounted it, taking off the barrel and cylinder, and cleaned it thoroughly before putting it together again. Pierre and Gresham had just started on the Colts when he slipped the revolver out of sight and rejoined them.

It took over a half-hour to finish; when they had gotten completely around the collection, Rand had a list of twenty-six missing items, including four cased sets. At a conservative estimate, the missing pistols were worth ten to twelve thousand dollars, dealer's list value; the stuff that had been moved in to replace them might have a value of two or three hundred, but no serious collector would buy any of it at any price. There had been no attempt to replace the cased items; the cases had been merely rearranged on the table to avoid any conspicuous vacancies.

"See that thing?" Pierre asked, tapping a small .25 Webley & Scott automatic with his finger. Rand looked at it; it had been fitted with an English-made silencer. "That thing," Pierre said, "is the one illustrated in Pollard's book. The identical pistol; it used to be in the Pollard collection."

"Lane had a lot of stuff from some famous collections," Gresham said. "Pollard collection, Sawyer collection, Fred Hines collection, Meeks collection, even the old Mark Field collection, that was sold at Libbie Galleries in 1911. His own could rank with any of them. Think you can get any of this stuff back?"

"I hope so. By the way, where does this fellow Umholtz, the fabricator of spurious Whitneyville Walker Colts, hang out? I believe he ought to be looked into."

"Say, that's an idea!" Pierre ejaculated. "He might have bought the pistols, instead of Rivers. Why, he has a gunshop at Kingsville, on Route 22, about fifteen miles west of here, just this side of the village. He had a big sign along the road, and his shop's in the barn, behind the house."

"I'll have to check up on him. But first, I want to see if any of this stuff's at Rivers's shop. I won't ask you to come along," he told Gresham. "No use you sticking your head into the lion's mouth. I've talked the State Police temporarily off your trail, but I still have Farnsworth to worry about."

"He'd like to prosecute a big corporation lawyer, if he thought he had any chance of getting a conviction," Pierre said. "Make a nice impression on the proletarian vote in the south end of the county."

"You're a member of the Mohawk Club in New Belfast, aren't you?" Rand asked Gresham. "Well, go there and stay there for a couple of days, till the heat's off. Pierre, you can come with me to Rivers's; I'll run you home in my car when we're through."

Gresham let himself out the front door; Pierre and Rand went out through the garage and got into Rand's car.

"You have any idea, so far, about who could have killed Rivers?" the ex-Marine asked, as they coasted down the drive to the highway.

"I haven't even the start of an idea," Rand said. He ran briefly over what he knew, or at least those items which were likely to become public knowledge soon. "From what I've observed at the shop, and from what I know of Rivers's character, I'd think that he'd been in some kind of a crooked deal with somebody, and got double-crossed, or else the other man caught Rivers double-crossing him. Or else, Rivers and somebody else had some secret in common, and the other man wanted a monopoly on it and killed Rivers as a security measure."

"Think it might be the Fleming pistols?"

"That depends. I'll have to see whether any of the Fleming pistols turn up anywhere in Rivers's former possession. Personally, I've about decided that the man who was drinking with Rivers killed him. There aren't any indications that anybody else was in the shop afterward. If that's the case, I doubt if the killer was Walters. You know what a snobbish guy Rivers was. And from what I know of him, he seems to have had a thoroughly Aristotelian outlook; he identified individuals with class-labels. Walters, of course, would be identified with the label 'butler,' and I can't imagine Rivers sitting down and drinking with a 'butler.' He would only drink with people whom he thought of as his equals, that is, people whom he identified with class-labels of equal social importance to his own labels of 'antiquarian' and 'businessman.'"

"That sounds like Korzybski," Pierre said, as they turned onto Route 19 in the village and headed east. "You've read *Science and Sanity?*"

Rand nodded. "Yes. I first read it in the 1933 edition, back about 1936; I've been rereading it every couple of years since. The principles of General Semantics come in very handy in my business, especially in criminal-investigation work, like this. A consciousness of abstracting, a realization that we can only know something about a thin film of events on the surface of any given situation, and a habit of thinking structurally and of individual things, instead of verbally and of categories, saves a lot of blind-alley chasing. And they suggest a great many more avenues of investigation than would be evident to one whose thinking is limited by intensional, verbal, categories."

"Yes. I find General Semantics helpful in my work, too," Pierre said. "I can use it in plotting a story.... Oh-oh!"

"The Gentlemen of the Press," Rand said, looking ahead as the car approached the Rivers house and shop. "There hasn't been a good, sensational, murder story for some time; this is a gift from the gods."

A swarm of cars were parked in front and beside the red-brick house. Among them, Rand spotted a gold-lettered green sedan of the New Belfast *Dispatch* and *Evening Express*, a black coupé bearing the blazonry of the New Belfast *Mercury*, cars from a couple of papers at Louisburg, the state capital, and cars from papers as far distant as Pittsburgh, Buffalo, and Cincinnati. In front of the shop, a motley assemblage of journalists was interviewing and photographing an undersized runt in a tan Chesterfield topcoat and a gray Homburg hat, whom they were addressing as Mr. Farnsworth. The District Attorney of Scott County had a mustache which failed miserably to make him look like Tom Dewey; he impressed Rand as the sort of offensive little squirt who compensates for his general insignificance by bad manners and loud-mouthed self-assertion. Corporal Kavaalen, standing in the doorway of the shop, caught sight of Rand and his companion as they got out of the car and came to meet them, hustling them around the crowd and into the shop before anybody could notice and recognize them.

"That was a good tip, about the telephone," he said softly. "Mick checked at the Rosemont exchange. Rivers got a long-distance call from Topeka last night; ten fifteen to ten seventeen. We got the night long distance operator out of bed, and she confirmed it; Rivers took the call himself. He gets a lot of long distance calls in the evenings; she knew his voice." He corrected himself, shifting to the past tense and glancing, as he did, at the chalk outline on the floor, now scuffed by many feet, and the dried bloodstains. "You say this puts Gresham in the clear?"

"Absolutely," Rand assured him. "He was at home from nine twenty-two on." He introduced Pierre Jarrett, and explained their mission. "You find anything except what's here in the shop?"

"Only Rivers's own .38 Smith & Wesson, in his room, and a lot of pistols out in the garage, that look like junk to me," Kavaalen said. "I'll show them to you."

Rand nodded. "Pierre, you look around the shop; I'll see what this other stuff is."

He followed Kavaalen through a door at the rear of the shop; the same one through which Cecil Gillis had carried the Kentucky rifle the afternoon before. Beside Rivers's car, there was a long workbench in the garage, and piles of wood and cardboard cartons, and stacks of newspapers, and a barrel full of excelsior, all evidently used in preparing arms for shipment. There was also a large pile of old pistols, and a number of long-arms.

Rand pawed among the pistols; they were, as the State Police corporal had said, all junk. The sort of things a dealer has to buy, at times, in order to get something really good. Many of them had been partially dismantled for parts. When he was certain that the heap of junk-weapons didn't conceal anything of value, he returned to the shop. Pierre was waiting for him by Rivers's desk.

He shook his head. "Not a thing," he reported. "I found a couple of out-and-out fakes, and about ten or fifteen that had been altered in one way or another, and a lot of reblued stuff, but nothing from Fleming's collection. What did you find?"

Rand laughed. "I found Rivers's scrap-heap, and some pistols that probably contributed parts to some of the stuff you found," he said. "Of course, all we can say is that the stuff isn't here; Rivers could have bought it, and stored it outside somewhere. But even so, I'm not taking the Fleming butler too seriously as a suspect for the murder."

"What's this about Fleming's butler?" a voice broke in. "Have you been withholding information from me?"

Rand turned, to find that Farnsworth had left the press conference in front and crepe-soled up on him from behind.

"I withheld a theory, which seems to have come to nothing," he replied.

Kavaalen told the D.A. who Rand was. "He's cooperating with us," he added. "Sergeant McKenna instructed us to give him every consideration."

"It seems that a number of valuable pistols were stolen from the collection of the late Lane Fleming," Rand said. "We suspected that the butler had stolen them and sold them to Rivers; I thought it possible that he might also have killed Rivers to silence him about the transaction." He shrugged. "None of the stolen items have turned up here, so there's nothing to connect the thefts with the death of Rivers."

"Good heavens, you certainly didn't suspect a prominent and respected citizen like Mr. Rivers of receiving stolen goods?" Farnsworth demanded, aghast.

"Who respects him?" Rand hooted. "Rivers was a notorious swindler; he had that reputation among arms-collectors all over the country. He was expelled from membership in the National Rifle Association for misrepresentation and fraud. Why, he even swindled Lane Fleming on a pair of fake pistols, a week or so before Fleming's death. And the very reason why your man Olsen was inclined to suspect Stephen Gresham was that he had had trouble with Rivers about a crooked deal Rivers had put over on him. Fortunately, Mr. Gresham has since been cleared of any suspicion, but —"

"Who says he's been cleared?" Farnsworth snapped. "He's still a suspect."

"Sergeant McKenna says so," Corporal Kavaalen declared. "He has been cleared. I guess we just didn't get around to telling you about that." He went on to explain about the long distance call that had furnished Stephen Gresham's alibi.

"And Gresham was at home from nine twenty-two on," Rand added. "There are eight witnesses to that: His wife and daughter; myself; Captain Jarrett, here; and his fiancée, Miss Lawrence; Philip Cabot; Adam Trehearne; Colin MacBride."

Farnsworth looked bewildered. "Why wasn't I told about that?" he demanded sulkily.

"Sergeant McKenna's been too busy, and I didn't think of it," Kavaalen said insolently. "I'm not supposed to report to you, anyhow. Why didn't your man Olsen tell you; he was with us when we checked with the telephone company."

Farnsworth tried to ignore that by questioning Pierre about the time of Gresham's arrival home, then turned to Rand and wanted to know what the latter's interest in the case was.

Rand told him about his work in connection with the Fleming collection, producing Humphrey Goode's letter of authorization. Farnsworth seemed impressed in about the same way as the coroner, Kirchner, but he was still puzzled.

"But I understood that you had been retained by Stephen Gresham, to investigate this murder," he said.

"So you did talk to Olsen, after I saw him," Rand pounced. "Odd he didn't mention this telephone thing.... Why, yes; that's true. My agency handles all sorts of business. The two operations aren't mutually exclusive; for a while, I even thought they might be related, but now —" He shrugged.

"Well, you believe, now, that Rivers had nothing to do with the pistols you say were stolen from the Fleming collection?" Farnsworth asked. Rand shook his head ambiguously; Farnsworth took that for a negative answer to his question, as he was intended to. "And you say Mr. Gresham has been completely cleared of any suspicion of complicity in this murder?"

"Mr. Rand's helping us; we want him to stick around till the case is closed," Corporal Kavaalen threw in, perceiving the drift of Farnsworth's questions. "He and Sergeant McKenna have worked together before; he's given us a lot of good tips."

"You understand," Rand took over, "Mr. Gresham didn't retain me merely to help him clear himself. I don't accept that kind of retainers. I was retained to find the murderer of Arnold Rivers, and I intend to continue working on this case until I do. I hope that the same friendly spirit of mutual cooperation will exist between your office and my agency as exists between me and the State Police. I certainly don't want to have to work at cross purposes with any of the regular law-enforcement agencies."

"Oh, certainly; of course." Farnsworth didn't seem to like the idea, but there was no apparent opening for objection. He and Rand exchanged mendacious compliments, pledged close cooperation, and did practically everything but draw up and sign a treaty of alliance. Then Farnsworth and Corporal Kavaalen accompanied Rand and Pierre Jarrett to the front door.

Some of the reporters who were ravening outside must have spotted Rand as he had entered; they were all waiting for him to come out, and set up a monstrous ululation when he appeared in the doorway. With Farnsworth beaming approval, Rand assured the Press that he was no more than a mere spectator, that the State Police and the efficient District Attorney of Scott County had the situation well in hand, and that an arrest was expected within a matter of hours. Then he and Pierre hurried to his car and drove away.

Chapter 14

Neither of them spoke for a moment or two. Then, after they had left the criminological-journalistic uproar at the Rivers place behind and were approaching the village of Rosemont, Pierre turned to Rand.

"You know," he said, "for a disciple of Korzybski, you came pretty close to confusing orders of abstraction, a couple of times, back there. You showed that Stephen was at home while Rivers was taking that phone call, a little after ten. But when you talk about clearing him completely, aren't you overlooking the possibility that he came back to Rivers's after you and Philip Cabot left the Gresham place?"

Rand eased the foot-pressure on the gas and spared young Jarrett a side-glance before returning his attention to the road ahead.

"Understand," Pierre hastened to add, "I don't believe that Stephen was fool enough to kill Rivers over that fake North & Cheney, but weren't you producing inferences that hadn't been abstracted from any descriptive data?"

"Pierre, when I'm working on a case like this, any resemblance between my opinions and the statements I may make is purely due to conscious considerations of policy," Rand told him. "I don't want Farnsworth or Mick McKenna going around bitching this operation up for me. If they feel justified in eliminating Gresham on the strength of that phone call, I'm satisfied, regardless of the semantics involved. Right now, the thing that's worrying me is the ease with which I seem to have talked Farnsworth into laying off Gresham. He and Olsen both have single-track minds. They may just dismiss that telephone alibi, such as it is, as mere error of the mortal mind, and go right ahead building some kind of a ramshackle case against Gresham. Since they picked him for their entry, they won't want to have to scratch him....Damn, I wish I could think of where Walters could have sold those pistols!"

"Well, if Rivers wasn't involved somehow, why was he killed?" Pierre wondered. "Hey! Maybe Walters sold the pistols to Umholtz! He's just as big a crook as Rivers was, only not quite so smart."

Rand nodded thoughtfully. "Maybe so. And suppose Rivers found out about it, and tried to declare himself in on it. That stuff would be worth at least ten thousand; I doubt if whoever bought it paid Walters more than two. In the Umholtz-Rivers income bracket, the difference might be worth killing for."

"That's right. And Umholtz was in the infantry, in the other war; he served in the Twenty-eighth Division. He was trained to use a bayonet. And he'd pick that short Mauser; it has about the same weight and balance as a 1903 Springfield."

"Well, you know, the killer wouldn't need to have been trained to use a bayonet," Rand pointed out. "Mick McKenna made that point, this afternoon. There have been a lot of war-movies that showed bayonet fighting; pretty nearly everybody knows about the technique that was used. And against an unarmed and probably unsuspecting victim like Rivers, a great deal of proficiency wouldn't be needed." He slowed the car. "Up this road?" he asked.

"Yes. That's my place, over there."

Pierre pointed to a white-walled, red-roofed house that lay against a hillside, about a mile ahead, making a vivid spot in the dull grays and greens of the early April landscape. It consisted of a square two-story block, with one-story wings projecting to give it an L-shaped floorplan. It reminded Rand of farmhouses he had seen in Sicily during the War.

"Come on in and see my stuff, if you have time," Pierre invited, as Rand pulled to a stop in the driveway. "I think I told you what I collect-personal combat arms, both firearms and edge-weapons."

They entered the front door, which opened directly into a large parlor, a brightly colored, cheerful room. A woman rose from a chair where she had been reading. She was somewhere between forty-five and fifty, but her figure was still trim, and she retained much of what, in her youth, must have been great beauty.

"Mother, this is Colonel Rand," Pierre said. "Jeff, my mother."

Rand shook hands with her, and said something polite. She gave him a smile of real pleasure.

"Pierre has been telling me about you, Colonel," she said. There was a faint trace of French accent in her voice. "I suppose he brought you here to show you his treasures?"

"Yes; I collect arms too. Pistols," Rand said.

She laughed. "You gun-collectors; you're like women looking at somebody's new hat....Will you stay for dinner with us, Colonel Rand?"

"Why, I'm sorry; I can't. I have a great many things to do, and I'm expected for dinner at the Flemings'. I really wish I could, Mrs. Jarrett. Maybe some other time."

They chatted for a few minutes, then Pierre guided Rand into one of the wings of the house.

"This is my workshop, too," he said. "Here's where I do my writing." He opened a door and showed Rand into a large room.

On one side, the wall was blank; on the other, it was pierced by two small casement windows. The far end was of windows for its entire width, from within three feet of the floor almost to the ceiling. There were bookcases on either long side, and on the rear end, and over them hung Pierre's weapons. Rand went slowly around the room, taking everything in. Very few of the arms were of issue military type, and most of these showed alterations to suit individual requirements. As Pierre had told him the evening before, the emphasis was upon weapons which illustrated techniques of combat.

At the end of the room, lighted by the wide windows, was a long desk which was really a writer's assembly line, with typewriter, reference-books, stacks of notes and manuscripts, and a big dictionary on a stand beside a comfortable swivel-chair.

"What are you writing?" Rand asked.

"Science-fiction. I do a lot of stories for the pulps," Pierre told him. "*Space-Trails*, and *Other Worlds*, and *Wonder-Stories*; mags like that. Most of it's standardized formula-stuff; what's known to the trade as space-operas. My best stuff goes to *Astonishing*. Parenthetically, you mustn't judge any of these magazines by their names. It seems to be a convention to use hyperbolic names for science-fiction magazines; a heritage from what might be called an earlier and ruder day. What I do for *Astonishing* is really hard work, and I enjoy it. I'm working now on one for them, based on J. W. Dunne's time-theories, if you know what they are."

"I think so," Rand said. "Polydimensional time, isn't it? Based on an effect Dunne observed and described-dreams obviously related to some waking event, but preceding rather than following the event to which they are related. I read Dunne's *Experiment with Time* some years before the war, and once, when I had nothing better to do, I recorded dreams for about a month. I got a few doubtful-to-fair examples, and two unmistakable Dunne-Effect dreams. I never got anything that would help me pick a race-winner or spot a rise in the stock market, though."

"Well, you know, there's a case on record of a man who had a dream of hearing a radio narration of the English Derby of 1933, including the announcement that Hyperion had won, which he did," Pierre said. "The dream was six hours before the race, and tallied very closely with the phraseology used by the radio narrator. Here." He picked up a copy of Tyrrell's *Science and Psychical Phenomena* and leafed through it.

"Did this fellow cash in on it?" Rand asked.

"No. He was a Quaker, and violently opposed to betting. Here." He handed the book to Rand. "Case Twelve."

Rand sat down on the edge of the desk, and read the section indicated, about three pages in length.

"Well, I'll be damned!" he said, as he finished. The idea of anybody passing up a chance like that to enrich himself literally smote him to the vitals. "I see the British Society for Psychical Research checked that case, and got verification from a couple of independent witnesses. If the S.P.R. vouches for a story, it must be the McCoy; they're the toughest-minded gang of confirmed skeptics anywhere in Christendom. They take an attitude toward evidence that might be advantageously copied by most of the district attorneys I've met, the one in this county being no exception.... What's this story you're working on?"

"Oh, it's based on Dunne's precognition theories, plus a few ideas of my own, plus a theory of alternate lines of time-sequence for alternate probabilities," Pierre said. "See, here's the situation..."

Half an hour later, they were still arguing about a multidimensional universe when Rand remembered Dave Ritter, who should be at the Rosemont Inn by now. He looked at his watch, saw that it was five forty-five, and inquired about a telephone.

"Yes, of course; out here." Pierre took him back to the parlor, where he dialed the Inn and inquired if a Mr. Ritter, from New Belfast, were registered there yet.

He was. A moment later he was speaking to Ritter.

"Jeff, for Gawdsake, don't come here," Ritter advised. "This place is six-deep with reporters; the bar sounds like the second act of *The Front Page*. Tony Ashe and Steve Drake from the

Dispatch and *Express*; Harry Bentz, from the *Mercury*; Joe Rawlings, the AP man from Louisburg; Christ only knows who all. This damn thing's going to turn into another Hall-Mills case! Look, meet me at that beer joint, about two miles on the New Belfast side of Rosemont, on Route 19; the white-with-red-trimmings place with the big Pabst sign out in front. I'll try to get there without letting a couple of reporters hide in the luggage-trunk."

"Okay; see you directly."

Rand hung up, spent the next few minutes breaking away from Pierre and his mother, and went out to his car. Trust Dave Ritter, he thought, to pick some place where malt beverages were sold, for a rendezvous.

Dave's coupé was parked inconspicuously beside the red-trimmed roadhouse. Opening his glove-box, Rand took out the two percussion revolvers and shoved them under his trench coat, one on either side, pulling up the belt to hold them in place. As he went into the roadhouse, he felt like Damon Runyon's Twelve-Gun Tweeney. He found Ritter in the last booth, engaged in finishing a bottle of beer. Rand ordered Bourbon and plain water, and Ritter ordered another beer.

"I have the stuff Tip left with Kathie," Ritter said, taking out a couple of closely typed sheets and handing them across the table. "He said this was the whole business."

Rand glanced over them. Tipton had neatly and concisely summarized the provisions of Lane Fleming's will, and had also listed all Fleming's life insurance policies, with beneficiaries, including a partnership policy on the lives of Fleming, Dunmore, and Anton Varcek, paying each of the survivors $25,000.

"I see Gladys and Geraldine and Nelda each get a third of Fleming's Premix stock," Rand commented. "But before they can have the certificates transferred to them, they have to sign over their voting-power to the board of directors. Evidently Fleming didn't approve of the feminine touch in business."

"Yeah, isn't that a dandy?" Ritter asked. "The directors are elected by majority vote of the stockholders. They now have the voting-power of a majority of the stock; that makes the present board self-perpetuating, and responsible only to each other."

"So it does, but that wasn't what I was thinking of. According to Tip, the board is one hundred per cent in favor of the merger with National Milling & Packaging. We'll have to suppose Fleming knew that; there must have been considerable intramural acrimony on the subject while he was still alive. Now, since he opposed the merger, if he had intended committing suicide, he would have made some other arrangement, wouldn't he? At least, one would suppose so. Well, then," Rand asked, "why, since he is so worried about these suicide rumors, doesn't Goode use the one argument which would utterly disprove them? Or is there some reason why he doesn't want to call attention to the fact that Fleming's death is what makes the merger possible?"

"Well, that would be calling attention to the fact that the merger made Fleming's death necessary," Ritter pointed out. He poured more beer into his glass. "While we're on it, what's the angle on this butler's livery I was supposed to bring? I brought my tux, and I borrowed a striped vest from the Theatrical Property Exchange, and I brought that Dago .380 of yours. But what makes you think the Flemings are going to be needing a new butler? You going to poison the one they have?"

"The one they have has been exceeding his duties," Rand said. "He was supposed to clean the pistol-collection. Not content with that, he's been cleaning it out. I know it was the butler." He went, at length, into his reasons for thinking so, and described the *modus operandi* of the thefts. "Now, all this is just theory, so far, but when I'm able to prove it, I'm going to put the arm on this Walters, if it's right in the middle of dinner and he only has the roast half served. And I want you ready to step into the vacancy thus created. I'm going to be busy as a pup in a fireplug factory with this Rivers thing, and I'll need some checking-upping done inside the Fleming household."

He went on, in meticulous detail, to explain about the Rivers murder. "I'll have some work for you, before you're ready to start buttling, too." Disencumbering himself of the two percussion revolvers, he laid them on the table. "I want you to take these and show them to this barbecue man. Get from him a positive statement, preferably in writing, as to which, if either, he sold to Lane Fleming. You might show your Agency card and claim to be checking up on some stolen pistols that have been recovered. Then, if he identifies the Leech & Rigdon, take the Colt and show it to Elmer Umholtz. You want to be careful how you handle him; we may want him for puncturing Rivers, though I'm inclined to doubt that, as of now. Get him to tell you, yes or no, whether he reblued it and replated the back-strap and trigger-guard, and if he did it for Rivers; and if so, when. I know that's been done; the bluing is too dark for a Civil War period job; the frame, which ought to be case-hardened in colors, has been blued like the barrel and cylinder, the cylinder-engraving is almost obliterated, and you can see a few rust-pits that have been blued over. But I want to know if this gun was ever in Rivers's shop; that's the important thing."

"Uh-huh. Got the addresses?"

Rand furnished them, and Ritter noted them down. The waitress wandered back to see if they wanted anything else; she gave a small squeak of surprise when she saw the two big six-shooters on the table. Rand and Ritter repeated their orders, and when she brought back the drinks, the Colt and the Leech & Rigdon were out of sight.

"The way I see it, everybody who's within a light-year of this Rivers killing is trying to pin the medal on somebody else," Ritter was saying. "The Lawrence girl was afraid young Jarrett had done it; right away, she sicced you onto Gillis. Gillis didn't lose any time putting McKenna and Farnsworth onto Gresham. Gresham's the only one who didn't have a pasty ready; you're supposed to dig one up for him. And Jarrett, the first chance he gets, introduces Umholtz." He stared into his beer, as though he thought Ultimate Verity might be lurking somewhere under the suds. "Do you think it might be possible that Rivers bumped Fleming off, in spite of his getting killed later?" he asked.

"Anything's possible," Rand replied, "except where some structural contradiction is involved, like scoring thirteen with one throw of a pair of dice. Yes, he could have. The way the Flemings leave their garage open as long as any of the cars are out, anybody could have sneaked into the house from the garage, and gone up from the library to the gunroom. The only question in my mind is whether Rivers would have known about that. That lawsuit and criminal action that Fleming was going to start-and that's been verified from sources independent of Goode-was a good sound motive. And say he took the Leech & Rigdon away, after leaving the Colt in Fleming's hand; selling it to some collector who'd put it in with a hundred or so other pistols would be a good way of disposing of it. And I can understand his trying to buy the Colt, to get it out of circulation." Rand sipped his Bourbon. "But that leaves us with the question of who killed Rivers, and why."

"Well, because Fleming is dead-and it doesn't matter whether he was murdered or died of old age-Walters starts robbing the collection. He sells the pistols to Rivers," Ritter reconstructed. "And, as Rivers doesn't want them around his shop till they've had time to cool off, he stores them with this Umholtz character, who seems to have been in plenty of crooked deals with Rivers in the past. The pistols are worth about ten grand, and nobody knows where they are but Rivers and Umholtz, and if Rivers drops dead all of a sudden, nobody will know where they are except Umholtz, and in a couple of years he can get them sold off and have the money all to himself."

"Yes, Dave; that's good sound murder, too. And Rivers would sit down and drink with Umholtz, and Umholtz could take that Mauser out of the rack right in front of Rivers and Rivers wouldn't suspect a thing till it was too late. Of course, it depends upon two unverified assumptions: One, that the pistols were sold to Rivers, and, two, that Rivers stored them with Umholtz."

"And, three, that Walters stole the pistols in the first place," Ritter added. "You know, it's possible that somebody else in that house might have stolen them."

"Yes. As I said, anything's possible, within structural limits, but possibilities exist on different orders of probability. We can't try to consider all the possibilities in any case, because they are indefinitely numerous; the best we can do is screen out all the low-order probabilities, list the high-order probabilities, and revise our list when and as new data comes to light. Well, I've told you why I think Walters is a good suspect. From what I've seen of that household, I think Walters was personally loyal to Lane Fleming, and I don't believe he feels any loyalty to anybody else there, with the exception of Gladys Fleming. He might keep quiet about the missing pistols if she were the thief; if Dunmore, or Varcek, or either of the girls had done the stealing, he'd tell Gladys, and she'd pass it on to me. She would be glad of anything that could be used against any of the others. And if, on the other hand, she had stolen the pistols herself, she wouldn't have wanted me poking around, and wouldn't have brought me in, at least not to handle the collection." Rand looked regretfully at his empty glass and decided against ordering another. "Dave, I just thought of something," he said. "How do you think this would work?"

He told Ritter what he had thought of. Ritter drank beer slowly and meditatively.

"It just might work," he considered. "I've seen that gag work a hundred times: hell, I've used something like that, myself, at least fifty times, and so have you. And I don't think Walters would be familiar enough with dick-practice to see what you were doing. But if it turns out that Walters didn't sell the pistols to Rivers at all, what then?"

"Well, if he sold them to Umholtz, Pierre Jarrett's theory is still valid until disproved," Rand said. "And if he didn't sell them either to Rivers or Umholtz, we'll have to conclude that Rivers and Fleming were killed by the same person, the Rivers killing being a security measure. That is, unless we find that Rivers was killed by Pierre Jarrett, which is a sort of medium-high-order probability. Jarrett and the girl left Gresham's early enough for him to have killed Rivers; they were both pretty hard hit by that twenty-five-grand blockbuster Rivers had dropped on them.... Give me back that Colt, Dave. All you have to do is get an identification on the Leech & Rigdon from the barbecue man. I'm going to let Mick McKenna handle Umholtz, one way or another, after we've concluded the Walters experiment. Until then, we don't want to stir Umholtz up, at all."

Chapter 15

Parking in the drive, Rand entered the Fleming house by the front door. The butler must have been busy with his pre-dinner tasks in the rear; it was Gladys herself who admitted him.

"Stay out of there," she warned him, taking his arm and guiding him away from the parlor doorway. "Nelda and Geraldine are in there, ignoring each other. If you go in, they'll start talking to you, and then they'll start talking at each other through you, and the air will be full of tomahawks in a jiffy. Let's go up in the gunroom; that's out of the battle zone."

"What started the hostilities this time?" Rand asked, going up the stairway with her.

"Oh, Geraldine lost Nelda's place-marker out of the Kinsey Report, or something." She shrugged. "Mainly reaction to Rivers's death. That was a great blow to all of us; twenty-five thousand dollars' worth of blow. It was a blow to me, too, but I'm not letting it throw me.... What were you doing all afternoon?"

"Trying to keep the rest of our prospects out of jail. This sixteenth-witted District Attorney you have in this county had the idea he could charge Stephen Gresham with the killing. I had a time talking him out of it, and I'm still not sure how far I succeeded. And I was trying to get a line on where those pistols got to."

"Ssssh!" They reached the top of the stairs, and Rand saw Walters approaching down the hall. "It was Colonel Rand, Walters; I let him in myself. Are Mr. Varcek and Mr. Dunmore here, yet?"

"Mr. Dunmore is in the library, ma'am, and Mr. Varcek is upstairs, in his laboratory. Dinner will be ready in three-quarters of an hour."

"Have you mixed the cocktails? You'd better do that. Serve them in about twenty minutes. And you'd better go up and warn Mr. Varcek not to become involved in anything messy before dinner."

Walters yes-ma'am'd her and started toward the attic stairway. Rand and Gladys went into the gunroom; Rand turned to the left, picked a pistol from the wall, and carried it with him as he guided Gladys toward the desk in the corner.

"You think Walters stole them?" she asked.

"So far, I'm inclined to. Have you told any of the others, yet?"

"Oh, Lord, no! They'd all be sure that I stole them myself. I'm counting on you to get them back with as little fuss as possible. Do you think that was why Rivers was killed? After all, when a lot of valuable pistols disappear, and a crooked dealer is murdered, I'd expect there to be a connection."

"There could be. Did you ever hear any stories about Mrs. Rivers and this young fellow Gillis who works in Rivers's shop?"

Gladys laughed. "Is that rearing its ugly head in public, now?" she asked. "Well, there's nothing like a good murder to shake the skeletons out of the closets. Not that this particular skeleton was ever exactly hidden. The stories are numerous, and somewhat repetitious; Cecil and Mrs. Rivers would be seen together, at roadhouses and so on, at what they imagined was a safe distance from Rosemont, and it was said that when Rivers was away over night, Cecil was never seen to leave the Rivers place in the evenings. Might this be relevant to Rivers's sudden demise?"

"It could be." Rand was keeping one eye on the hall door and the other on the head of the spiral stairway. "Don't mention outside what I told you about Farnsworth having this brain-storm about Stephen Gresham. If it got out, it might hurt Gresham professionally. The fact is, Gresham has just retained me to investigate the Rivers murder for him. That won't interfere to any great extent with the work I'm doing here; if necessary, I'll bring a couple of my men in from New Belfast to help me on the Rivers operation." He broke off abruptly, catching a movement at the head of the spiral, and lifted the pistol in his hand, as though showing it to Gladys. "See," he went on, "it has two hammers and two nipples, but only one barrel. It was loaded with two charges, one on top of the other; the bullet of the rear charge acted as the breech-plug for the front charge....Oh, Walters!" He affected to catch sight of the butler for the first time. "Bring me that .36 Walch revolver, will you?"

"Yes, sir." Walters, crossing the room, veered to the right and went to the middle wall, bringing a revolver over to the desk. It was a percussion weapon with an abnormally long cylinder. "The cocktails are served," he announced.

"We'll be down in a moment; you can put these back where they belong when you find time," Rand told him. "Now, here," he said to Gladys. "This is the same idea, in a revolver. Six chambers, two charges in each. In theory, it was a good idea, but in actual practice..."

Walters went out the hall door, presumably to call Varcek. Rand continued talking about the superposed-load principle, as used in the Lindsay pistol and the Walch revolver, until he was sure the butler was out of hearing. Gladys was looking at him in appreciative if slightly punch-drunk delight.

"I wondered why you brought that thing over here with you," she said. "Brother, was that a quick shift!...You're really sure he's the one?"

"I'm not really sure of anything, except of my own existence and eventual extinction," Rand told her. "It pretty nearly has to be somebody inside this house. I don't think anybody else here, yourself included, would know enough about arms to rob this collection as selectively as it has been robbed. Did you see what just happened, here? I asked him for one of the most uncommon arms here, and he went straight and got it. He knows this collection as well as your husband did, and I assume he knows values almost as well....And, of course, there was a musket, too; Mr. Fleming didn't collect long-arms, or he'd have had one. It embodied the same principle as the pistol. The legend is that this man Lindsay's brother was a soldier; he was supposed to have been killed by Indians who drew the fire of the detail he was with and then charged them when their muskets were empty." Rand shrugged. "Actually, the superposed-load principle is ancient; there's a sixteenth-century wheel lock pistol in the Metropolitan Museum, in New York, firing two shots from the same barrel."

Varcek and the butler, who had entered by the hall door, went across the gunroom and down the spiral. Rand laid down the pistol and escorted Gladys after them.

Dunmore and Geraldine were in the library when they went down. Geraldine, mildly potted, was reclining in a chair, sipping her drink. Dunmore was still radiating his synthetic cheerfulness.

"Get many of the pistols listed, Colonel?" he hailed Rand, with jovial condescension.

"No." Rand poured two cocktails, handing one to Gladys. "I went to Arnold Rivers's place this morning, on a little unfinished business, and damn near tripped over Rivers's corpse. I spent the rest of the day getting myself disinvolved from the ensuing uproar," he told Dunmore. "You heard about it, of course."

"Yes, of course. Horrible business. I hope you didn't get mixed up in it any more than you had to. After all, you're working for us, and if the police knew that, we'd be bothered, too.... Look here, you don't think some of these other people who were after the collection might have killed Rivers, to keep him from outbidding them?"

Nelda, entering from the hallway, caught the last part of that.

"Good God, Fred!" she shrieked at him. "Don't say things like that! Maybe they did, but wait till they've bought the collection and paid for it, before you start accusing them!"

"I'm not accusing anybody," Dunmore growled back at her. "I don't know enough about it to make any accusations. All I'm saying is —"

"Well, don't say it, then, if you don't know what you're talking about," his wife retorted.

In spite of this start, dinner passed in relative quiet. For the most part, they talked about the remaining chances of selling the collection, about which nobody was optimistic. Rand tried to build up morale with pictures of large museums and important dealers, all fairly slavering to get their fangs into the Fleming collection, but to little avail. A pall of gloom had settled, and he was forced to concede that he had at last found somebody who had a valid reason to mourn the sudden and violent end of Arnold Rivers.

Dinner finished, he went up to the gunroom and began compiling his list. He found a yardstick, and thumbtacked it to the edge of the desk to get over-all and barrel lengths, and used a pair of inside calipers and a decimal-inch rule from the workbench to get calibers. Sticking a sheet of paper into the portable, he began on the wheel locks, leaving spaces to insert the description of the stolen pistols, when recovered. When he had finished the wheel locks, he began on the snaphaunces, then did the miguelet-locks. He had begun on the true flintlocks when Walters, who had finished his own dinner, came up to help him. Rand put the butler to work fetching pistols from the racks, and replacing those he had already listed. After a while, Dunmore strolled in.

"You say you found Rivers's body yourself, Colonel Rand?" he asked.

Rand nodded, finished what he was typing, and looked up.

"Why, yes. There were a few details I wanted to clear up with him, and I called at his shop this morning. I found him lying dead inside." He went on to describe the manner in which Rivers had met his death. "The radio and newspaper accounts were accurate enough, in the main; there were a few details omitted, at the request of the police, of course."

"Well, you didn't get involved in it, though?" Dunmore inquired anxiously. "I mean, you're not taking any part in the investigation? After all, we don't want to be mixed up in anything like this."

"In that case, Mr. Dunmore, let me advise you not to discuss the matter of Rivers's offer to buy this collection with anybody outside," Rand told him. "So far, the police and the District

Attorney's office both seem to think that Rivers was killed by somebody whom he'd swindled in a business deal. Of course, they know about the collection being for sale, and Rivers's offering to buy it."

"They do?" Dunmore asked sharply. "Did you tell them that?"

"Naturally. I had to account for my presence at Rivers's shop, this morning," Rand replied. "I don't know if the idea has occurred to them that somebody might have killed Rivers to eliminate a rival bidder for the collection or not; I wouldn't say anything, if I were you, that might give them the idea."

The extension phone rang shrilly. Walters picked it up, spoke into it, and listened for a moment.

"Yes, Miss Lawrence; he's right here. You wish to speak to him?" He handed the phone across the desk to Rand. "Miss Karen Lawrence, for you, Colonel Rand."

Rand took the phone. Before he had time to say "hello," the antique-shop girl demanded of him:

"Colonel Rand, you must tell me the truth. Did you have anything to do with Pierre Jarrett's being arrested?"

"*What?*" Rand barked. Then he softened his voice. "No; on my honor, Miss Lawrence. I knew nothing about it until this moment. Who did it? Olsen?"

"I don't know what his name was. He was a State Police sergeant," she replied. "He and another State Policeman came to the Jarrett house about half an hour ago, charged Pierre with the murder of Arnold Rivers, and took him away. His mother phoned me about it a few minutes ago."

"That God-damned two-faced Jesuitical bastard!" Rand exploded. "Where are you now?"

"Here at my shop. Mrs. Jarrett is coming here. She's afraid the reporters will be coming out to the house as soon as they hear about it, and she doesn't want to talk to them."

"All right. I'll be there as soon as I can. If there's anything I can do to help you, you can count on me for it."

He hung up, and turned to Walters. "Is my car still out front?" he asked. "It is? Good. I'll be gone for a while; tell the others I have something to attend to."

"What's happened now?" Dunmore asked sourly.

"Just what I was speaking about. The Gestapo gathered up Pierre Jarrett; they seem to have gotten the idea, now, that the motive may have been competition for the collection. Next thing, Farnsworth will think he has a case against Carl Gwinnett, and he'll land in the jug, too. I hope you realize that every time something like this happens, it peels a thousand or so off the price I'll be able to get for you people for these pistols."

Dunmore didn't try to ask how that would happen, for which Rand was duly thankful; he accepted the statement uncritically. Walters was staring at Rand in horror, saying nothing. Rand picked up the outside phone and dialed the same number he had called from the Rivers place that morning.

"Is Sergeant McKenna about?... He is? Fine; I'd like to speak to him.... Oh, hello, Mick; Jeff Rand."

McKenna chuckled out of the receiver. "Sort of slipped one over on you, didn't I?" he gloated. "Why, I was checking up on those people who were at Gresham's, last evening, and they all agreed that young Jarrett and the Lawrence girl had left the party about ten. So I had a talk with Miss Lawrence, and she tried to tell me that Jarrett was with her at her apartment, over the antique shop, from about ten fifteen until about twelve, when another girl she rooms with got home from a date. I'd of took that, too, only right across the street from the antique shop there is one of these old hens like you find in every neighborhood, the kind that keeps their nose flattened on the window between the curtains, checking up on the neighbors. I spotted her when I came out of the antique shop, so I slipped around to see her, and she told me that young Jarrett went into the apartment with the girl at about quarter past ten, stayed inside for about twenty minutes, then came out and drove away. She says Jarrett came back in about half an hour, and stayed till this girl who shares the Lawrence girl's apartment —a Miss Dupont, who teaches sixth grade at Thaddeus Stevens School-got home, about twelve. So there you are."

"Uh-huh. Dave Ritter said this was going to turn into another Hall-Mills case; well, now you have your Pig Woman," Rand said. "Miss Lawrence shouldn't have lied to you, Mick. I suppose she got worried when you started asking questions, and there's nothing like a good murder in the neighborhood to make liars out of people."

"And damn well I know that!" McKenna agreed. "But that isn't all. It seems our cruise-car crew spotted Jarrett's car standing in Rivers's drive, about eleven. Just when he was away from the antique-shop, and about when the M.E. figures Rivers was getting the business."

"Did they get the number?" Rand asked. "Or how did they identify the car?"

"Oh, they knew it; see, our boys shoot a lot with the Scott County Rifle & Pistol Club, and they've all seen Jarrett's car at the range, different times," McKenna said. "A gray 1947 Plymouth coupé. Like I say, they knew the car, and they knew Jarrett collects guns, and the lights were on inside the shop and the shades were drawn, so they didn't think anything of it, at the time. See, they went to bed about ten this morning, and didn't get up till after five, so I didn't find out about it till after supper."

Rand shrugged, and managed to get some of the shrug into his voice. "Can be, at that," he said. "I hope you're not making a mistake, Mick; if you are, his lawyer's going to crucify you. What are you using for a motive?"

"Rivers was outbidding this crowd Jarrett and the girl were in with. They all told me about that," McKenna said. "And he and the girl were planning to use their end of the collection to go into the arms business, after they got married. Rivers got in the way." McKenna, at the other end of the line, must have shrugged, too. "After all, for about four years, they'd been training Jarrett to overcome resistance with the bayonet, so he did just that."

"Maybe so. You find out anything about that other matter I was interested in?"

"You mean the pistols? Huh-unh; we went over Rivers's place with a fine-tooth comb, and questioned young Gillis about it, and we didn't get a thing. You sure those pistols went to Rivers?"

"I'm not sure of anything at all," Rand replied, looking at his watch. "You going to be in, say in a couple of hours? I want to have a talk with you."

"Sure. I'll be around all evening," McKenna assured him. "If we don't have another murder."

Rand hung up. He pulled the sheet out of the typewriter, laid it face down on the other sheets he had finished, and laid a long seventeenth-century Flemish flintlock on top for a paperweight, memorizing the position of the pistol relative to the paper under it.

"Put those pistols back on the wall," he told Walters, indicating several he had laid aside after listing. "Leave the others there; I'm not finished with them yet. I'll be back before too long. If I don't find any more bodies."

Chapter 16

It was raining again as Rand parked his car about a hundred yards up the street from Karen Lawrence's antique-shop. The windows were dark, but Karen was waiting inside the door for him. He entered quickly, mindful of the All-Seeing Eye across the street, and followed her to a back room, where Mrs. Jarrett and Dorothy Gresham were. All three women regarded him intently, as though trying to decide whether he was friend or enemy. There was a long silence before Mrs. Jarrett spoke, and when she did, her words were almost the same as Karen's when she had spoken over the phone.

"Colonel Rand," she began, obviously struggling with herself, "you must tell me the truth. Did you have anything to do with my son's being arrested?"

Rand shook his head. "Absolutely nothing, Mrs. Jarrett," he told her, unbuckling the belt of his raincoat and taking it off. "I have never seriously suspected your son of the Rivers murder, I had no idea that McKenna was contemplating arresting him, and if I had, I would have advised him against it. Besides causing annoyance to innocent people, McKenna's made a serious tactical error. He was misled by appearances, and he was afraid I'd break this case before he did, which I intend to do." He turned to Karen Lawrence. "I talked to McKenna after you called me; he as much as admitted making that arrest to get in ahead of me."

"I told you," Dorothy Gresham flashed at the others. "I knew Jeff wouldn't stoop to anything as contemptible as pretending to be Pierre's friend and then getting him arrested!"

Rand permitted himself a wry inward smile. He hoped she would not have an opportunity to observe his stooping capabilities before he had finished his various operations at Rosemont.

"I certainly hoped not." Mrs. Jarrett relaxed, smiling faintly at Rand. "Pierre likes you, Colonel. I hated the thought that you might have betrayed him. Are you working on the Rivers case, too?"

Rand nodded again, turning to Dot Gresham. "Your father retained me to make an investigation," he said. "After that trouble he had with Rivers about that spurious North & Cheney, he wanted the murderer caught before somebody got around to accusing him."

"You mean there's a chance Dad might be suspected?" Dot was scared.

Rand nodded. The girl was beginning to look suspiciously at Karen and Mrs. Jarrett. Getting ready to toss Pierre to the wolves if her father were in danger, Rand suspected. He hastened to reassure her.

"Rivers was still alive when your father reached home, last evening," he told her. "That's been established."

She breathed her obvious relief. If Gresham had left home after Rand's departure with Philip Cabot, she didn't know it.

Karen, on the other hand, was growing more and more worried.

"Look, Colonel," she began. "They didn't just pull Pierre's name out of a hat. They must have had something to suspect him about."

"Yes. You shouldn't have lied to McKenna. He checked up on your story; the woman across the street told him about seeing Pierre leave here a little before eleven and come back about half an hour later."

"I was afraid of that," Karen said. "I forgot all about that old hag. There's nothing that can go on around here that she doesn't know about; Pierre calls her Mrs. G2."

"And then," Rand continued, "McKenna claims that a car like Pierre's was seen parked in Rivers's drive about the time Pierre was away from here."

Mrs. Jarrett moaned softly; her face, already haggard, became positively ghastly. Karen gasped in fright.

"They only identified it as to model and make; they didn't get the license number ... Where did Pierre go, while he was away from here?"

"He went out for cigarettes," Karen said. "When we came here from Greshams', we made some coffee, and then sat and talked for a while, and then we found out that we were both out of cigarettes and there weren't any here. So Pierre said he'd go out and get some. He was gone about half an hour; when he came back, he had a carton, and some hot pork sandwiches. He'd gotten them at the same place as the cigarettes-Art Igoe's lunch-stand."

"Could Igoe verify that?"

"It wouldn't help if he did. Igoe's place isn't a five-minute drive from Rivers's, farther down the road."

"Has Pierre a lawyer?" Rand asked.

"No. Not yet. We were just talking about that."

"Dad would defend him," Dot suggested. "Of course, he's not a criminal lawyer —"

"Carter Tipton, in New Belfast," Rand told them. "He's my lawyer; he's gotten me out of more jams than you could shake a stick at. Where's the telephone? I'll call him now."

"You think he'd defend Pierre?"

"Unless I'm badly mistaken, Pierre isn't going to need any trial defense," Rand told them. "He will need somebody to look after his interests, and we'll try to get him out on a writ as soon as possible."

He looked at his watch. It was ten minutes to nine. It was hard to say where Carter Tipton would be at the moment; his manservant would probably know. Karen showed him the phone and he started to put through a person-to-person call.

It was eleven o'clock before he backed his car into the Fleming garage, and the rain had turned to a wet, sticky snow. All the Fleming cars were in, but Rand left the garage doors open. He also left his hat and coat in the car.

After locating and talking to Tipton and arranging for him to meet Dave Ritter at the Rosemont Inn, he had gone to the State Police substation, where he had talked at length with Mick McKenna. He had been compelled to tell the State Police sergeant a number of things he had intended keeping to himself. When he was through, McKenna went so far as to admit that he had been a trifle hasty in arresting Pierre Jarrett. Rand suspected that he was mentally kicking himself with hobnailed boots for his premature act. He also submitted, for McKenna's approval, the scheme he had outlined to Dave Ritter, and obtained a promise of cooperation.

When he entered the Fleming library, en route to the gunroom, he found the entire family assembled there; with them was Humphrey Goode. As he came in, they broke off what had evidently been an acrimonious dispute and gave him their undivided attention. Geraldine, relaxed in a chair, was smoking; for once, she didn't have a glass in her hand. Gladys occupied another chair; she was smoking, too. Nelda had been pacing back and forth like a caged tiger; at Rand's entrance, she turned to face him, and Rand wondered whether she thought he was Clyde Beatty or a side of beef. Goode and Dunmore sat together on the sofa, forming what looked like a bilateral offensive and defensive alliance, and Varcek, looking more than ever like Rudolf Hess, stood with folded arms in one corner.

"Now, see here, Rand," Dunmore began, as soon as the detective was inside the room, "we want to know just exactly for whom you're working, around here. And I demand to know where you've been since you left here this evening."

"And I," Goode piped up, "must protest most strongly against your involvement in this local murder case. I am informed that, while in the employ of this family, you accepted a retainer from another party to investigate the death of Arnold Rivers."

"That's correct," Rand informed him. Then he turned to Gladys. "Just for the record, Mrs. Fleming, do you recall any stipulation to the effect that the business of handling this pistol-collection should have the exclusive attention of my agency? I certainly don't recall anything of the sort."

"No, of course not," she replied. "As long as the collection is sold to the best advantage, I haven't any interest in any other business of your agency, and have no right to have." She turned to the others. "I thought I made that clear to all of you."

"You didn't answer my question!" Dunmore yelled at him.

"I don't intend to. You aren't my client, and I'm not answerable to you."

"Well, you carry my authorization," Goode supported him. "I think I have a right to know what's being done."

"As far as the collection's concerned, yes. As for the Rivers murder, or my armored-car service, or any other business of the Tri-State Agency, no."

"Well, you made use of my authorization to get that revolver from Kirchner —" Goode began.

"Aah!" Rand cried. "So that concerns the Rivers murder, does it? Well! When did you find that out, now? When Kirchner called you, you had no objection to his giving me that revolver. What changed your mind for you? Didn't you know that Rivers was dead, then?" Rand watched Goode trying to assimilate that. "Or didn't you think I knew?"

Goode cleared his throat noisily, twisting his mouth. The others were looking back and forth from him to Rand, in obvious bewilderment; they realized that Rand had pulled some kind of a rabbit out of a hat, but they couldn't understand how he'd done it.

"What I mean is that since then you have allowed yourself to become involved in this murder case. You have let it be publicly known that you are a private detective, working for the Fleming family," Goode orated. "How long, then, will it be before it will be said, by all sorts of irresponsible persons, that you are also investigating the death of Lane Fleming?"

"Well?" Rand asked patiently. "Are you afraid people will start calling that a murder, too?"

Gladys was looking at him apprehensively, as though she were watching him juggle four live hand grenades.

"Is anybody saying that now?" Varcek asked sharply.

"Not that I know of," Rand lied. "But if Goode keeps on denying it, they will."

"You know perfectly well," Goode exploded, "that I am alluding to these unfounded and mischievous rumors of suicide, which are doing the Premix Company so much harm. My God, Mr. Rand, can't you realize —"

"Oh, come off it, Goode," Varcek broke in amusedly. "We all-Colonel Rand included-know that you started those rumors yourself. Very clever-to start a rumor by denying it. But scarcely original. Doctor Goebbels was doing it almost twenty years ago."

"My God, is that true?" Nelda demanded. "You mean, he's been going around starting all these stories about Father committing suicide?" She turned on Goode like an enraged panther. "Why, you lying old son of a bitch!" she screamed at him.

"Of course. He wants to start a selling run on Premix," Varcek explained to her. "He's buying every share he can get his hands on. We all are." He turned to Rand. "I'd advise you to buy some, if you can find any, Colonel Rand. In a month or so, it's going to be a really good thing."

"I know about the merger. I am buying," Rand told him. "But are you sure of what Goode's been doing?"

"Of course," Gladys put in contemptuously. "I always wondered about this suicide talk; I couldn't see why Humphrey was so perturbed about it. Anything that lowered the market price of Premix, at this time, would be to his advantage." She looked at Goode as though he had six legs and a hard shell. "You know, Humphrey, I can't say I exactly thank you for this."

"Did you know about it?" Nelda demanded of her husband. "You did! My God, Fred, you are a filthy specimen!"

"Oh, you know; anything to turn a dishonest dollar," Geraldine piped up. "Like the late Arnold Rivers's ten-thousand offer. Say! I wonder if that mightn't be what Rivers died of? Raising the price and leaving Fred out in the cold!"

Dunmore simply stared at her, making a noise like a chicken choking on a piece of string.

"Well, all this isn't my pidgin," Rand said to Gladys. "I only work here, *Deo gratias*, and I still have some work to do."

With that, he walked past Goode and Dunmore and ascended the spiral stairway to the gunroom. Even at the desk, in the far corner of the room, he could hear them going at it, hammer-and-tongs, in the library. Sometimes it would be Nelda's strident shrieks that would dominate the bedlam below; sometimes it would be Fred Dunmore, roaring like a bull. Now and then, Humphrey Goode would rumble something, and, once in a while, he could hear Gladys's trained and modulated voice. Usually, any remark she made would be followed by outraged shouts from Goode and Dunmore, like the crash of falling masonry after the whip-crack of a tank-gun.

At first Rand eavesdropped shamelessly, but there was nothing of more than comic interest; it was just a routine parade and guard-mount of the older and more dependable family skeletons, with special emphasis on Humphrey Goode's business and professional ethics. When he was satisfied that he would hear nothing having any bearing on the death of Lane Fleming, Rand went back to his work.

After a while, the tumult gradually died out. Rand was still typing when Gladys came up the spiral and perched on the corner of the desk, picking up a long brass-barreled English flintlock and hefting it.

"You know, I sometimes wonder why we don't all come up here, break out the ammunition, pick our weapons, and settle things," she said. "It never was like this when Lane was around. Oh, Nelda and Geraldine would bare their teeth at each other, once in a while, but now this place has turned into a miniature Iwo Jima. I don't know how much longer I'm going to be able to take it. I'm developing combat fatigue."

"It's snowing," Rand mentioned. "Let's throw them out into the storm."

"I can't. I have to give Nelda and Geraldine a home, as long as they live," she replied. "Terms of the will. Oh, well, Geraldine'll drink herself to death in a few years, and Nelda will elope with a prize-fighter, sometime."

"Why don't you have the house haunted? The Tri-State Agency has an excellent house-haunting department. Anything you want; poltergeists; apparitions; cold, clammy hands in the dark; footsteps in the attic; clanking chains and eldritch screams; banshees. Any three for the price of two."

"It wouldn't work. Geraldine is so used to polka-dotted dinosaurs and Little Green Men from Mars that she wouldn't mind an ordinary ghost, and Nelda'd probably try to drag it into bed with her." She laid down the pistol and slid off the desk. "Well, pleasant dreams; I'll see you in the morning."

After she had left the gunroom, Rand looked at his watch. It was a very precise instrument; a Swiss military watch, with a sweep second hand, and two timing dials. It had formerly been the property of an *Obergruppenführer* of the S.S., and Rand had appropriated it to replace his own, broken while choking the *Obergruppenführer* to death in an alley in Palermo. He zeroed the timing dials and pressed the start-button. Then he stood for a time over the old cobbler's bench, mentally reconstructing what had been done after Lane Fleming had been shot, after which he hurried down the spiral and along the rear hall to the garage, where he snatched his hat and coat from the car. He threw the coat over his shoulders like a cloak, and went on outside. He made his way across the lawn to the orchard, through the orchard to the lawn of Humphrey Goode's house, and across this to Goode's side door. He stood there for a few seconds, imagining himself opening the door and going inside. Then he stopped the timing hands and returned to the Fleming house, locking the garage doors behind him. In the garage, he looked at the watch.

It had taken exactly six minutes and twenty-two seconds. He knew that he could move more rapidly than the dumpy lawyer, but to balance that, he had been moving over more or less unfamiliar ground. He left his hat and trench coat in the car and went upstairs.

Undressing, he went into the bathroom in his dressing-gown, spent about twenty minutes shaving and taking a shower, and then returned to his own room.

Chapter 17

When he rose, the next morning, Rand noticed something which had escaped his eye when he had gone to bed the night before. His .38-special, in its shoulder-holster, was lying on the dresser; he had not bothered putting it on when he had gone to see Rivers the morning before, and it had lain there all the previous day. He distinctly remembered having moved it, shortly after dinner, when he had gone to his room for some notes he had made on the collection.

However, between that time and the present it had managed to flop itself over; the holster was now lying back-up. Intrigued by such a remarkable accomplishment in an inanimate object, Rand crossed the room in the dress-of-nature in which he slept and looked more closely at it, receiving a second and considerably more severe surprise. The revolver in the holster was not his own.

It was, to be sure, a .38 Colt Detective Special, and it was in his holster, but it was not the Detective Special he had brought with him from New Belfast. His own gun was of the second type, with the corners rounded off the grip; this one was of the original issue, with the square Police Positive grip. His own gun had seen hard service; this one was in practically new condition. There was a discrepancy of about thirty thousand in the serial numbers. His gun had been loaded in six chambers with the standard 158-grain loads; this one was loaded in only five, with 148-grain mid-range wad-cutter loads.

Rand stood for some time looking at the revolver. The worst of it was that he couldn't be exactly sure when the substitution had been made. It might have happened at any time between eight o'clock and twelve, when he had gone to bed. He rather suspected that it had been accomplished while he had been in the bathroom, however.

Dumping out the five rounds in the cylinder, he inspected the changeling carefully. It was, he thought, the revolver Lane Fleming had kept in the drawer of the gunroom desk. There was no obstruction in the two-inch barrel, the weapon had not been either fired or cleaned recently, the firing-pin had not been shortened, the mainspring showed the proper amount of tension, and the mechanism functioned as it should. There was a chance that somebody had made up five special hand-loads for him, using nitroglycerin instead of powder, but that didn't seem likely, as it would not necessitate a switch of revolvers. There were four or five other possibilities, all of them disquieting; he would have been a great deal less alarmed if somebody had taken a shot at him.

Getting a box of cartridges out of his Gladstone, he filled the cylinder with 158-grain loads. When he went to the bathroom, he took the revolver in his dressing-gown pocket; when he dressed, he put on the shoulder-holster, and pocketed a handful of spare rounds.

Anton Varcek was loitering in the hall when he came out; he gave Rand good-morning, and fell into step with him as they went toward the stairway.

"Colonel Rand, I wish you wouldn't mention this to anybody, but I would like a private talk with you," the Czech said. "After Fred Dunmore has left for the plant. Would that be possible?"

"Yes, Mr. Varcek; I'll be in the gunroom all morning, working." They reached the bottom of the stairway, where Gladys was waiting. "Understand," Rand continued, "I never really studied biology. I was exposed to it, in school, but at that time I was preoccupied with the so-called social sciences."

Varcek took the conversational shift in stride. "Of course," he agreed. "But you are trained in the scientific method of thought. That, at least, is something. When I have opportunity to explain my ideas more fully, I believe you will be interested in my conclusions."

They greeted Gladys, and walked with her to the dining-room. As usual, Geraldine was absent; Dunmore and Nelda were already at the table, eating in silence. Both of them seemed self-conscious, after the pitched battle of the evening before. Rand broke the tension by offering Humphrey Goode in the role of whipping-boy; he had no sooner made a remark in derogation of the lawyer than Nelda and her husband broke into a duet of vituperation. In the end, everybody affected to agree that the whole unpleasant scene had been entirely Goode's fault, and a pleasant spirit of mutual cordiality prevailed.

Finally Dunmore got up, wiping his mouth on a napkin.

"Well, it's about time to get to work," he said. "We might as well save gas and both use my car. Coming, Anton?"

"I'm sorry, Fred; I can't leave, yet. I have some notes upstairs I have to get in order. I was working on this new egg-powder, last evening, and I want to continue the experiments at the plant laboratory. I think I know how we'll be able to cut production costs on it, about five per cent."

"And boy, can we stand that!" Dunmore grunted. "Well, be seeing you at the plant."

Rand waited until Dunmore had left, then went across to the library and up to the gunroom. As soon as he entered the room above, he saw what was wrong. The previous thefts had been masked by substitutions, but whoever had helped himself to one of the more recent metallic-cartridge specimens, the night before, hadn't bothered with any such precaution, and a pair of vacant screwhooks disclosed the removal. A second look told Rand what had been taken: the little .25 Webley & Scott from the Pollard collection, with the silencer.

The pistol-trade which had been imposed on him had disquieted him; now, he had no hesitation in admitting to himself, he was badly scared. Whoever had taken that little automatic had had only one thought in mind-noiseless and stealthy murder. Very probably with one Colonel Jefferson Davis Rand in mind as the prospective corpse.

He sat down at the desk and started typing, at the same time trying to keep the hall door and the head of the spiral stairway under observation. It was an attempt which was responsible for quite a number of typographical errors. Finally, Anton Varcek came in from the hallway, approached the desk, and sat down in an armchair.

"Colonel Rand," he began, in a low voice, "I have been thinking over a remark you made, last evening. Were you serious when you alluded to the possibility that Lane Fleming had been murdered?"

"Well, the idea had occurred to me," Rand understated, keeping his right hand close to his left coat lapel. "I take it you have begun to doubt that it was an accident?"

"I would doubt a theory that a skilled chemist would accidentally poison himself in his own laboratory," Varcek replied. "I would not, for instance, pour myself a drink from a bottle labeled HNO3 in the belief that it contained vodka. I believe that Lane Fleming should be credited with equal caution about firearms."

"Yet you were the first to advance the theory that the shooting had been an accident," Rand pointed out.

"I have a strong dislike for firearms." Varcek looked at the pistols on the desk as though they were so many rattlesnakes. "I have always feared an accident, with so many in the house. When I saw him lying dead, with a revolver in his hand, that was my first thought. First thoughts are so often illogical, emotional."

"And you didn't consider the possibility of suicide?"

"No! Absolutely not!" The Czech was emphatic. "The idea never occurred to me, then or since. Lane Fleming was not the man to do that. He was deeply religious, much interested in church work. And, aside from that, he had no reason to wish to die. His health was excellent; much better than that of many men twenty years his junior. He had no business worries. The company is doing well, we had large Government contracts during the war and no reconversion problems afterward, we now have more orders than we have plant capacity to fill, and Mr. Fleming was consulting with architects about plant expansion. We have been spared any serious labor troubles. And Mr. Fleming's wife was devoted to him, and he to her. He had no family troubles."

Rand raised an eyebrow over that last. "No?" he inquired.

Varcek flushed. "Please, Colonel Rand, you must not judge by what you have seen since you came here. When Lane Fleming was alive, such scenes as that in the library last evening would have been unthinkable. Now, this family is like a ship without a captain."

"And since you do not think that he shot himself, either deliberately or inadvertently, there remains the alternative that he was shot by somebody else, either deliberately or, very improbably, by inadvertence," Rand said. "I think the latter can be safely disregarded. Let's agree that it was murder and go on from there."

Varcek nodded. "You are investigating it as such?" he asked.

"I am appraising and selling this pistol collection," Rand told him wearily. "I am curious about who killed Fleming, of course; for my own protection I like to know the background of situations in which I am involved. But do you think Humphrey Goode would bring me here to stir up a lot of sleeping dogs that might awake and grab him by the pants-seat? Or did you think that uproar in the library last evening was just a prearranged act?"

"I had not thought of Humphrey Goode. It was my understanding that Mrs. Fleming brought you here."

"Mrs. Fleming wants her money out of the collection, as soon as possible," Rand said. "To reopen the question of her husband's death and start a murder investigation wouldn't exactly expedite things. I'm just a more or less innocent bystander, who wants to know whether there is going to be any trouble or not.…Now, you came here to tell me what happened on the night of Lane Fleming's death, didn't you?"

"Yes. We had finished dinner at about seven," Varcek said. "Lane had been up here for about an hour before dinner, working on his new revolver; he came back here immediately after he was through eating. A little later, when I had finished my coffee, I came upstairs, by the main stairway. The door of this room was open, and Lane was inside, sitting on that old shoemaker's-bench, working on the revolver. He had it apart, and he was cleaning a part of it. The round part, where the loads go; the drum, is it?"

"Cylinder. How was he cleaning it?" Rand asked.

"He was using a small brush, like a test-tube brush; he was scrubbing out the holes. The chambers. He was using a solvent that smelled something like banana-oil."

Rand nodded. He could visualize the progress Fleming had made. If Varcek was telling the truth, and he remembered what Walters had told him, the last flicker of possibility that Lane Fleming's death had been accidental vanished.

"I talked with him for some ten minutes or so," Varcek continued, "about some technical problems at the plant. All the while, he kept on working on this revolver, and finished cleaning out the cylinder, and also the barrel. He was beginning to put the revolver together when I left him and went up to my laboratory.

"About fifteen minutes later I heard the shot. For a moment, I debated with myself as to what I had heard, and then I decided to come down here. But first I had to take a solution off a Bunsen burner, where I had been heating it, and take the temperature of it, and then wash my hands, because I had been working with poisonous materials. I should say all this took me about five minutes.

"When I got down here, the door of this room was closed and locked. That was most unusual, and I became really worried. I pounded on the door, and called out, but I got no answer. Then Fred Dunmore came out of the bathroom attached to his room, with nothing on but a bathrobe. His hair was wet, and he was in his bare feet and making wet tracks on the floor."

From there on, Varcek's story tallied closely with what Rand had heard from Gladys and from Walters. Everybody's story tallied, where it could be checked up on.

"You think the murderer locked the door behind him, when he came out of here?" Varcek asked.

"I think somebody locked the door, sometime. It might have been the murderer, or it might have been Fleming at the murderer's suggestion. But why couldn't the murderer have left the gunroom by that stairway?"

Varcek looked around furtively and lowered his voice. Now he looked like Rudolf Hess discussing what to do about Ernst Roehm.

"Colonel Rand; don't you think that Fred Dunmore could have shot Lane Fleming, and then have gone to his room and waited until I came downstairs?" he asked.

Here we go again! Rand thought. Just like the Rivers case; everybody putting the finger on everybody else.…

"And have undressed and taken a bath, while he was waiting?" he inquired. "You came down here only five minutes after the shot. In that time, Dunmore would have had to wipe his fingerprints off the revolver, leave it in Fleming's hand, put that oily rag in his other hand, set the deadlatch, cross the hall, undress, get into the bathtub and start bathing. That's pretty fast work."

"But who else could have done it?"

"Well, you, for one. You could have come down from your lab, shot Fleming, faked the suicide, and then gone out, locking the door behind you, and made a demonstration in the hall until you were joined by Dunmore and the ladies. Then, with your innocence well established, you could have waited until your wife prompted you, as she or somebody else was sure to, and then have gone down to the library and up the spiral," Rand said. "That's about as convincing, no more and no less, as your theory about Dunmore."

Varcek agreed sadly. "And I cannot prove otherwise, can I?"

"You can advance your Dunmore theory to establish reasonable doubt," Rand told him. "And if Dunmore's accused, he can do the same with the theory I've just outlined. And as long as reasonable doubt exists, neither of you could be convicted. This isn't the Third Reich or the Soviet Union; they wouldn't execute both of you to make sure of getting the right one. Both of you had a motive in this Mill-Pack merger that couldn't have been negotiated while Fleming lived. One or the other of you may be guilty; on the other hand, both of you may be innocent."

"Then who...?" Varcek had evidently bet his roll on Dunmore. "There is no one else who could have done it."

"The garage doors were open, if I recall," Rand pointed out. "Anybody could have slipped in that way, come through the rear hall to the library and up the spiral, and have gone out the same way. Some of the French Maquis I worked with, during the war, could have wiped out the whole family, one after the other, that way."

A look of intense concentration settled upon Varcek's face. He nodded several times.

"Yes. Of course," he said, his thought-chain complete. "And you spoke of motive. From what you must have heard, last evening, Humphrey Goode was no less interested in the merger than Fred Dunmore or myself. And then there is your friend Gresham; he is quite familiar with the interior of this house, and who knows what terms National Milling & Packaging may have made with him, contingent upon his success in negotiating the merger?"

"I'm not forgetting either of them," Rand said. "Or Fred Dunmore, or you. If you did it, I'd advise you to confess now; it'll save everybody, yourself included, a lot of trouble."

Varcek looked at him, fascinated. "Why, I believe you regard all of us just as I do my fruit flies!" he said at length. "You know, Colonel Rand, you are not a comfortable sort of man to have around." He rose slowly. "Naturally, I'll not mention this interview. I suppose you won't want to, either?"

"I'd advise you not to talk about it, at that," Rand said. "The situation here seems to be very delicate, and rather explosive....Oh, as you go out, I'd be obliged to you for sending Walters up here. I still have this work here, and I'll need his help."

After Varcek had left him, Rand looked in the desk drawer, verifying his assumption that the .38 he had seen there was gone. He wondered where his own was, at the moment.

When the butler arrived, he was put to work bringing pistols to the desk, carrying them back to the racks, taking measurements, and the like. All the while, Rand kept his eye on the head of the spiral stairway.

Finally he caught a movement, and saw what looked like the top of a peak-crowned gray felt hat between the spindles of the railing. He eased the Detective Special out of its holster and got to his feet.

"All right!" he sang out. "Come on up!"

Walters looked, obviously startled, at the revolver that had materialized in Rand's hand, and at the two men who were emerging from the spiral. He was even more startled, it seemed, when he realized that they wore the uniform of the State Police.

"What....What's the meaning of this, sir?" he demanded of Rand.

"You're being arrested," Rand told him. "Just stand still, now."

He stepped around the desk and frisked the butler quickly, wondering if he were going to find a .25 Webley & Scott automatic or his own .38-Special. When he found neither, he holstered his temporary weapon.

"If this is your idea of a joke, sir, permit me to say that it isn't...."

"It's no joke, son," Sergeant McKenna told him. "In this country, a police-officer doesn't have to recite any incantation before he makes an arrest, any more than he needs to read any Riot Act before he can start shooting, but it won't hurt to warn you that anything you say can be used against you."

"At least, I must insist upon knowing why I am being arrested," Walters said icily.

"Oh! Don't you know?" McKenna asked. "Why, you're being arrested for the murder of Arnold Rivers."

For a moment the butler retained his professional glacial disdain, and then the bottom seemed to drop suddenly out of him. Rand suppressed a smile at this minor verification of his theory. Walters had been expecting to be accused of larceny, and was prepared to treat the charge with contempt. Then he had realized, after a second or so, what the State Police sergeant had really said.

"Good God, gentlemen!" He looked from Mick McKenna to Corporal Kavaalen to Rand and back again in bewilderment. "You surely can't mean that!"

"We can and we do," Rand told him. "You stole about twenty-five pistols from this collection, after Mr. Fleming died, and sold them to Arnold Rivers. Then, when I came here and started checking up on the collection, you knew the game was up. So, last evening, you took out the station-wagon and went to see Rivers, and you killed him to keep him from turning state's evidence and incriminating you. Or maybe you killed him in a quarrel over the division of the loot. I hope, for your sake, that it was the latter; if it was, you may get off with second degree murder. But if you can't prove that there was no premeditation, you're tagged for the electric chair."

"But ... But I didn't kill Mr. Rivers," Walters stammered. "I barely knew the gentleman. I saw him, once or twice, when he was here to see Mr. Fleming, but outside of that...."

"Outside of that, you sold him about twenty-five of these pistols, and got a like number of junk pistols from him, for replacements." He took the list Pierre Jarrett and Stephen Gresham had compiled out of his pocket and began reading: "Italian wheel lock pistol, late sixteenth- or early seventeenth-century; pair Italian snaphaunce pistols, by Lazarino Cominazo...." He finished the list and put it away. "I think we've missed one or two, but that'll do, for the time."

"But I didn't sell those pistols to Mr. Rivers," Walters expostulated. "I sold them to Mr. Carl Gwinnett. I can prove it!"

That Rand had not expected. "Go on!" he jeered. "I suppose you have receipts for all of them. Fences always do that, of course."

"But I did sell them to Mr. Gwinnett. I can take you to his house, if you get a search warrant, and show you where he has them hidden in the garret. He was afraid to offer them for sale until after this collection had been broken up and sold; he still has every one of them."

McKenna spat out an obscenity. "Aren't we ever going to have any luck?" he demanded. "Jarrett out on a writ this morning, and now this!"

"But he ain't in the clear," Kavaalen argued. "Maybe he didn't sell Rivers the pistols, but maybe he did kill him."

"Dope!" McKenna abused his subordinate. "If he didn't sell Rivers the pistols, why would he kill him?"

"He's only said he sold them to Gwinnett," Rand pointed out. Then he turned to Walters. "Look here; if we find those pistols in Gwinnett's possession, you're clear on this murder charge. There's still a slight matter of larceny, but that doesn't involve the electric chair. You take my advice and make a confession now, and then accompany these officers to Gwinnett's place and show them the pistols. If you do that, you may expect clemency on the theft charge, too."

"Oh, I will, sir! I'll sign a full confession, and take these police-officers and show them every one of the pistols...."

Rand put paper and carbon sheets in the typewriter. As Walters dictated, he typed; the butler listed every pistol which Gresham and Pierre Jarrett had found missing, and a cased presentation pair of .44 Colt 1860's that nobody had missed. He signed the triplicate copies willingly; he didn't seem to mind signing himself into jail, as long as he thought he was signing himself out of the electric chair.

The book in which Fleming had recorded his pistols he still had; he had removed it from the gunroom and was keeping it in his room. He said he would get it, along with the things he would need to take to jail with him. When it was finished, they all went down the spiral stairway into the library.

Nelda was standing at the foot of it. Evidently she had been listening to what had been going on upstairs.

"You dirty sneak!" she yelled, catching sight of Walters. "After all we've done for you, you turn around and rob us! I hope they give you twenty years!"

Walters turned to McKenna. "Sergeant, I am willing to accept the penalty of the law for what I have done, but I don't believe, sir, that it includes being yapped at by this vulgar bitch."

Nelda let out an inarticulate howl of fury and sprang at him, nails raking. Corporal Kavaalen caught her wrist before she could claw the prisoner.

"That's enough, you!" he told her. "You stop that, or you'll spend a night in jail yourself."

She jerked her arm loose from his grasp and flung out of the library. As she went out, Gladys entered; Rand, who had been bringing up in the rear, stepped down from the stairway.

"He confessed," he said softly. "We had to bluff it out of him, but he came across. Sold the pistols to Carl Gwinnett. We're going, now, to pick up Gwinnett and the pistols."

"I'm glad you found the pistols," she told him. "But what're we going to do, over the week-end, for a butler...."

Rand snapped his fingers. "Dammit, I never thought of that!" He allowed his brow to furrow with thought. "I won't promise anything, but I may be able to dig up somebody for you, for a day or so. Some of my friends are visiting their son, in a Naval hospital on the West Coast, and their butler may be glad for a chance to pick up a little extra money. Shall I call him and find out?"

"Oh, Colonel Rand, would you? I'd be eternally grateful!"

It was just as easy as that.

Chapter 18

Dave Ritter, driving his small coupé, kept his eye on the white State Police car ahead. Rand, who had come away from the Fleming home in the white car, had called Ritter from the office of the Justice of the Peace while waiting for Walters to put up bail, after his hearing. Now, en route to Gwinnett's, he was briefing his assistant on what had happened.

"So everything's set," he concluded. "Mrs. Fleming jumped at it; she knows you're coming in your own car, which you may keep in the garage there. You've left New Belfast about now; if you show up around three, you'll be safe on the driving time. Your name is Davies; I decided on that in case I suffer a *lapsus linguæ* and call you Dave in front of somebody."

"Yeah. I'll have to watch and not call you Jeff, Colonel Rand, sir." He nodded toward the glove-box. "That Leech & Rigdon's in there; you'd better get it out before I go to the Flemings'. The guy at the drive-in made a positive identification; it's the one he sold Fleming. I saw the rest of the pistols he has there; don't waste time looking him up about them. They stink. And I saw Tip this morning. He got young Jarrett sprung on a writ." He thought for a moment. "What does this do to the Rivers and Fleming murders?"

"We can look for one man for both jobs, now," Rand said. "Probably the motive for Fleming was that merger he was so violently opposed to, and the Rivers killing must have been a security measure of some sort. There; that must be Gwinnett's, now."

The State Police car had pulled up in front of a large three-story frame house with faded and discolored paint and jigsaw scrollwork around the cornices, standing among a clump of trees beside the road. McKenna and Kavaalen got out, with Walters between them, and started up the path to the front steps. Ritter stopped behind the white sedan, and he and Rand got out. By that time, Walters and the two policemen were on the front porch.

Suddenly Ritter turned and sprinted around the right side of the house. Rand stood looking after him for a moment, then started to follow more slowly; as he did, a shot slammed in the rear. Jerking out the changeling .38-special, he whirled and ran around the left side of the house, arriving at the rear in time to see Gwinnett standing on a boardwalk between the house and the stable-garage behind, with his hands raised. There was a fresh bullet-scar on the boardwalk at his feet. Ritter was covering him from the corner of the house with the .380 Beretta.

Rand strolled over to Gwinnett, frisked him, and told him to put his hands down.

"Nice, Dave," he complimented. "I thought of that, too, about a minute too late. As soon as he saw Walters coming up the walk with the police, he knew what had happened. Come on, Gwinnett; we'll go through the house and let them in."

Gwinnett's eyes darted from side to side, like the eyes of a trapped animal. "I don't know what you're talking about," he said, stiff-lipped. "What is this, a stick-up?"

Nobody bothered to tell him to stop kidding. They marched him through the kitchen, where a Negro girl, her arms white with flour, was dithering in fright, and into the front hall. A woman in a faded housedress had just admitted the two officers and the former Fleming butler.

"You goddam rat!" Gwinnett yelled at Walters, as soon as he saw him.

"For God's sake, Carl," the woman begged. "Don't make things any worse than they are. Keep quiet!"

"All right, Gwinnett," McKenna said. "We're arresting you: receiving stolen goods, and accessory to larceny. We have a search warrant. Want to see it?"

"So you have a search warrant," Gwinnett said. "So go ahead and search; if you don't find anything, you'll plant something. I want to call my lawyer."

"That's your right," McKenna told him. "Aarvo, take him to a phone; let him call the White House if he wants to." He turned to Walters. "Now, where would he have this stuff stashed?"

"In the garret, sir. I know the way."

As Kavaalen accompanied Gwinnett to the phone, Walters started upstairs. Rand and McKenna followed, with Mrs. Gwinnett bringing up the rear. During the search of the attic, she stood to one side, watching the ex-butler dig into a pile of pistols.

"This is one, gentlemen," Walters said, producing a Springfield 1818 Model flintlock. "And here is the Walker Colt, and the .40-caliber Colt Paterson, and the Hall...."

Eventually, he had them all assembled, including the five cased sets. Rand found a couple of empty bushel baskets and laid the pistols in them, between layers of old newspapers. He picked up one, and McKenna took the other, while Walters piled the five flat hardwood cases into his arms like cordwood. Still saying nothing, her eyes stony with hatred, the woman followed them downstairs.

The rest of the afternoon was consumed with formalities. Gwinnett was given a hearing, at which he was represented by a lawyer straight out of a B-grade gangster picture. Rand had a heated argument with an over-zealous Justice of the Peace, who wanted to impound the pistols and jackknife-mark them for identification, but after hurling bloodthirsty threats of a damage suit for an astronomical figure, he managed to retain possession of the recovered weapons.

Ritter left at a little past three, to report for duty in the Fleming household. Rand rode with McKenna and Kavaalen to the State Police substation, where the pistols were transferred to McKenna's personal car, in which they and Rand were to be transported back to the Fleming place.

It was five o'clock before Rand had finished telling the sergeant and the corporal everything he felt they ought to know.

"When we get to the Flemings', I'll give you that revolver I got from the coroner," he finished. "One of your boys can take it to this fellow Umholtz, and get him to identify it. You might also show it to young Gillis, and see what he knows about it. Gillis might even give you a name for who got it from Rivers. I'm not building any hopes on that, and the reason I'm not is that Gillis is still alive. If he knew, I don't think he would be."

"Yeah. I can see that," McKenna nodded. "Fact is, I can see everything, now, except one thing. This pistol-switch somebody gave you; what's the idea of that?"

"Why, that's because I'm on the spot," Rand told him. "I'm to be killed, and somebody else is to be killed along with me. The .25 automatic will be used on me, and the .38 will be used on the other fellow, and we'll be found dead about five feet apart, and I'll be holding my own gun, and the other fellow will be holding the .25, and it will look as though we shot it out and scored a double knockout. That way, my mouth will be shut about what I've learned since I came here, and the man who's supposed to have killed me will take the rap for Fleming and Rivers both. Nothing to stop an investigation like a couple of corpses who can't tell their own story and can take the blame for everything."

"*Zhee-zus!*" Kavaalen's eyes widened. "That must be just it!"

"Well, you got your nerve about you, I'll say that," McKenna commented. "You sit there and talk about it like it was something that was going to happen to Joe Doakes and Oscar Zilch." He looked at Rand intently. "You want us to keep an eye on you?"

Rand leaned over and spat into the brass cuspidor, a gesture of braggadocio he had picked up among the French maquis.

"Hell, no! That's the last thing I do want!" he said. "I want him to try it. You realize, don't you, that all this is pure assumption and theory? We don't have a single fact, as it stands, that proves anything. We could go and pick this fellow up, and he's one of three men, so we could grab all three of them, and even if we found the .25 Webley & Scott and my .38 in his pockets, we couldn't charge him with anything. Fact is, right now we can't even prove that Lane Fleming's death was anything but the accident it's on the books as being. But let him take a shot at me...."

"And then you'll have another nice, clear case of self-defense." McKenna frowned. "God-dammit, Jeff, you've had to defend yourself too many times, already. This'll be-well, how many will it be?"

"Counting Germans?" Rand grinned. "Hell, I don't know; I can't remember all of them."

"One thing," Kavaalen said solemnly, "you never hear of any lawyers springing people out of cemeteries on writs."

"Look, Jeff," McKenna said, at length. "If it's the way you think, this guy won't dare kill you instantly, will he? Seems to me, the way the script reads, this other guy shoots you, and you shoot back and kill him, and then you die. Isn't that it?"

Rand nodded. "I'm banking on that. He'll try to give me a fatal but not instantly fatal wound, and that means he'll have to take time to pick his spot. The reason I've managed to survive these people against whom I've had to defend myself has been that I just don't give a damn where I shoot a man. A lot of good police officers have gotten themselves killed because they tried to wing somebody and took a second or so longer about shooting than they should have."

"Something in that, too," McKenna agreed. "But what I'm getting at is this: I think I know a way to give you a little more percentage." He rose. "Wait a minute; I'll be right back."

Chapter 19

There was less feuding at dinner that evening than at any previous meal Rand had eaten in the Fleming home. In the first place, everybody seemed a little awed in the presence of the new butler, who flitted in and out of the room like a ghost and, when spoken to, answered in a heavy B.B.C. accent. Then, the women, who carried on most of the hostilities, had re-erected their *front populaire* and were sharing a common pleasure in the recovery of the stolen pistols. And finally, there was a distinct possibility that the swift and dramatic justice that had overtaken Walters and Gwinnett at Rand's hands was having a sobering effect upon somebody at that table.

Dunmore, Nelda, Varcek, Geraldine and Gladys had been intending to go to a party that evening, but at the last minute Gladys had pleaded indisposition and telephoned regrets. The meal over, Rand had gone up to the gunroom, Gladys drifted into the small drawing-room off the dining-room, and the others had gone to their rooms to dress.

Rand was taking down the junk with which Walters had infiltrated the collection and was listing and hanging up the recovered items when Fred Dunmore, wearing a dressing-gown, strolled in.

"I can't get over the idea of Walters being a thief," he sorrowed. "I wouldn't have believed it if I hadn't seen his signed confession.... Well, it just goes to show you...."

"He took his medicine standing up," Rand said. "And he helped us recover the pistols. If I were you, I'd go easy with him."

Dunmore shook his head. "I'm not a revengeful man, Colonel Rand," he said, "but if there's one thing I can't forgive, it's a disloyal employee." His mouth closed sternly around his cigar. "He'll have to take what's coming to him." He stood by the desk for a moment, looking down at the recovered items and the pile of junk on the floor. "When did you first suspect him?"

"Almost from the first moment I saw this collection." Rand explained the reasoning which had led him to suspect Walters. "The real clincher, to my mind, was the fact that he knew this collection almost as well as Lane Fleming did, and wouldn't be likely to be deceived by these substitutions any more than Fleming would. Yet he said nothing to anybody; neither to Mrs. Fleming, nor Goode, nor myself. If he weren't guilty himself, I wanted to know his reason for keeping silent. So I put the pressure on him, and he cracked open."

"Well, I want you to know how grateful we all are," Dunmore said feelingly. "I'm kicking hell out of myself, now, about the way I objected when Gladys brought you in here. My God, suppose we'd tried to sell the collection ourselves! Anybody who'd have been interested in buying would have seen what you saw, and then they'd have claimed that we were trying to hold out on them." He hesitated. "You've seen how things are here," he continued ruefully. "And that's something else I have to thank you for; I mean, keeping your mouth shut till you got the pistols back. There'd have been a hell of a row; everybody would have blamed everybody else.... How did you get him to confess, though?"

Rand told him about the subterfuge of the trumped-up murder charge. Dunmore had evidently never thought of that hoary device; he chuckled appreciatively.

"Say, that *was* smart! No wonder he was so willing to admit everything and help you get them back." He looked at the pistols on the desk and moved one or two of them. "Did you get the one the coroner had? Goode said something —"

"Oh, yes; I got that yesterday." Rand turned and went to the workbench, bringing back the Leech & Rigdon, which he handed to Dunmore. "That's it. I fired out the other five charges, and cleaned it at the State Police substation." He watched Dunmore closely, but there seemed to be no reaction.

"So that's it." Dunmore looked at it with a show of interest and honest sorrow, and handed it back, then shifted his cigar across his mouth. "Look here, Colonel; I've been wanting to ask you something. Did Gladys just get you to come here to appraise and sell the collection, or are you investigating Lane's death, too?"

"Well, now, you're asking me to be disloyal to my employer," Rand objected. "Why don't you ask her that? If she wants you to know, she'll tell you."

"Dammit, I can't! Suppose she's satisfied that it really was an accident; would I want to start her worrying and imagining things?"

"No, I suppose you wouldn't," Rand conceded. "You're not at all satisfied on that point yourself, are you?"

"Well, are you?" Dunmore parried.

That sort of fencing could go on indefinitely. Rand determined to stop it. After all, if Dunmore was the murderer of Lane Fleming, he would already know how little Rand was deceived by the fake accident; the Leech & Rigdon had told him that already. If he weren't, telling him would do no harm at this point, and might even do some good.

"Why, I think Fleming was murdered," Rand told him, as casually as though he were expressing an opinion on tomorrow's weather. "And I further believe that whoever killed Fleming also killed Arnold Rivers. That, by the way, is where I come in. Stephen Gresham has retained me to find the Rivers murderer; to do that, I must first learn who killed Lane Fleming. However, I was not retained to investigate the Fleming murder, and as far as I know from anything she has told me, Gladys Fleming is quite satisfied that her husband shot himself accidentally." In a universe of ordered abstractions and multiordinal meanings, the literal truth, on one order of abstraction, was often a black lie on another. "Does that answer your question?" he asked, with open-faced innocence.

Dunmore nodded. "Yes, I get it, now. Look here, do you think Anton Varcek could have done it? I know it's a horrible idea, and I want you to understand that I'm not making any accusations, but we always took it for granted that he'd been up in his lab, and had come downstairs when he heard the shot. But suppose he came down and shot Fleming, and then went out in the hall, and made that rumpus outside after locking the door behind him?"

"That's possible," Rand agreed. "You were taking a bath when you heard the shot, weren't you?"

Dunmore shook his head. "I suppose so. I didn't hear any shot, to tell the truth. All I heard was Anton pounding on the door and yelling. I suppose I had my head under the shower, and the noise of the water kept me from hearing the shot." He stopped short, taking his cigar from his mouth and pointing it at Rand. "And, by God, that would have been about five minutes before he started hammering on the door!" he exclaimed. "Time enough for him to have fixed things to look like an accident, set the deadlatch, and have gone out in the hall, and started making a noise. And another thing. You say that whoever killed Lane also killed this fellow Rivers. Well, on Thursday night, when Rivers was killed, Anton didn't get home till around twelve."

"Yes, I'd thought of that. You know, though, that the murderer doesn't have to be Varcek, or anybody else who was in the house at the time. The garage doors were open —I'm told that your wife was out at the time-and anybody could have sneaked in the back way, up through the library, and out the same way. There are one or two possibilities besides you and Anton Varcek."

Dunmore's eyes widened. "Yes, and I can think of one, without half trying, too!" He nodded once or twice. "For instance, the man who was afraid you were investigating Fleming's death; the man who started that suicide story!" He looked at Rand interrogatively. "Well, I got to go; Nelda'll be out of the bathroom by now. I want to talk to you about this some more, Colonel."

After Dunmore had gone out, Rand mopped his face. The room seemed insufferably hot. He found an electric fan over the workbench and plugged it in, but it made enough noise to cover any sounds of stealthy approach, and he shut it off. He had finished revising his list to include the recovered pistols for as far as it was completed, and was hanging them back on the wall when Ritter came in.

"House is clear, now," his assistant said, stepping out of his P. G. Wodehouse character. "Both pairs left in the Packard, Dunmore driving. Man, what a cat-and-dog show this place is! It's a wonder our client isn't nuts."

"You haven't seen anything; you ought to have been here last night ... Where is our client, by the way?"

"Downstairs." Ritter fished a cigarette out of his livery and appropriated Rand's lighter. "If we hear her coming, you can grab this." He brushed a couple of Paterson Colts to one side and sat down on the edge of the desk, taking a deep drag on the cigarette. "What's the regular law doing, now that young Jarrett is out?"

"I had a long talk with Mick McKenna," Rand said. "Fortunately, Mick and I have worked together before. I was able to tell him the facts of life, and he'll be a good boy now. When last heard from, Farnsworth was beginning to blow his hot breath on the back of Cecil Gillis's neck."

Ritter picked up the big .44 Colt Walker and tried the balance. "Man, this even makes that Colt Magnum of mine feel light!" he said. "Say, Jeff, if Farnsworth's going after Gillis, it's probably on account of those stories about him and Mrs. Rivers. At least, all that stuff would come out if he arrested him. Maybe we could get a fee out of Mrs. Rivers."

"I'd thought of that. Unfortunately, Mrs. Rivers had a very convenient breakdown, when she heard the news; she is now in a hospital in New York, and won't be back until after the funeral. Prostrated with grief. Or something. And this case is due to blow up like Hiroshima before then. Well, we can't get fees from everybody." That, of course, was one of the sad things of life to which one must reconcile oneself. "I got a call from Pierre Jarrett; Tip's staying at the Jarrett place tonight. I thought it would be a good idea to have him within reach for a while."

The private outside phone rang shrilly. Ritter let it go for several rings, then picked it up.

"This is the Fleming residence," he stated, putting on his character again. "Oh, yes indeed, sir. Colonel Rand is right here, sir; I'll tell him you're calling." He put a hand over the mouthpiece. "Humphrey Goode."

Rand took the phone and named himself into it.

"I would like to talk to you privately, Colonel Rand," the lawyer said. "On a subject of considerable importance to our, shall I say, mutual clients. Could you find time to drop over, sometime this evening?"

"Well, I'm very busy, at the moment, Mr. Goode," Rand regretted. "There have been some rather deplorable developments here, lately. The butler, Walters, has been arrested for larceny. It seems that since Mr. Fleming's death, he has been systematically looting the pistol-collection. I'm trying to get things straightened out, now."

"Good heavens!" Goode was considerably shaken. "When did you discover this, Colonel Rand? And why wasn't I notified before? And are there many valuable items missing?"

"I discovered it as soon as I saw the collection," Rand began answering his questions in order. "Neither you, nor anybody else was notified, because I wanted to get evidence to justify an arrest first. And nothing is missing; everything has been recovered," he finished. "That's what I'm so busy about, now; getting my list revised, and straightening out the collection."

"Oh, fine!" Goode was delighted. "I hope everything was handled quietly, without any unnecessary publicity? But this other matter; I don't care to go into it over the phone, and it's imperative that we discuss it privately, at once."

"Well, suppose you come over here, Mr. Goode," Rand suggested. "That way, I won't have to interrupt my work so much. There's nobody at home now but Mrs. Fleming, and as she's indisposed, we'll be quite alone."

"Oh; very well. I think that's really a good idea; much better than your coming over here. I'll see you directly."

Ritter was grinning as Rand hung up. "That's the stuff," he approved. "The old Hitler technique; make them come to you, and then you can pound the table and yell at them all you want to."

"You go let him in," Rand directed. "Show him up here, and then take a plant on that spiral stairway out of the library, just out of sight. I don't think this it, but there's no use taking chances." He mopped his face again. "Damn, it's hot in here!"

Ten minutes later, Ritter ushered in Humphrey Goode, and inquired if there would be anything further, sir? When Rand said there wouldn't, he went down the spiral. Just as Rand had expected, Goode began peddling the same line as Varcek and Dunmore before him. They all came to see him in the gunroom with a common purpose. After easing himself into a chair, and going through some prefatory huffing and puffing, Goode came out with it. Did Rand believe that Lane Fleming had really been murdered, and was he investigating Fleming's death, after all?

"I have always believed that Lane Fleming was murdered," Rand replied. "I also believe that his murderer killed Arnold Rivers, as well. I am investigating the Rivers murder, and the Fleming murder may be considered as a part thereof. But what brings you around to discuss that, now? Did you learn something, since last evening, that leads you to suspect the same thing?"

"Well, not exactly. But this afternoon, Fred Dunmore and Anton Varcek came to my office, separately, of course, and each of them wanted to know if I had any reason to suspect that the, uh, tragedy, was actually a case of murder. Both had the impression that you were conducting an investigation under cover of your work on the pistol collection, and wanted to know whether Mrs. Fleming or I had employed you to do so."

"And you denied it, giving them the impression that Mrs. Fleming had?" Rand asked. "I hope you haven't put her in any more danger than she is now, by doing so."

Goode looked startled. "Colonel Rand! Do you actually mean that...?" he began.

"You were Lane Fleming's attorney, and board chairman of his company," Rand said. "You can probably imagine why he was killed. You can ask yourself just how safe his principal heir is now." Without giving Goode a chance to gather his wits, he pressed on: "Well, what's your opinion about Fleming's death? After all, you did go out of your way to create a false impression that he had committed suicide."

Goode, still bewildered by Rand's deliberately cryptic hints and a little frightened, had the grace to blush at that.

"I admit it; it was entirely unethical, and I'll admit that, too," he said. "But.... Well, I'm buying all the Premix stock that's out in small blocks, and so are Mr. Dunmore and Mr. Varcek. We all felt that such rumors would reduce the market quotation, to our advantage."

Rand nodded. "I picked up a hundred shares, the other day, myself. Your shenanigans probably chipped a little off the price I had to pay, so I ought to be grateful to you. But we're talking about murder, not market manipulation. Did either Varcek or Dunmore express any opinion as to who might have killed Fleming?"

The outside telephone rang before Goode could answer. Rand scooped it up at the end of the first ring and named himself into it. It was Mick McKenna calling.

"Well, we checked up on that cap-and-ball six-shooter you left with me," he said. "This gunsmith, Umholtz, refinished it for Rivers last summer. He showed the man who was to see him the entry in his job-book: make, model, serials and all."

"Oh, fine! And did you get anything out of young Gillis?" Rand asked.

"The gun was in Rivers's shop from the time Umholtz rejuvenated it till around the first of November. Then it was sold, but he doesn't know who to. He didn't sell it himself; Rivers must have."

"I assumed that; that's why he's still alive. Well, thanks, Mick. The case is getting tighter every minute."

"You haven't had any trouble yet?" McKenna asked anxiously. "How's the whoozis doing?"

"About as you might expect," Rand told him, mopping his face again. "Thanks for that, too."

He hung up and turned back to Goode. "Pardon the interruption," he said. "Sergeant McKenna, of the State Police. The officer who made the arrest on Walters and Gwinnett. Well, I suppose Dunmore and Varcek are each trying to blame the other," he said.

"Well, yes; I rather got that impression," Goode admitted.

"And which one do you like for the murderer? Or haven't you picked yours, yet?"

"You mean.... Yes, of course," Goode said slowly. "It must have been one or the other. But I can't think.... It's horrible to have to suspect either of them." For a moment, he stared unseeingly at the litter of high-priced pistols on the desk. Then:

"Colonel Rand, Lane Fleming is dead, and nothing either of us can do will bring him back. To expose his murderer certainly won't. But it would cause a scandal that would rock the Premix Company to its very foundations. It might even disastrously affect the market as a whole."

"Oh, come!" Rand reproved. "That's like talking about starting a hurricane with a palm-leaf fan."

"But you will admit that it would have a dreadful effect on Premix Foods," Goode argued. "It would probably prevent this merger from being consummated. Look here," he said urgently. "I don't know how much Gladys Fleming is paying you to rake all this up, but I'll gladly double her fee if you drop it and confine yourself to the matter of the collection."

Even in his colossal avarice, that was one kind of money Jeff Rand had never been tempted to take. An offer of that sort invariably made him furious. At the moment, he managed to choke down his anger, but he rejected Goode's offer in a manner which left no room for further discussion. Goode rose, shaking his head sadly.

"I suppose you realize," he said, sorrowfully, "that you're wrecking a ten-million-dollar corporation. One in which you, yourself, are a stockholder."

Rand brightened. "And the biggest wrecking jobs I ever did before were a couple of petrol dumps and a railroad bridge." He got to his feet along with the lawyer. "No need to call the butler; I'll let you out myself."

He accompanied Goode down the front stairway to the door. Goode was still gloomy.

"I made a mistake in trying to bribe you," he said. "But can't I appeal to your sense of fairness? Do you want to inflict serious losses on innocent investors merely to avenge one crime?"

"I don't approve of murder," Rand told him. "Least of all, to paraphrase Clausewitz, as an extension of business by other means. You know, if we let Lane Fleming's killer get away with it, somebody might take that as a precedent and bump you off to win a lawsuit, sometime. Ever think of that?"

When he returned to the gunroom, he found Gladys Fleming occupying the chair lately vacated by the family attorney. She blew a smoke-ring at him in greeting as he entered.

"Now what was Hump Goode up to?" she wanted to know.

"I'm taking too much on myself," Rand evaded. "Maybe I should have turned Walters over for trial by family court-martial. How do you like Davies, by the way?"

"Oh, he's cute," Gladys told him. "One of your operatives, isn't he?"

"Now what in the world gave you an idea like that?" he asked, as though humoring the vagaries of a child.

"Well, I suspected something of the sort from the alacrity with which you produced him, before Walters was out of the house," she said. "And nobody could be as perfect a stage butler as he is. But what really convinced me was coming into the library, a little while ago, and finding him squatting on the top of the spiral, covering Humphrey Goode with a small but particularly evil-looking automatic."

Rand chuckled. "What did you do?"

"Oh, I climbed up and squatted beside him," she replied. "I got there just as you were telling Goode what he could do with his bribe. You know, with one thing and another, Goode's beginning to become unamusing." She smoked in silence for a moment. "I ought to be indignant with you, filling my house with spies," she said. "But under the circumstances, I'm afraid I'm thankful, instead. Your op's a good egg, by the way; he's on his way to bring us some drinks."

"I ought to be sore at you, retaining me into a mess like this and telling me nothing," Rand told her. "What was the idea, anyhow? You wanted me to investigate your husband's murder, all along, didn't you?"

"I—I hadn't a thing to go on," she replied. "I was afraid, if I came out and told you what I suspected, that you'd think it was just another case of feminine dam-foolishness, and dismiss it as such. I knew it wasn't an accident; Lane didn't have accidents with guns. And if he'd wanted to kill himself, he'd have done it and left a note explaining why he had to. But I didn't have a single fact to give you. I thought that if you came here and started working on the collection, you'd find something."

"You should have taken a chance and told me what you suspected," Rand said. "I've taken a lot of cases on flimsier grounds than this. The fact is, you practically told me it was murder, when you were talking to me in my office."

"Jeff, I never was what the soap-operas call being 'in love' with Lane," she continued. "But he was wonderful to me. He gave me everything a girl who grew up in a sixteen-dollar apartment over a fruit store could want. And then somebody killed him, just as you'd step on a cockroach, because he got in the way of a business deal. I'm glad to be able to spend money to help catch whoever did it. It won't help him, but it'll make me feel a lot better....You will catch him, won't you?"

Rand nodded. "I don't know whether he'll ever go to trial and be convicted," he said. "I don't think he will. But you can take my word for it; he won't get away with it. Tomorrow, I think the lid's going to blow off. Maybe you'd better be away from home when it does. Take Nelda and Geraldine with you, and go somewhere. There's likely to be some uproar."

"Well, Nelda and Geraldine and I are going to church, in the morning," Gladys said. "It's a question of face. We have a rented pew-Lane was quite active in church work-and none of us are willing to let ourselves get squeezed out of it. We all go; even Geraldine manages to drag herself to the Lord's House through an alcoholic fog. And we'll have to be back in time for dinner. It would look funny if we weren't."

"Well, if nothing's happened by the time you get back, I want you to talk the girls into going somewhere with you in the afternoon, and stay away till evening. And don't get the idea that you could help me here," he added, stopping an objection. "I know what I'm talking about. The presence of any of you here would only delay matters and make it harder for me."

Then Ritter came in, a cigarette in one corner of his mouth, carrying a tray on which were a bottle of Bourbon, a bottle of Scotch, a siphon and a couple of bottles of beer.

Chapter 20

The dining-room was empty, when Rand came down to breakfast the next morning. Taking the seat he had occupied the evening before, he waited until Ritter came out of the kitchen through the pantry.

"Good morning, Colonel Rand," the Perfect Butler greeted him unctuously. "If I may say so, sir, you're a bit of an early riser. None of the family is up yet, sir."

Rand jerked a thumb toward the kitchen. "Who's out there?" he hissed.

"Just the cook; frying sausage and flipping pancakes. Premix pancakes, of course. The maid sleeps out; she hasn't gotten here yet. How'd it go last night? You put a dummy under the covers and sleep on the floor?"

"No, last night I was safe. The blow-off isn't due till this morning, when the women are at church, and he'll have to catch me and the fall-guy together."

"What do you want me to do?" Ritter asked, giving an un-butler-like hitch at his shoulder-holster. "I can stand on my official dignity, and get out of any cleaning-up work till after dinner, and I won't have any buttling to do till the women get home from church."

"Case Varcek and Dunmore, when they come in; see if either of them is rod-heavy. Find anything, last night?"

Ritter shook his head. "I searched Varcek's lab, after everybody was in bed, and I searched the cars in the garage, and a lot of other places. I didn't find them. Whoever he is, the chances are he has them in his room."

"Did you look back of the books in the library?" Rand asked. When Ritter shook his head, he continued: "That's probably where they are. Not that it makes a whole lot of difference."

"If I'd found them, it'd of given me something to watch; then I'd know when the fun was going to start." Ritter broke off suddenly. "Yes, sir. Will you have your coffee now, or later, sir?"

Gladys entered, wearing the blue tailored outfit she had worn to Rand's office, on Wednesday.

"At ease, at ease," she laughed, dropping into her chair. "Anything new?"

Rand shook his head. "We'll have to wait. I'm expecting some action this morning; I hope it'll be over before you're home from church."

She looked at him seriously. "Jeff, you're using yourself as murder-bait," she said. "Aren't you?"

"More or less. He knows I'm onto him. He's pretty sure I haven't any real proof, yet, but he doesn't know how soon I will have. He realizes that I'm cat-and-mousing him, the way I did Walters. So he'll try to kill me before I pounce, and when he does, he'll convict himself. What he doesn't realize is that as long as he sits tight, he's perfectly safe."

Neither of them mentioned the obvious corollary, that conviction and execution would be almost simultaneous. It must have been uppermost in Gladys's mind; she leaned over and put her hand on Rand's arm.

"Jeff, would it help any if I stayed home, instead of going to church?" she asked. "I'm a pretty fair pistol-shot. Lane taught me. I can stay over ninety at slow fire, and in the eighties at timed-and-rapid. If I hid somewhere with a target pistol —"

"Absolutely not!" Rand vetoed emphatically. "I'm not saying that because I'm afraid you might stop a slug yourself. You're a big girl, now; you can take your own chances. But if you stayed home, he wouldn't make a move. You and Geraldine and Nelda have to be out of the house before he'll feel safe coming out of the grass."

"Watch it!" Ritter warned. "Yes, ma'am; at once, ma'am."

Nelda came in and sat down. Ritter held her chair and fussed over her, finding out what she wanted to eat. He was bringing in her fruit when Varcek and Geraldine entered. Nelda was inquiring if Rand wanted to come to church with them.

"No; I'm one of the boys the chaplain couldn't find in the foxholes," Rand said. "I'm going to put in a quiet morning on the collection. If nobody gets murdered or arrested in the meantime, that is."

Geraldine looked woebegone; her hands were trembling. "My God, do I have a hangover!" she moaned. "Walters, for heaven's sake, fix me up something, quick!" Then she saw Ritter. "Who the devil are you?" she demanded. "Where's Walters?"

"Out on bail," Rand told her. "Don't you remember?"

"Oh, you did this to me!" she accused. "Walters could always fix me up, in the morning. Now what am I going to do?"

"You might stop drinking," her husband suggested mildly.

"Oh, just stop breathing; that would be better all around," Nelda interposed.

Ritter coughed delicately. "Begging your pardon, ma'am, but I've always rawther fawncied myself for an expert on morning-awfter tonics. If you'll wait a moment —"

He departed on his errand of mercy, returning shortly with a highball glass filled with some dark, evil-looking potion. He set it on the table in front of the sufferer and poured her a cup of coffee.

"Now, ma'am; just try this. Take it gradually, if I may suggest. Don't attempt to gulp it; it's quite strong, ma'am."

Geraldine tasted it and pulled a Gorgon-face. Encouraged by Ritter, she managed to down about half of the mixture.

"Splendid, ma'am; splendid!" he cheered her on. "Now, drink your coffee, ma'am, and then finish it. That's right, ma'am. And now, more coffee."

Geraldine struggled through with the black draft and drank the second cup of coffee. As she set down the empty cup, she even managed to smile.

"Why, that's wonderful!" She lit a cigarette. "What is it? I feel as though I might live, after all."

"A recipe of my own, a variant on the old Prairie Oyster, but without the raw egg, which I consider a needless embellishment, ma'am. I learned it in the household of a former employer, a New York stockbroker. Poor man: he did himself in in the autumn of 1929."

"Well, it's too bad you won't be with us permanently, Davies," Nelda said. "Your recipe seems to be just what Geraldine needs. With a dash of prussic acid added, of course."

That got the bush-fighting off to a good start. When Dunmore came in, a few minutes later, the two sisters were stalking one another through the jungle, blow-gunning poison darts back and forth. The newcomer sat down without a word; throughout the meal, he and Varcek treated one another with silent and hostile suspicion. Finally Gladys looked at her watch and called a truce to the skirmishing by announcing that it was time to start for church. Rand left the room with the ladies; in the hall, Gladys brushed against him quickly and gripped his left arm.

"Do be careful, Jeff," she whispered.

"Don't worry; I will," Rand assured her. Then he turned into the library and went up the spiral to the gunroom, while the three women went down to the garage.

He was standing at the window as the big Packard moved out onto the drive. Nelda was at the wheel, and Gladys, beside her on the front seat, raised a white-gloved hand in the thumbs-up salute. Rand gave it back, and watched the car swing around the house. Then he mopped his face with a wad of Kleenex and went over to the room-temperature thermostat, turning it down to sixty.

Sitting down at the desk, he dialed Humphrey Goode's number on the private outside line. A maid answered; a moment later he was talking to the Fleming lawyer.

"Rand, here," he identified himself. "Mr. Goode, I've been thinking over our conversation of last evening. There is a great deal to be said for the position you're taking in the matter. As you reminded me, I'm a small, if purely speculative, stockholder in Premix, myself, and even if I weren't, I should hate to be responsible for undeserved losses by innocent investors."

"Yes?" Goode's voice fairly shook. "Then you're going to drop the investigation?"

"No, Mr. Goode; I can't do that. But I believe a formula could be evolved which would keep the Premix Company and its affairs out of it. In fact, I think that the whole question of the death of Lane Fleming might possibly be kept in the background. Would that satisfy you? It would require some very careful manipulation on my part, and your cooperation."

"But.... See here, if you're investigating the death of Mr. Fleming, how can that be kept in the background?" Goode wanted to know.

"The murderer of Lane Fleming is also guilty of the murder of Arnold Rivers," Rand stated. "I know that positively, now. Murder is punished capitally, and one of the peculiarities of capital punishment is that it can be inflicted only once, on no matter how many counts. If our man goes to the chair for the death of Rivers, the death of Fleming might even remain an accident. I can hardly guarantee that; I have my agency license to think of, among other things. But I feel reasonably safe in saying that I could keep the Premix Company from figuring in the case. Would that satisfy you?"

"It most certainly would, Colonel Rand!" Goode's voice shook even more. "Are you sure?"

"I'm not sure of anything. It'll cost the Premix Company some money to get this done —I'll have certain expenses, for one thing, which could not very gracefully be itemized-and I will have to have your cooperation. Now, I want you to remain at home, where I can reach you at any moment, for the rest of the day. I'll call you later."

He listened to Goode babble his gratitude for a while, then terminated the call and hung up. Then he transferred the Colt .38 to the side pocket of his coat, picked up one of the sheets on which he had been listing the collection, and sat for almost fifteen minutes pretending to study it, keeping his eyes shifting from the hall door to the spiral stairway and back again.

Finally, the hall door opened, and Anton Varcek came in. Rand half rose, covering the Czech from his side pocket; Varcek came over and sat down in an armchair near the desk. He was looking more than ever like Rudolf Hess. Rudolf Hess on the morning of the Beer Hall Putsch.

"Colonel Rand," he began. "There has, within the last half hour, been a most important development. I am at a loss to define its significance, but its importance is inescapable."

Rand nodded. He had been expecting somebody to give birth to an important development; the steps toward gunfire were progressing in logical series.

"Well?" He smiled encouragingly. "What happened?"

"After you and the ladies left the dining-room," Varcek said, "Fred Dunmore turned to me and apologized for harboring unjust suspicions of me in the matter of Lane Fleming's death. He said that he had been unable to understand who else could have murdered Lane, until you had pointed out to him that the house could have been entered from the garage, and the gunroom from the library. Then, he said, he had had a conversation with some unnamed gentleman at the party last evening, and had learned that Lane had discovered that Humphrey Goode was deceiving him, and had been about to have him dismissed from his position with the company, and to sever his personal connections with him."

"The devil, now!" Rand gave a good imitation of surprise. "What sort of jiggery-pokery was Goode up to?"

"Fred said that his informant told him that Lane had proof that Goode had accepted a bribe from Arnold Rivers, to misconduct the suit which Lane was bringing against Rivers about a pair of pistols he had bought from Rivers. It seems that Goode was Rivers's attorney, also, and had been involved with him in a number of dishonest transactions, although the connection had been kept secret."

"That's a new angle, now," Rand said. "I suppose that he killed Rivers in order to prevent the latter from incriminating him. Why didn't Fred come to me with this?" he asked.

"Eh?" Evidently Varcek hadn't thought of that. "Why, I suppose he was concerned about the possibility of repercussions in the business world. After all, Goode is our board chairman, and maybe he thought that people might begin thinking that the murder had some connection with the affairs of the company."

"That's possible, of course," Rand agreed. "And what's your own attitude?"

"Colonel Rand, I cannot allow these facts to be suppressed," the Czech said. "My own position is too vulnerable; you've showed me that. Except for the fact that somebody could have entered the house through the garage, the burden of suspicion would lie on me and Fred Dunmore."

"Well, do you want me to help you with it?" Rand asked.

"Yes, if you will. It would be helping yourself, also, I believe," Varcek replied. "Fred is down-stairs, now, in the library; I suggest that you and I go down and have a talk with him. Maybe you could show him the folly of trying to suppress any facts concerning Lane's death."

"Yes, that would be both foolish and dangerous." Rand got to his feet, keeping his hand on the .38 Colt. "Let's go down and talk to him now."

They walked side by side toward the spiral, Rand keeping on the right and lagging behind a little, lifting the stubby revolver clear of his pocket. Yet, in spite of his vigilance, it happened before he could prevent it.

A lance of yellow fire jumped out of the shadows of the stairway, and there was a soft cough of a silenced pistol, almost lost in the *click-click* of the breech-action. Rand felt something sledge-hammer him in the chest, almost knocking him down. He staggered, then swung up the Colt he had drawn from his pocket and blazed two shots into the stairway. There was a clatter, and the sound of feet descending into the library. He rushed forward, revolver poised, and then a shot boomed from below, followed by three more in quick succession.

"Okay, Jeff!" Ritter's voice called out. "War's over!"

He managed, somehow, to get down the steep spiral. The little .25 Webley & Scott was lying on the bottom step; he pushed it aside with his foot, and cautioned Varcek, who was following, to avoid it. Ritter, still looking like the Perfect Butler in spite of the .380 Beretta in his hand, was standing in the hall doorway. On the floor, midway between the stairway and the door, lay Fred Dunmore. His tan coat and vest were turning dark in several places, and Rand's own Detective Special was lying a few inches from his left hand.

"He came in here and shut the door," Ritter reported. "I couldn't follow him in, so I took a plant in the hall. When I heard you blasting upstairs, I came in, just in time to see him coming down. You winged him in the right shoulder; he'd dropped the .25, and he had your gat in his left hand. When he saw mine, he threw one at me and missed; I gave him three back for it. See result on floor."

"Uh-uh; he'd have gotten away, if you hadn't been on the job," he told Ritter. Then he picked up his own revolver and holstered it. After a glance which assured him that Fred Dunmore was beyond any further action of any sort, he laid the square-butt Detective Special on the floor beside him. "You did all right, Dave," he said. "Now, nobody's going to have a chance to bamboozle a jury into acquitting him." He thought of his recent conversation with Humphrey Goode. "You did just all right," he repeated.

"So it was Fred, then," he heard Varcek, behind him, say. "Then he was lying about this evidence against Goode." The Czech came over and stood beside Rand, looking down at the body of his late brother-in-law. "But why did he tell me that story, and why did he shoot at us when we were together?"

"Both for the same general reason." Rand explained about the two pistols and the planned double-killing. "With both of us dead, you'd be the murderer, and I'd be a martyr to law-and-order, and he'd be in the clear."

Varcek regarded the dead man with more distaste than surprise. Evidently his experiences in Hitler's Europe had left him with few illusions about the sanctity of human life or the extent of human perfidy. Ritter holstered the Beretta and got out a cigarette.

"I hope you didn't leave your lighter upstairs," he told Rand.

Rand produced and snapped it, holding the flame out to his assistant. "Dave," he lectured, "the Perfect Butler always has a lighter in good working order; lighting up the mawster is part of his duties. Remember that, the next time you have a buttling job."

Ritter leaned forward for the light. "Dunmore was a better shot with his right hand than he was with his left," he commented. "He didn't come within a yard of me, and he scored a twelve-o'clock center on you. Right through the necktie."

Rand glanced down. Then he burst into a roar of obscene blasphemy.

"Seven dollars and fifty cents I paid for that tie, not three weeks ago," he concluded. "Does your grandmother make patchwork quilts? If she does, she can have it."

"My God!" Varcek stared at Rand unbelievingly. "Why, he hit you! You're wounded!"

"Only in the necktie," Rand reassured him. "I have a hole in my shirt, too." He reached under the latter garment and rummaged, as though to evict a small trespasser. When he brought out his hand, he was holding a battered .25-caliber bullet. He held it out to show to Varcek and Ritter.

"Sure," Ritter grinned at Varcek. "Didn't you know? Superman."

"I'm wearing a bulletproof vest; Mick McKenna loaned it to me yesterday," Rand enlightened Varcek. "I never wore one of the damn things before, and if I can help it, I'll never wear one again. I'm damn near stewed alive in it."

"Think how hot you'd be, right now, if you hadn't been wearing it," Ritter reminded him.

"Then you knew, since yesterday, that he would do this?" Varcek asked.

"I knew one or the other of you would," Rand replied. "I had quite a few reasons for thinking it might be Dunmore, and one good one for not suspecting you."

"You mean my dislike for firearms?"

"That could have been feigned, or it could have been overcome," Rand replied. "I mean your knowledge of biology and biochemistry. If you'd killed Lane Fleming, there'd have been no clumsy business of fake accidents; not as long as both of you ate at the same table. He'd have just died, an unimpeachably natural death." He turned to Ritter. "Dave, I'm going upstairs; I want to get out of this damned coat of mail I'm wearing. While I'm doing it, I want you to call Carter Tipton, at the Jarrett place, and Humphrey Goode, and Mick McKenna, in that order. Tell Goode to get over here as fast as he can, and come up to my room; tell him we have to consider ways and means of implementing my suggestion to him."

Chapter 21

In the month which followed, events transpired through a thickening miasma of rumors, official communiques, journalistic conjectures, and outright fabrications, fitfully lit by the glare of newsmen's photo-bulbs, bulking with strange shapes, and emitting stranger noises. There were the portentous rumblings of prepared statements, and the hollow thumps of denials. There were soft murmurs of, "Now, this is strictly off the record ..." followed by sibilant whispers. The unseen screws of political pressure creaked, and whitewash brushes slurped suavely. And there was an insistent yammering of bewildered and unanswered questions. Fred Dunmore really had killed Arnold Rivers, hadn't he? Or had he? Arnold Rivers had been double-crossing Dunmore ... or had Dunmore been double-crossing Rivers? Somebody had stolen ten-or was it twenty-five —thousand dollars' worth of old pistols? Or was it just twenty-five thousand dollars? Or what, if anything, had been stolen? Was somebody being framed for something ... or was somebody covering up for somebody ... or what? And wasn't there something funny about the way Lane Fleming got killed, last December?

The surviving members of the Fleming family issued a few noncommittal statements through their attorney, Humphrey Goode, and then the Iron Curtain slammed down. Mick McKenna gave an outraged squawk or so, then subsided. There was a series of pronunciamentos from the office of District Attorney Charles P. Farnsworth, all full of high-order abstractions and empty of meaning. The reporters, converging on the Fleming house, found it occupied by the State Police, who kept them at bay. Harry Bentz, of the New Belfast *Evening Mercury*, using a 30-power spotting-'scope from the road, observed Dave Ritter, whom he recognized, wearing a suit of butler's livery and standing in the doorway of the garage, talking to Sergeant McKenna, Carter Tipton and Farnsworth; the *Mercury* exploited this scoop for all it was worth.

On the whole, the Rosemont Bayonet Murder was, from a journalistic standpoint, an almost complete bust. There had been no arrest, no hearing, no protracted trial, no sensational revelations. Only one monolithic fact, officially attested and indisputable, loomed out of the murk: "... and the said Frederick Parker Dunmore, deceased, did receive the aforesaid gunshot-wounds, hereinbefore enumerated, at the hands of the said Jefferson Davis Rand and at the hands of the said David Abercrombie Ritter ..." and "... the said Jefferson Davis Rand and the said David Abercrombie Ritter, being in mortal fear for their several lives, did so act in defense of their several persons..." and, finally, "... the said Frederick Parker Dunmore did die."

The *Evening Mercury*, which sheet the said Jefferson Davis Rand had once cost the loss of an expensive libel-suit and exposed in certain journalistic malpractices verging upon blackmail, promptly burst into print with an indignant editorial entitled *Trial by Pistol*. The terms: "legalized slaughter," and "flagrant whitewash," were used, and mention was made of "the well known preference of a certain notorious private detective for the procedure of *habeas* cadaver." The principal result of this outcry was to persuade an important New Belfast manufacturer, who had hitherto resisted Rand's sales pressure, to contract with the Tri-State Agency for the protection of his payroll deliveries.

Then, at the other end of the state, the professor of Moral Science at a small theological seminary caught his wife in *flagrante delicto* with one of the fourth-year students and opened fire upon them, at a range of ten feet, with a 12-gauge pump-gun. The Rosemont Bayonet Murder, already pretty well withered on the vine, passed quietly into limbo.

Summer, almost a month before its official opening, was already a *fait accompli*. The trees were in full leaf and invaded by nesting birds, the air was fragrant with flower scents, and the mercury column of the thermometer was stretching itself up toward the ninety mark.

They were all outside, where the long shadow of the Fleming house fell across the lawn and driveway, gathered about the five parked cars. The new Fleming butler, a short and somewhat globular Negro with a gingerbread-crust complexion and an air of affable dignity, was helping

Pierre Jarrett and Karen Lawrence put a couple of cartons and a tall peach-basket into Pierre's Plymouth. Colin MacBride, a streamer of pipe-smoke floating back over his shoulder, was peering into his luggage-compartment to check the stowage of his own cargo, while his twelve-year-old son, Malcolm, another black Highlander like his father, was helping Philip Cabot carry a big laundry hamper full of newspaper-wrapped pistols to his Cadillac. Pierre's mother, and the stylish-stout Mrs. Trehearne, and Gladys Fleming, obviously detached from the bustle of pre-departure preparations, were standing to one side, talking. And Rand had finished helping Adam Trehearne pack the last container of his share of the Fleming collection into his car.

"I see Colin's about ready to leave, and I'm in his way," Trehearne said. He extended his hand to Rand. "No need hashing over how we all feel about this. If it hadn't been for you, that offer of Kendall's would have had us stopped as dead as Rivers's had. Five hundred dollars deader, in fact."

Stephen Gresham, carrying a package-filled orange crate, joined him, setting down his burden. His wife and daughter, with another crate between them, halted beside him.

"Haven't you got your stuff packed yet, Jeff?" Gresham asked.

"Jeff's been helping everybody else," Irene Gresham burst out. "Come on, everybody; let's go help Jeff pack! You're going to have dinner with us, aren't you, Jeff?"

"Oh, sorry. I have some more details to clear up; I'm having dinner here, with Mrs. Fleming," Rand regretted. "I'll pack my stuff later."

Mrs. Jarrett, Mrs. Trehearne, and Gladys came over; one by one the rest of the group converged upon them. Then, when the good-by's had been said, and the promises to meet again had been given, they parted. One by one the cars moved slowly down the driveway to the road. Only Gladys and Rand, standing at the foot of the front steps, and the gingerbread-brown butler were left.

"My, my; that was some party!" the Negro chuckled, gathering up three empty pasteboard cartons and telescoping them together. "Dinner'll be ready in about half an hour, Mrs. Fleming. Shall I go mix the cocktails now?"

"Yes; do that, Reuben. In the drawing-room." She watched the servant carry the discarded containers around the house, then turned to Rand. "You know, not the least of your capabilities is your knack of finding servant-replacements on short notice," she told him.

"My general factotum, Buck Pendexter, is a prominent personage in New Belfast colored lodge circles," Rand said. "When your cook and maid quit on you, the day of the blow-up, all I had to do was phone him, and he did the rest." He got out his cigarettes, offered them, and snapped his lighter. "I notice you're having cocktails in the drawing-room now."

"Yes. I suppose, in time, I'll stop imagining I see Fred Dunmore's blood on the library floor. I got used to what had happened in the gunroom last December. Shall we go in?" she asked, taking Rand's arm.

The cocktails were waiting when they entered the drawing-room, off the dining-room. The butler poured for them and put the glasses and the shaker on a low table by a lounge.

"I'm afraid dinner's going to be a little later than I said, Mrs. Fleming," he apologized. "Things were kind of stirred up, today, with all those people here."

"That's all right; we can wait," she replied. "We won't need anything more, Reuben."

Motioning Rand down on the lounge beside her, she handed him a glass and lifted her own.

"Now," she began. "Just what sort of skulduggery has been going on? As of Friday, the top offer for the collection was twenty-five thousand five hundred, from some dealer up in Massachusetts. And then, on Saturday, you came bounding in with Stephen Gresham's certified check for twenty-six thousand. And I seem to recall that the late unlamented Rivers's offer of twenty-five thousand straight had them stopped. Not that I'm inclined to look askance at an extra five hundred —I can buy a new hat with my share of that, even after taxes-but I would like to know what happened. And I might add, that's only one of many things I'd like to know."

"The client is entitled to a full report," Rand said, tasting his cocktail. It was a vodka Martini, and very good. "You know, none of that crowd are millionaires. Adam Trehearne, who's the plutocrat of the bunch, isn't so filthy rich he doesn't know what to do with all his money-what the tax-collectors leave of it-and the rest of them have to figure pretty closely. The most they could possibly scratch together was twenty-two thousand. So I put four thousand into the pot, myself, bringing the total to five hundred over the Kendall offer, and hastily declared the collection sold. Of course, my getting into it meant that much less for everybody else, but five-sixths of a collection is better than no pistols at all. I imagine Colin MacBride is honing up his *sgian-dhu* for me because I got that big Whitneyville Walker Colt, but what the hell; he got the cased pair of Paterson .34's, and the Texas .40 with the ramming-lever."

"Why, I think the division was fair enough," Gladys said. "They'd agreed to take your valuation, hadn't they? And all that slide-rule and comptometer business....But Jeff-four thousand dollars?" she queried. "You only got five from me, and you can't run a detective agency on old pistols."

Rand grinned as he set down his empty glass. Gladys refilled it from the shaker.

"My dear lady, that five thousand I unblushingly accepted from you was only part of it," he confessed.

"There was also a fee of three thousand from Stephen Gresham, for pulling the bloodhounds of the D.A.'s office off his back in the matter of Arnold Rivers, and there was five thousand from Humphrey Goode, which I suppose he'll get the Premix Company to repay him, for engineering the suppression of a lot of facts he wanted suppressed. And, finally, my connection with this business brought that merger to my attention, and I picked up a hundred shares of Premix at 73-1/4, and now I have two hundred shares of Mill-Pack, worth about twenty-nine thousand, which I can report for my income tax as capital gains. I'd say I could afford to treat myself to a few old pistols for my collection."

"Well!" She raised both eyebrows over that. "Don't anybody tell me crime doesn't pay."

"Yes. In my ghoulish way, I generally manage to bear myself in mind, on an operation like this. I make no secret of my affection for money." He lifted his glass and sipped slowly. "Look here, Gladys; are you satisfied with the way this was handled?"

She shrugged. "I should be. When I started out as Lane's blood-avenger, I suppose I expected things to end somewhere out of sight, in a nice, antiseptic death-chamber at the state penitentiary. You must admit that that business in the library was really bringing it home. There's no question that you got the man who killed Lane, and if you hadn't, I'd never have been at peace with myself. And I suppose all that chicanery afterward was necessary, too."

"It was, if you wanted that merger to go through, and unless you wanted to see the bottom drop out of your Premix stock," Rand assured her. "If the true facts of Mr. Fleming's death had gotten out, there'd have been a simply hideous stink. The Mill-Pack people would have backed out of that merger like a bear out of an active bee-tree....You know what the situation really was, don't you?"

She shook her head. "I know Mill-Pack wanted to get control of the Premix Company, and Lane refused to go in with them. I don't fully understand his reasons, though."

"They weren't important; they were mainly verbal, and unrelated to actuality," Rand said. "The important thing is that he did refuse, and Mill-Pack wanted that merger so badly that it could be tasted in every ounce of food they sold. They got Stephen Gresham to negotiate it for them, and he was just on the point of reporting it to be an impossibility when Fred Dunmore came to him with a proposition. Dunmore said he thought he could persuade or force Mr. Fleming to consent, and he wanted a contract guaranteeing him a vice-presidency with Mill-Pack, at forty thousand a year, if and when the merger was accomplished. The contract was duly signed about the first of last November."

"Well, good Lord!" Gladys Fleming's eyes widened. "When did you hear about that?"

"I got that out of Gresham, a couple of days after the blow-up, when it was too late to be of any use to me," Rand said. "If I'd known it from the beginning, it might have saved me some work. Not much, though. Gresham was just as badly scared about the facts coming out as

Goode was. I can't prove collusion between him and Goode, but Gresham was helping spread the suicide story, too."

"Nice friends Lane had! But didn't anybody think there was something odd about that accident, immediately after that contract was signed?"

"Of course they did, but try and get them to admit it, even to themselves. Nobody likes to think that the new vice president of the company murdered his way into the position. So everybody assumed the attitudes of the three Japanese monkeys, and made respectable noises about what a great loss Mr. Fleming was to the business world, and how lucky Dunmore was that he had that contract."

She looked at him inquiringly for a moment. "Jeff, I want you to tell me exactly how everything happened," she said. "I think I have a right to know."

"Yes, you have," he agreed. "I'll tell you the whole thing, what I actually know, and what I was forced to guess at:

"When this merger idea first took shape, last summer, Dunmore saw how unalterably opposed to it Mr. Fleming was, and he began wishing him out of the way. Some time later, he decided to do something about it. I suppose Anton Varcek gave him the idea, in the first place, with his jabber about the danger of a firearms accident. Dunmore decided he'd fix one up for Mr. Fleming. First of all, he'd need a firearm, collector's type and in good working order. It couldn't be one of the guns in the collection. He'd have to keep it loaded all the time, waiting for an opportunity to use it; he couldn't take a weapon out of the collection, because it would be missed, and he couldn't load one and hang it up again, because that would be discovered. So he had to get one of his own, and he got it from Arnold Rivers."

"You know that? I mean, that's not just a guess?"

"I know it. The gun he got from Rivers was a .36 Colt, 1860 Navy-model, serial number 2444," Rand told her. "Rivers had that gun last summer. He had it refinished by a gunsmith named Umholtz. After Umholtz refinished it, the gun was in Rivers's shop until November of last year, when it was sold by Rivers personally. And that was the revolver that was found in Lane Fleming's hand, and the one I got from the coroner, with a letter vouching for the fact that it had been so found."

He finished his cocktail. Gladys picked up the shaker mechanically and refilled his glass.

"Now we have Dunmore with this .36 Colt, loaded with powder, caps and bullets from the ammunition supply in the gunroom, waiting for a chance to use it. And also, he has this Mill-Pack contract in his safe deposit box at the bank. That takes care of the weapon and the motive; only the opportunity is needed, and that came on the 22nd of December, when Mr. Fleming brought home that Confederate Leech & Rigdon .36 he had just bought. It was just a piece of luck that both revolvers were alike in caliber and general type, but it wouldn't have made a lot of difference. Nobody was paying much attention to details, and Dunmore was on the scene to misdirect any attention anybody would pay to anything.

"Now, we come to the mechanics of the thing; the *modus operandi*, or, as it is professionally known, the M.O. You remember what happened that evening. Nelda had gone out. You and Geraldine were listening to the radio in the parlor, over there. Varcek had gone up to his lab. Mr. Fleming was alone in the gunroom, working on his new revolver. And Fred Dunmore said he was going to take a bath. What he did, of course, was to draw a tub full of water, undress, put on his bathrobe and slippers, hide the .36 Colt under the bathrobe, and then go across the hall to the gunroom, where he found Mr. Fleming sitting on that cobbler's bench, putting the finishing touches on the Leech & Rigdon. So he fired at close range, wiped the prints off the Colt with an oily rag, put it in Lane Fleming's right hand, put the rag in his left, grabbed up the Leech & Rigdon, and scuttled back to his bathroom, deadlatching and shutting the gunroom door as he went out. This last, of course, was a delaying tactic, to give him time to establish his bathtub alibi."

He lifted the cocktail glass to his lips. These vodka Martinis were strong, and three of them before dinner was leaning way over backward maintaining the tradition of the hard-drinking private eye, but Gladys was working on her third, and no client was going to drink him under.

"So, in the privacy of his bathroom, he kicked out of his slippers, threw off his robe, hid the Leech & Rigdon, probably in a space between the tub and the wall that I found while we were searching the house, the night before the shooting of Dunmore, and jumped into the tub, there to await developments. As soon as he heard Varcek's uproar in the hall, he could emerge, dripping bathwater and innocence, to find out what the fuss was all about....Do you know anything about something called General Semantics?" he asked suddenly.

"Yes. Before I married Lane, I went around with a radio ad-writer," she told him. "He was a nice boy, but he'd get drunker than a boiled owl about once a month, and weep about his crimes against sanity and meaning. He'd recite long excerpts from his professional creations, and show how he had been deliberately objectifying words and identifying them with the things for which they stood, and confusing orders of abstraction, and juggling multiordinal meanings. He was going to lend me his Koran, a book called *Science and Sanity*, and then he took a job with an ad agency in Chicago, and I got married, and —"

Rand nodded. "Then you realize that the word is not the thing spoken of, and that the inference is not the description, and that we cannot know 'all' about anything. Etcetera," he added hastily, like a Papist signing himself with the Cross. "Well, some considerable disregard of these principles seems to have existed in this case. Dunmore is seen in a bathrobe, his feet bare and making wet tracks on the floor, his hair wet, etcetera. Straightaway, one and all appear to have assumed that he was in the tub, splashing soapsuds around, while Lane Fleming was being shot. And Anton Varcek, who can be taken as an example of what S. I. Hayakawa was talking about when he spoke of people behaving like scientists inside but not outside their laboratories, saw Lane Fleming dead, with an object labeled 'revolver' in his hand, and, because of his verbal identifications and semantic reactions, immediately included the inference of an accident in his description of what he had seen. That was just an extra dividend of luck for Dunmore; it got the whole crowd of you thinking in terms of accidental shooting.

"Well, from there out, everything would have been a wonderful success for Dunmore, except for one thing. Arnold Rivers must have heard, somehow, that Lane Fleming had been shot with a Confederate .36 that he'd bought somewhere that day, and that the revolver was in the hands of this coroner of yours. So Arnold, with his big chisel well ground, went to see if he could manage to get it out of the coroner for a few dollars. And when he saw it, lo! it was the .36 Colt that he'd sold to Dunmore about a month before."

Gladys set down her glass. "So!" she said. "Things begin to explain themselves!"

"You may say so, indeed," Rand told her. "And what do you suppose Rivers did with this little item of information? Why, as nearly as I can reconstruct it, he did a very foolish thing. He tried to blackmail a man who had committed a murder. He told Fred Dunmore he'd keep his mouth shut about the .36 Colt, if Dunmore would get him the Fleming collection. He wanted that instead of cash, because he could get more out of it, in a few years, than Dunmore could ever scrape, and in the meantime, the prestige of handling that collection would go a long way toward repairing his rather dilapidated reputation. Fred should have bumped him off, right then; it would have been the cheapest and easiest way out, and he'd probably be alive and uncaught today if he had. But he was willing to pay ten thousand dollars to save himself the trouble, and that's what he told you Rivers had offered for the collection. The ten thousand Dunmore told you Rivers was willing to pay was really the ten thousand he was willing to pay, himself, to keep Rivers quiet.

"Then I was introduced into the picture, and, as you know, one of my first acts was to go to Rivers's shop and sneer scornfully at Rivers's supposed offer of ten thousand. And, right away, Rivers upped it to twenty-five thousand. You'll recall, no doubt, that Mr. Fleming had a life-insurance policy, one of these partnership mutual policies, which gave both Dunmore and Varcek exactly twenty-five thousand apiece. I assume that Rivers had found out about that.

"I thought, at the time, that it was peculiar that Rivers would jump his own offer up, without knowing what anybody else was offering for the collection. I see, now, that it wasn't his own money he was being so generous with. And there was another incident, while I was at Rivers's shop, that piqued my curiosity. Rivers had in his shop a .36 Leech & Rigdon revolver, and I had been informed that it was a revolver of that type that Mr. Fleming had brought home the evening he was killed. I thought at the time that it was curious that two Confederate arms of the same type and make should show up this far north, but my main idea in buying it was the possibility that I might use it, in some way as circumstances would permit, to throw a scare into somebody. Rivers was quite willing to let me have it until he found out that I would be staying at this house, and then he tried to back out of the sale and offered me seventy-five dollars' credit on anything else in the shop, if I'd return it to him. Well, I'd known that Mr. Fleming had been about to start suit against Rivers over a crooked deal Rivers had put over on him, and I knew that if Mr. Fleming's death had been murder, there had been a substitution of revolvers. So I showed the gun I'd bought from Rivers to Philip Cabot, who had seen the revolver Mr. Fleming had bought, and he recognized it. It hasn't been established just how Rivers got the Leech & Rigdon, and never will be; the only people who knew were Rivers and Dunmore, and both are in the proverbial class of non-talebearers. I assume that Dunmore gave it to Rivers as a sort of down payment on Rivers's silence, and to get rid of it.

"Well, you remember Dunmore's angry incredulity when I told him that Rivers was offering twenty-five thousand instead of ten thousand. One would have thought, on the face of it, that he would have been glad; as Nelda's husband, he would share in the higher price being paid for the collection. But when you realize that Rivers was buying the collection out of Dunmore's pocket, his reaction becomes quite understandable. I daresay I signed Arnold Rivers's death-warrant, right there."

"I'll bet your conscience bothers you about that," Gladys remarked.

"Oh, sure; it's been gnawing hell out of me, ever since," Rand told her cheerfully. "But, right away, Dunmore decided to kill Rivers. He called him on the phone as soon as he left the table-here I'm speaking by the book; I walked in on him, in the gunroom, as he was completing the call, though I didn't know it at the time-and arranged to see him that evening. Probably to devise ways and means of dealing with the Jeff Rand menace, for an ostensible reason.

"So that night, Dunmore killed Rivers, with a bayonet. And here we have some more Aristotelian confusion of orders of abstraction. The bayonet is defined, verbally, as a 'soldier's weapon,' so Farnsworth and Mick McKenna and the rest of them bemused themselves with suspects like Stephen Gresham and Pierre Jarrett, and ignored Dunmore, who'd never had an hour's military training in his life. I'd like to check up on what picture-shows Dunmore had been seeing in the week or so before the killing. I'll bet anything he'd been to one of these South-Pacific banzai-operas. And speaking of confusing orders of abstraction, Mick McKenna and his merry men pulled a classic in that line. They saw Dunmore's automobile, verbally defined as a 'gray Plymouth coupé' in Rivers's drive at the estimated time of the murder. Pierre Jarrett has a car of that sort, so they included the inferential idea of Pierre Jarrett's ownership of the car so described.

"Well, that's about all there is to it. Of course, I showed Fred Dunmore the Leech & Rigdon, and told him it was the gun I'd gotten from the coroner. That was all he needed to tell him that I was onto the murder, and probably onto him as the murderer. But he had evidently assumed that already; that was after he'd assembled my .38 and that .25 automatic, and was planning to double-kill me and Anton Varcek. At that, he'd have probably killed me, if I hadn't been wearing that bulletproof vest of McKenna's. I owe Mick for my life; I'll have to buy him a drink, sometime, to square that."

"Well, how about Walters, and the pistols he stole?" Gladys asked. "Didn't that have anything to do with it?"

"No. It was a result of Mr. Fleming's death, of course. I understand that the situation here had deteriorated rather abruptly after Mr. Fleming's death. Walters was about fed up on the way things were here, and he was going to hand in his notice. Then he decided that he ought to have a stake to tide him over till he could get another buttling job, so he started higrading the collection."

Gladys nodded. "I suppose he decided, after Lane's death, that he didn't owe anybody here anything. Too bad he didn't wait, though. The situation has remedied itself, and that's something else I owe you."

"Yes? I noticed that there was nobody here but you," Rand mentioned.

"Oh, Anton's gone to New York. The Rockefeller Foundation is financing the major part of his research work, and he's well enough off to finance the rest himself. Geraldine went with him. Nelda is still recuperating from the shock of her sudden bereavement at a high-priced sanatorium —I understand there's a very good-looking young doctor there. And she's been talking about going to New York herself, in order, as she puts it, to lead her own life. I don't know whether she was afraid I'd be a restraining influence, or a dangerous competitor, but she feels that her own life could be best led away from here." She set down her glass and leaned back comfortably. "Peace, it's wonderful!"

Reuben, the gingerbread butler, appeared in the dining-room doorway. "Dinner's served now, Mrs. Fleming," he announced.

Rand rose, and Gladys took his arm; together, they went into the dining-room.